The Stages

THOM SATTERLEE

The Stages
A Mystery

CROOKED
LANE

Copyright © 2013 by Thom Satterlee

Published in the United States by Crooked Lane Books, an imprint of The Quick Brown Fox & Company LLC.

Crooked Lane Books and its logo are trademarks of The Quick Brown Fox & Company LLC.

The Library of Congress Cataloging-in-Publication Data is available upon request.

978-1-62953-419-0

Cover design by Jonathan Bouw

Printed in the United States.

www.crookedlanebooks.com

Crooked Lane Books
2 Park Avenue, 10th Floor
New York, NY 10016

Second Edition: October 2015

10 9 8 7 6 5 4 3 2 1

For Kathy

CAST OF CHARACTERS
~by appearance~

Daniel Peters: The novel's narrator, an American translator living in Copenhagen

Mette Rasmussen (MET-ta RASS-moose-in): Former director of the Søren Kierkegaard Research Center

Carsten Rasmussen: Son of Mette and Peter Rasmussen, college student at Princeton

Jesper Olsen (YES-per OHL-son): Lutheran priest at Our Lady's Church, Copenhagen's cathedral

Søren Kierkegaard (SIR-in KEER-ka-gore): 19th-century Danish philosopher, considered the father of Existentialism

Anders (AHN-ers): Secretary at the Kierkegaard Center

Lona Brøchner (LOW-nah BROOK-ner): Head philologist at the Kierkegaard Center

Rebekah Wilcox: American post-doctoral student conducting research at the Kierkegaard Center

Ingrid Bendtner (ING-rithe BENT-ner): Homicide detective with the Copenhagen Police

N.F.S. Grundtvig (GROONT-vee): 19th-century priest, reformer, and hymn writer

Lars Andersen: Philologist at the Kierkegaard Center

Annette Rifbjerg (Ah-NET-ta RIFF-byair): Philologist at the Kierkegaard Center

Per Aage Simonsen (PEER-owe-ah SEE-men-sen): Philologist at the Kierkegaard Center

Birgit Fisker-Steensen (BEER-git FISK-er STEEN-sen): Director of the Copenhagen Museum

Erik Thorvaldsen (TORE-val-sen): Brother of Mette Rasmussen, Danish Member of Parliament

Morton Olsen: Branch chief of Danske Bank, Nytorv

Susannah Lindegaard (LIN-a-gore): Specialist in forgery detection at the Royal Library

Thorkild Grønkjær (TORE GRUN-care): Director of the Royal Library

Rolf Poulsen: Homicide Team Leader, Copenhagen Police

Sven Carlsen: Homicide Detective, Copenhagen Police

Torben Kvist: Copenhagen lawyer, former classmate of Daniel Peters

Fru Thorvaldsen (FREW TORE-val-sen): Mette Rasmussen and Eric Thorvaldsen's mother, a widow living alone on the western side of Denmark

"There are three stages in life: the Aesthetic, the Ethical, the Religious. . . . The Aesthetic is the stage of unmediatedness, the Ethical is responsibility . . . [and] the Religious is fulfillment, but note well, not the sort of 'fulfillment' as when one fills up an offering plate or a sack with gold coins, for repentance has instead created an unlimited space, and with it the religious contradiction: to float upon 70,000 fathoms of water and yet feel happy."

—SØREN KIERKEGAARD, *Stages on Life's Way*
(Transl., Daniel Peters)

STAGE I:

The Set-up

Chapter 1

A crowd has gathered outside Our Lady's Church. Some stand on the porch between the Roman columns, and others congregate on the steps or on the sidewalk below. Most are dressed in dark-colored overcoats, hats, and gloves—appropriate both for the ceremony they are about to attend and for the damp-cold weather of this mid-January morning. Seeing them from the other side of the street, I estimate that about a hundred people have come for Mette Rasmussen's funeral. They wait, like me, for the doors to be opened for family and friends. The casket is already inside the church—I know this because it is customary for mourners to file past the casket and also because I was one of six people who carried it into the church about an hour ago. I could have waited inside but instead I decided to do something I haven't done in years: smoke a cigarette. I bought a pack of Prince, the Danish brand that was our favorite back when Mette and I were teenagers in Kolding. I had to buy a lighter to go with them, it's been that long. Then I found this isolated spot in a parking lot across from the church and smoked three in rapid succession. At the moment I am feeling sick to my stomach. I can almost hear Mette's voice saying, "Daniel, what were you thinking?"

A sudden glare of light flashes off the glass doors as they are opened. The crowd begins to stir. Slowly the shape that was a mass begins to divide into separate bodies, separate pairs of legs marching toward the gap at the top of the stairs. It takes a couple of minutes before everyone is inside. I wait a while longer, watching. A bike passes in front of the church, the cyclist slowing down as if out of respect—or maybe simply curiosity. A young woman ducks her head out of the church door and looks both ways down the street. Her blonde hair is pulled back with a black headband and she wears a gray scarf bunched up under her chin. She is pretty, in the simple Danish style that Mette was pretty when I met her twenty-seven years ago. Then the girl is gone, back inside the church. For a few seconds the street is completely silent—no cars, no bikes, no one walking on the sidewalk—and it occurs to me that I could turn and walk to my apartment, that no one would miss me, that Mette would understand in whatever way the dead can understand. She would say, "*Det må du selv om,*" using the colloquialism that can almost be captured with the English "It's up to you." I feel a giddiness of freedom that passes instantly into dread. Because two things happen at once: I see Carsten, Mette's son, walking quickly around the corner, fumbling to put his cell phone in a jacket pocket and then reaching through the gap in his coat to adjust his tie. He takes the steps two at a time. And the other thing that happens is this: I remember that besides carrying the casket into the church, I am expected to carry it out. My stomach drops, the same way a corner of Mette's casket would if I were not there to hold it up. I cross the street and go inside.

The line of mourners stretches down the length of the center aisle, almost into the foyer. Carsten, I notice, is not at the back of it. He has probably gone around the side and taken his seat with the nearest of kin. I don't know the person immediately in front of me, but several places ahead is a colleague from work. She turns around and squints her eyes at me. Her look might be a question or a judgment, I'm not really sure. I glance away. No one in line is speaking. The only sound is an organ playing an adagio that I believe is from Brahms. The pipes are directly above my head, and when I look up into the organ loft I can see the organist's black pantleg, part of one arm, the profile of a face. I move forward slowly but steadily, concentrating on keeping a polite distance between myself and the person ahead, trying not to allow too much space between us, and avoiding eye contact with anyone.

Our Lady's Church is the official cathedral in Copenhagen, and it is what most people would call beautiful and awe-inspiring. From the vaulted ceiling hang circular chandeliers ringed with lights. Pillars and archways line the walls, evenly spaced and evenly paired. Between each of the arched balconies I see bas reliefs of cherubim with wings folded around their faces, and I can't miss the larger-than-life marble statues of *The Twelve Apostles* standing on slabs with their names carved into them, six on each side of the sanctuary. Matthew, I notice, is looking a bit confused, holding a pen above a tablet and gazing off into the distance, as if he can't find his thought, while a diminutive, curly-haired angel stands at his feet with her arms crossed over her chest—waiting, patiently, forever. Up ahead, in the first position on the left, Paul is more resolute. He holds one hand on the hilt of a sword and with the other hand gestures to a crowd. "Look," he seems to be saying, "we could reason together. If not, I have other means at my disposal." The tip of the sword is visible just behind his left leg.

I stop while the person ahead of me mounts a stair. We have come to the end of the pews and now approach the choir, where all the people who preceded us are sitting in chairs arranged in perfectly even rows, one section on either side of the altar. But before we get to them we must pass the casket, its closed lid covered in layers of white flowers. It is placed next to a statue of an angel kneeling and holding out a bowl: the baptismal font. I wait while the person ahead of me pauses beside the casket and touches it lightly, just grazing the wood with her fingertips. Then it is my turn. I feel suddenly self-conscious and awkward, like a performer who's forgotten his lines or no longer believes in them. The problem is, I have already touched the casket, when I carried it into the church, to this very spot, and I'll touch it again when I carry it out. Why should I do as the others have? It would be wrong to follow their rule, and wrong not to follow it. If I walked up to Mette's casket and touched it, just lightly as the woman ahead of me has done, I would feel like a liar to myself and Mette. But in front of me are a hundred people, and not all of them know that I am a pallbearer. To them I might look like a homeless person who's wandered into the church looking for a warm place to spend the morning. I'm conscious that I smell of cigarette smoke, that my coat has a stain on it, just under the left breast—but that doesn't mean I'm a slob, only that I stumbled this morning while walking down Strøget with a cup of coffee in my hand. These are not facts that I can communicate quickly to the strangers in front of me. Also I realize, shamefully, my hat and gloves are sticking out of my coat pockets—that there's something lewd about that. All the other mourners, sitting and looking at me, have taken whatever they found too warm to wear and tucked it neatly under their chairs. Alone and exposed, I stand frozen beside the casket of an old friend, an old girlfriend. I would stand here indefinitely, perhaps, if something didn't come to my rescue. It turns out to be the priest—the mere sight of him standing off to one side in his black robe and piped collar, looking at once serious and comical, like a clown in mourning, unsticks me from my spot. I spy an empty chair in the back row and walk toward it briskly. As soon as I sit down I feel better. I place my hat and gloves in a pile under my chair and begin to do what comes most naturally to me: be the observer and not the observed.

The priest's name is Jesper Olsen, and unlike me he has no hesitation about standing in front of a crowd of people, and no doubts about what he should do. I have seen him interviewed on TV news whenever a story involved religion, and he has always seemed confident, truthful, reasonable, kind, and well-spoken. He is the sort of clergyman that gives the State Church a good image and makes Danes wonder if they might want to attend a service more often than just Christmas and Easter. Why not, if the priests are as likable as Jesper? Seeing him in person for the first time, vested for a service, my only surprise is that he is such a slight man: his robe looks too big for him and the piped collar climbs up his neck like a lifesaver floating around the ears of a drowning man. And yet he manages to pull off his role by standing before us perfectly still with his hands pressed together at the fingertips. His gray hair is closely trimmed and looks like a "V" spreading outward from his forehead. He has a serious look on his face, but not stern, not angry—somber and one hundred percent appropriate for the occasion. When he invites us to stand for prayer, we all do, rising from our chairs with a communal creaking sound. His voice is thin, somewhat high-pitched, and yet it conveys authority. He is speaking to God for us, thanking Him for Mette's life, asking assistance in our sorrows, acknowledging the promises of resurrection. He prays in Danish, of course, and I catch most of it, though I haven't been to a Danish funeral in six years and the vocabulary is somewhat specialized and outside of my usual realm. Mostly what comes across is the man's earnestness and conviction. I doubt anyone in this church would want to trade places with him (I certainly wouldn't) and I am already at ease about how he will handle the eulogy, when that time comes around. He will know what to say, and more importantly what not to say.

The organ plays the prelude to "*Nu takker alle Gud.*" Soon, everyone around me begins to sing, but I don't join in. It's not that I don't want to participate, but that my mind simply goes elsewhere, to a place that Mette, if anyone, would understand. Like me, she loved to work with words, just as I am doing now as I look down at the hymn book and start translating in my head: "Now thank we all our God / With heart and mouth and hands . . ." As the organ plays on, taking its breath at the end of a line, then coming back strong again, and the voices rise and fall with the song's meter, I realize that the Danish word *hænder* ends with an unaccented syllable, giving the second line a feminine ending, so "hands" can't possibly work. Mette would have a suggestion. What would her suggestion be? At the same time as I'm thinking this, on another level of my mind, I am aware that although I am only one person in a group of many who've come to pay respect to

Mette, I feel especially close to her, as if I'm the closest. But am I? Am I closer to her than her son, her mother, her siblings, all of whom I can see seated in the row nearest to the flower-laden casket? I have no way of knowing what's going on in their minds. They have no way of knowing what's going on in mine. As the hymn ends, I realize we are a hundred different people with a hundred different relationships to the deceased. And now one man who didn't know her personally will speak of her. He will give what, in an older form of Danish, is called the "corpse talk," in English "eulogy"—from Greek *eu* (well) and *logos* (discourse)—and he will likely do a better job than any of the others of us could.

The longer he has stood before us, the more solid and reassuring Jesper Olsen has grown. His seventeenth-century priestly costume radiates dignity as he calmly tells us about Mette's life, how this third child of an old, wealthy, respected family showed early signs of unusual promise. She was a gifted musician, he tells us, had the soul of a poet, and was always curious to learn more. In time she focused her interests in a particular direction—to understanding and elucidating the life of an important countryman, none other than the great Søren Kierkegaard. Yes, that same Søren Kierkegaard who was born in this city almost two hundred years ago and who regularly attended this very church, even delivering sermons quite near the spot where Mette's casket now stands. For more than two decades she carried on the work of scholars who'd come before her, side by side with her husband, who died a few years ago, just as they were nearing the end of a major project. Though grieved at her loss, she continued on, and the work prospered. As recently as last month, she made an unprecedented discovery that would shape the future of all Kierkegaard research. She had found a new manuscript, entirely unknown, and confirmed it as Kierkegaard's. As those close to her knew, she spent countless hours poring over this new work. Her final days, indeed her life, were full of purpose and dedicated to a good cause. Her life ended tragically too soon, but it was not without meaning.

When he finishes his talk, Jesper Olsen faces the family members sitting in the front row. He offers them his personal condolences and tells them that the church is a place of much comfort and is always open to them. He lifts his eyes and scans across both sides of the choir, repeating his invitation to the rest of us. When he reaches me, he seems to pause and look directly into my eyes, although this is probably the effect he has on many. I glance away. When I look back, he is holding a small pail and a shovel. Even though I have seen this rite performed before, it still strikes me as absurd. The pail and shovel look too much like a child's toys for building a sand castle, and they clash with the use for which they are about to be made. And yet somehow Jesper Olsen pulls it off. In his black robe and protruding white collar, he stands up straight and sinks the shovel into the pail, pulling out a heap of rich, black dirt.

"From earth you have come, to earth you will return," he says, pronouncing the words in an even, perfectly balanced manner. Then he scatters dirt over the coffin, directly on top of the white flowers. A few clods dribble off the side and land on the floor, but Jesper ignores them. As he scoops another shovelful, someone cries out and I look around to see who it might be. Mette's mother holds a handkerchief to her nose and slowly shakes her head. One of her sons reaches over and takes her hand. All, I think, is well, is as it should be. A mother should cry at her daughter's funeral. Her son should comfort her. This is how people close to the deceased grieve and give comfort to each other. But then I notice the figure on the other side of Mette's mother. It's Carsten, sitting with his coat draped over his lap and his elbows propped on his thighs. Sometime during the service he has loosened his tie and rolled up the sleeves of his dress shirt. For the first time today I look directly into his face and see that something is wrong. I have seen Carsten look this way before, but not in a while, not since his father died and, according to Mette, Carsten finally cleaned up his act. The muscles in his face seem too relaxed, too at ease, and his lips are stuck in a slightly upturned position, almost a grin. Sweat has matted his hair to his forehead. I realize suddenly that he has either been drinking or taking drugs, or possibly both. The reaction inside me is violent, but I stay perfectly still. What can I do? He's on the other side of the choir, within steps of his mother's casket, the priest's back turned to us while he places the second shovelful of dirt onto the flowers and utters the required words, "From earth you have come, to earth you will return."

As the priest scatters the third and final shovelful of dirt and repeats the sad, true words, Carsten Rasmussen stands up, places his coat on his seat, and walks slowly toward the casket. His grandmother and uncles watch him cautiously. Several people steal glances at each other. Here and there whispers rise, and a general sense of concern and helplessness grips us all. We were not expecting this. We do not know what is about to happen. And with Carsten, it could be anything.

It's not until he has set down the pail and shovel that Jesper Olsen turns and sees Carsten standing before him. The priest shows no surprise. He merely leans an ear towards the young man's mouth and nods his head while the other speaks words the rest of us can't hear.

After a few seconds, Jesper places his hand on Carsten's shoulder and squeezes it lightly.

"Mette's son will now speak a few words," he says.

The priest steps off to the side, leaving Carsten alone beside the casket. Everyone looks at him, waiting for what he will say. His grandmother has removed the handkerchief from her nose and now holds it on her lap, folding it into a smaller and smaller square. One of his uncles, I notice, sits on the edge of his chair with one foot in front of the other, a position from which he could quickly spring and subdue his nephew if the situation proves necessary. I actually take comfort from the fact that this uncle is a large and athletic man, and against him Carsten would not stand a chance.

"I hadn't planned on speaking today," Carsten says.

He stands with his arms hanging loose at his sides and stares down at the floor. He looks like a little boy called out in front of the adults for some crime he committed, and is already sorry for, and is too shy to speak about. But everyone in this room knows Carsten Rasmussen. We all know his reputation for the exact opposite of shyness. Although he's passed his twenty-first birthday and presumably left his years of teenage rebellion behind him, Carsten is remembered throughout this city for childish acts splashed across newspaper headlines. There was the time he shot fireworks off the deck of his parents' yacht and a stray missile ignited a fire on the thatched roof of a cottage north of the city. There was the party he attended with members of a motorcycle gang, and though the investigation showed that Carsten had acquired the high-quality drugs himself and generously distributed them to his new friends, he was found alone and badly beaten inside a graffiti-sprayed warehouse in Nørrebro, tied to a table and wearing nothing but his underwear. For a time there were so many news stories about him and his rich-kid escapades that the standard expression among parents wanting to curb their children's unruliness was, "Now don't you go pulling a Carsten on me." For Mette's sake, I pray that he hasn't saved one final embarrassing moment for now. When I look over at Carsten's uncle, I can see that he is concerned, too. He grips the sides of his chair as if he were just about to launch himself out of it.

"My mom," says Carsten. "What can I say that the priest hasn't already? She was a trusting person. She trusted me, even when I lied to her. Which happened sometimes. And she trusted the people she worked with at the Center. She was always telling me how she could count on her staff."

Carsten lifts his head and takes a step closer to the choir, the scolded child already growing bold. He glances across the group before him and smiles.

"It's funny. Maybe ironic is the word. Ever since I was a kid, she wanted me to be more careful about the company I kept. Like I should hang around with people at the Center. But I wanted to have fun, not spend my evenings talking about Søren Kierkegaard! She was sure I'd end up getting myself killed. But now look what's happened to her."

Carsten glances over at the casket, then turns and holds us with his gaze. It can't be more than a second or two, but time seems suspended and I feel the way I do when I sense that someone is about to disobey a crossing light and step off the curb, possibly into the path of a bicycle or car.

"She got herself killed," he says flatly. "Murdered."

The well-dressed, respectable people seated in the choir look down at their laps or shake their heads in disbelief. Murmurs of disapproval echo overhead. We are all thinking the same thing: Oh Carsten, not again. To my relief, his uncle stands up from his chair.

"It's okay, Carsten," he says. "We know. We all know."

He nods toward an empty chair, inviting Carsten to sit back down. But Carsten doesn't budge.

"Can a son not speak at his mother's funeral? I'm not finished yet. I was going to say something else. Something you don't know, Uncle. I spoke with the Police this morning, and they told me their investigation, their entire investigation, has been wrong from the beginning."

The uncle's reply is hardly more than a whisper. If it weren't for the church's acoustics, I wouldn't hear him.

"Please, Carsten. I know you're upset. Not now."

"And make all these people wait to read about it in the newspapers? But these are my mother's closest and most trusted friends. They deserve to be the first to know. This morning, as I was beginning to say, the Police informed me that the new Kierkegaard manuscript has been stolen."

Somewhere, someone in the crowd gasps. The two people immediately beside me exchange glances.

"It makes me wonder," Carsten says, "if the person who murdered her might also have stolen the manuscript. And maybe that person was not a stranger to my mother. It may have been someone who worked with her. Someone she trusted. Maybe someone here at her funeral, right now, pretending to be mourning her death. As her son—and this is the last thing I'll say, Uncle, so you can go ahead and sit down now—I promise we'll find that person, whoever it is."

Carsten makes his way back to his seat, and except for the sound of his footsteps on the stone floor the church is completely silent. No one seems to know what to do next. For a moment I wonder if the funeral is permanently stalled, but finally Jesper Olsen steps away from the far railing and walks up to Carsten. After shaking hands with him and speaking some private words, the priest instructs the pallbearers to take their positions. I stuff my hat and gloves into my pockets and join the others around the casket. As I bend down to grasp a brass handle, the organ plays "*Hvo ved hvornår mit liv har ende*," "Who Knows When My Life Will End," the same hymn that was sung at Kierkegaard's funeral one hundred and fifty seven years ago. Rising in sync with the five others, I lift the weight of Mette Rasmussen's body, her wooden casket, the sprays of white flowers, the three small shovelfuls of dirt, and walk slowly down the center aisle of Our Lady's Church. I concentrate on placing my feet properly—to trip now would be an awful thing. We pass through the front doors and carefully manage the stairs, sidestepping down them. A hearse is parked at the curb. We slide the casket into the back of it and step away. A driver in a black suit (but no overcoat) closes the door.

On the porch of the church, on the steps, and on the sidewalk below, a crowd has formed, just as it had less than an hour earlier. This time they train their eyes away from the building, and I watch with them as the hearse pulls out onto the road. That black car with tinted windows is headed not for a cemetery but for the crematorium, where the casket with the body inside it will be lowered into a furnace. In a week, perhaps two, the remains will be returned in an urn. I assume that Carsten will have it buried in the Assistens Cemetery, beside his father's, not very far from the spot where Søren Kierkegaard is buried. There will be a small service, but I don't know if I will be invited, or if I am whether I'll go. If Mette hadn't listed my name as one of the pallbearers, I might not have come to her funeral. Her mother and brothers, I know, are not very fond of me.

The crowd begins to disperse, one stream heading around the corner toward the university and another stream walking in the direction of Nytorv Square. A few others linger, holding handkerchiefs to their faces or embracing friends. Several people have taken out their cell phones, with which they're probably checking on Carsten's story. I'm curious, too, but I can wait. There will be a newspaper stand on the way back to my apartment, and when I return to work tomorrow everyone will be talking about what really happened to our former director, where the manuscript has gone, and what we're all to do about it.

Chapter 2

They're tearing holes into Copenhagen—holes and troughs and tunnels. On the other side of wooden barricades, jackhammers break up slabs of pavement and front loaders rumble through the demolition scooping up jagged hunks of what used to be road or sidewalk. The worst of the construction zones is right in the middle of my daily walk to work, and I can barely stand the barrage of noises. *Jut-jut-jut-jut. Beep-beep-beep-beep.* I understand why they're doing it: it's all part of a well-thought-out plan to extend the metro and beautify the area around Town Hall Square, but I can't keep myself from growing angry. I am more sensitive to loud noises than most people. Even knowing *why* I'm so sensitive to auditory stimulus doesn't keep me from wanting to scream. The only thing that helps is following a practice Mette taught me. It's called "re-focusing," and I don't think I could make it between my apartment and the Søren Kierkegaard Research Center without its help.

When I feel disturbed, as I certainly feel now, I switch my sensory attention. Forget the sounds, I tell myself. Focus on what you see. It's like closing one door and opening another. I still hear the jackhammers and earthmover machines, but gradually a new world of awareness dawns over me. How much more pleasant to watch people passing down Vester Voldgade on bicycles! At 8:00 a.m. it's still more dark out than light, and the cyclists have white headlights on their handlebars and flashing red reflector lights on their rear wheels. Some of the bikes are mounted with a child seat on the back; others have a one-wheeled wooden cart extending ahead of the front tire. It's all very Danish: a safe, simple, and functional solution to a daily problem. The parents are headed to work, but first they must drop off their children in day care—but why crowd the roads with more cars when you can achieve your purpose by biking, and get your exercise at the same time? The scene is also beautiful, at times touching. Seeing a toddler bundled up in a snowsuit and red scarf, wearing a knit hat and gloves, her sleepy head lolling off to one side, looking actually bored while her mother sits in the saddle with perfect posture and pumps the pedals in a steady up-and-down rhythm—how can I not relax, too? With somewhat greater calm, I make my way from sidewalk to sidewalk along my route to work. I enjoy the cool wind on my face. I smile at the cyclists as they pass by.

As I said, I have Mette to thank for teaching me this technique. She read about it in an article written to help people cope with Asperger's, a condition I didn't even know I had until six years ago, when I was already thirty-seven. According to Mette and the wealth of medical literature she shared with me, I've always *had* Asperger's; or, to put it another way, I've always *been* a person with Asperger's. The language here is tricky because Asperger's isn't a disease—it's not something you come down with and possibly die from. It's something you live with and die with. I'd always known I was different. People called me weird, antisocial, or (my personal favorite) a genius. I won the state spelling bee four years in a row (a record still unbroken), got a full ride to State College, scored 100% on the verbal section of the GRE, won a graduate school fellowship, and now find myself employed at an acclaimed international research center. Not exactly the life story of someone who, back in the '70s, would have been called a "retard." But as Mette once told me, "You can be a genius and still have Asperger's. It affects your social and emotional awareness, not your IQ." Albert Einstein had Asperger's, or at least some experts believe. I don't mind being in his company. Although, truthfully, I'd prefer to be alone. If he was like me, he'd have felt the same way.

As I make the turn off of Vester Voldgade and onto Farvergade, the street where the Søren Kierkegaard Research Center is located, I find myself wondering whether Mette would forgive me for not grieving over her death. I know that I should, and at her funeral I certainly saw people grieving, so I understand how it's done, but try as I might I have not been able to feel what they appear to feel—something so deep their limbs go limp, their faces contort, they cry or whimper until someone holds their hand or gives them a hug. But grief just isn't on my emotional spectrum. Mette would understand. She'd say, "Daniel, it's okay." How many times has she told me that! But, honestly, I don't want it to be okay. I don't want the only person I've ever loved to die, then not mourn for her. I don't want to be a person who doesn't grieve. I just don't know how to.

With this cheery thought in mind, I step off the sidewalk and pass through a stone archway. The passageway takes me into "Vartov," a complex of buildings arranged in a rectangle and sharing a cobbled-brick courtyard in the center. As on any weekday, a few cars are parked along the edge of the buildings and ranks of bikes stand with their front tires pressed inside metal bars bolted to walls; scores of other bikes lean against the walls, under windowsills, to the side of doorways, next to staircases, or wherever else space can be found. I tried riding a bike for a while myself, but I'm just too clumsy. In some of the literature Mette shared with me, poor motor skills is correlated to Asperger's Syndrome. It explains why I hated gym more than any other class at school and why, even now, I find myself tripping and falling down more often than any self-respecting middle-aged man should.

When I come to the door of my building, I take out a round metal key and wave it under a sensor. The door lock clicks open and I walk inside. The Center occupies the first floor of what was, in Kierkegaard's time, a hospital, but with modern renovations it now makes for perfect business space. What to do with all those old hospital rooms? Turn them into offices, naturally. Where beds and chamber pots once sat and patients recovered or died from tuberculosis, the rooms now have desks and computers, shelves of books, and here the scholars sit understanding their subject matter in original ways or dying from lack of insight. As I walk down the narrow hallway with its walls painted cream-white and the tall doors painted light blue, passing one office after another, I imagine nurses and doctors shuffling these same corridors, carrying vials of medicine, trying to put on a happy face for the patients they will see. I don my own mask, my work persona: Daniel Peters, American translator of the new, complete edition of Søren Kierkegaard's writings. I love my work here, and to be honest I've missed it more than I've missed Mette. I know that's a terrible thing to say, but it's true. Grief I cannot summon; attachment to a set routine, however, comes naturally. Forgive me, Mette.

As I enter the meeting room, I find three colleagues sitting together at the long conference table: Anders, the Center's secretary; Lona, the senior philologist; and Rebekah, an American post-doctoral student who grew up in Indiana but got her terminal degree from Princeton's School of Divinity. They drink coffee from white porcelain cups and enjoy the pastries that Anders brought from *Lagkagehuset*—I know Anders brought them because Tuesday is his day. Mine is Thursday.

There was a time, not very long ago, when I wouldn't sit with the others unless forced to do so for mandatory meetings. Instead I would simply disappear into my office as soon as I arrived, work all day and afternoon, then leave without so much as bidding my colleagues good morning or good night. But social interaction is one of the areas I have improved since my diagnosis. Mette and I worked out a program together. Little by little I have increased the length of time when I voluntarily socialize. Lately, I have managed to make polite company in unstructured settings for up to fifteen minutes. But it's not easy. Having fresh pastries on hand serves as an important incentive. Anders is sitting with his back to me, so I reach over his shoulders and snatch two pastries, one with each hand, then walk to a chair at the other end of the table. The two women smile. One of them offers me a plate, but I shake my head.

The others are speaking in English, out of deference to Rebekah, who's trying to learn conversational Danish but isn't quite there yet. I wish her luck. I've lived in Denmark for nearly twenty years (from 1985 to 1986, then from 1994 until now) and still my spoken Danish is unintelligible to all but a few Danes—those being the ones who taught me the language in the first place. In order to understand me, they must do some complicated form of translation in their heads, taking in what I say, remembering my mispronunciations from the past, matching my Danish to standard Danish, and quickly decoding my message so that they can have something to say in response. The segment of the world population that understands "Daniel Danish" (the name that one of Mette's brothers gave my language many years ago, claiming not to speak that foreign tongue himself) has of course dwindled of late. With Mette's death, I now have three people with whom I can reliably speak Danish. Naturally, if a shopkeeper doesn't speak English and all I need is an open-faced sandwich to go or something simple like that, I can make myself understood. But living in Copenhagen, where just about everyone speaks English, I seldom have to speak like a native, much to my relief and that of others.

It's different, of course, when it comes to reading the language. If you ask a Dane who their most difficult writer is, they will say Søren Kierkegaard. I can explain it this way: Think of the prose style of William Faulkner, those long sentences, sometimes pages long, but now replace all of the concrete nouns with abstract ones, trade action verbs for the passive voice, and on top of the American writer's one very simple theme of "inheritance by blood," pile on all manner of themes from philosophy, theology, and psychology. If you do this, you will have a close approximation of how Søren Kierkegaard wrote in Danish. To make matters more confusing, but also to get an appreciation of Kierkegaard's work, you must also account for the fact that Kierkegaard wrote most of his books under false names, pseudonyms, and these various made-up authors knew one another in some strange fictional way and referred to one another in their separate books, providing fictional reviews of fictional books. And then, toward the end of his life, when Kierkegaard takes off his mask, his other mask, his other mask, his other mask, and a few others behind that and addresses the question that must be burning in his reader's mind—"So, which of these 'authors' do you agree with most?"—the iconic, ironic Dane simply smiles slyly and says, in effect, "Aw heck, I don't even think of myself as their author. I'm more like their reader."

It is to this head-spinning universe of linguistic complexities that I come five days a week as English-language translator at the Søren Kierkegaard Research Center. What most Danes don't even try to understand, I have a pretty good grasp on. My reading comprehension of Danish, if we place Kierkegaard at the top of the difficulty scale, where he belongs, probably falls in the ninety-ninth percentile, with almost everyone else's falling below it. I don't mean to brag. But when you spend five days a week translating someone like Kierkegaard, you're bound to build up your reading muscles. I suppose the opposite is also true: being alone most of the time, I don't give myself many chances to speak Danish, and so those muscles have atrophied.

I finish my two pastries, both of which were delicious. One of them had melted chocolate inside its flaky crust shell, and the other had a thin layer of marzipan; both were topped with sliced almonds and coarse sugar glued on in some mysterious way, perhaps by an egg wash. Now I look at my watch and see that I have sat here for only five minutes. I come to the hardest part. With the pastries gone, nothing in this room interests me. But my work, which does interest me and is only a few steps down the hall, doesn't begin for another ten minutes. I wish there were a way to leap over time. When I look at the group, I notice that they have stopped talking and Rebekah is staring at me. The others seem to be looking at me, too, but less intensely.

"I saw you at the funeral yesterday," says Rebekah. "How are you holding up?"

I force myself to make eye contact with her, in order to be polite. It's one of the first lessons I learned in social interaction, and people seem to appreciate it.

"Ready to get back to work, that's all I can say!"

I give Rebekah a big smile. She smiles back and adjusts her red scarf. It amazes me how quickly she's learned to tie it just like Danish women do, with folds that fall both neatly and casually over her chest and with no sign of where the two ends of the scarf have disappeared to. Mette tried to teach me how to tie a scarf once—here, men wear them, too, even indoors—but it turned into a frustrating experience. I just couldn't get it; I couldn't understand the mechanics of scarf-tying, no matter how many times I tried. Given Rebekah's aptitude with scarfs, I believe she'll master spoken Danish in no time.

"Hey," I say, "your Danish is pretty good for being here just three months."

Lona and Anders look at each other, then they both look at Rebekah.

"But we weren't speaking in Danish," she says.

"No," I say, "but you've got the scarf thing down pat."

Rebekah nods her head. Anders and Lona laugh at something, I'm not sure what. It may be my use of the phrase "down pat," but I'm certain I've used it in the correct idiomatic fashion with the intent to further casual conversation among friends. Still, I may have gotten it wrong again—"it" being my effort to fit in with others. At the opposite end of the table, the three of them are grouped closely together, in the shape of a pyramid, with Anders at the tip and the two women on either side of the base. They sit less than ten feet away from me, but they may as well be in a different country, and not just Sweden. More like Saudi Arabia.

"Well, I know you were close to Mette," Rebekah says. "I just wanted to say I'm sorry."

I glance at my watch and see that it's almost time to leave. I scoot back my chair and start to stand up.

"You have some messages in your mailbox," says Anders.

"I'll check them later," I say. To my mind, there's no point in looking at them now. I've already walked past the main office, where the mailboxes are kept, and I'll be going that way when I leave for lunch. What's another few hours? And I want to get to work!

"Some of them are important," he says.

"They can wait."

The clock at Town Hall begins its half-hour chime.

"Okay," says Anders. "But you've got a guest coming at 8:30. I thought you might want to know about that."

His words reach me just as I am about to step through the doorway. I freeze, then turn back.

"Who?" I ask.

"I don't remember her name, but she's with the Police. From the Department of Personal and Violent Crime. She's been trying to reach you since yesterday morning. She couldn't believe it when I told her you don't have a cell phone."

"Or an email address," adds Lona.

I feel the floor underneath me giving away.

"I don't want to talk to her. Tell her to come back at 4:30, when I'm finished with my work."

The two women shake their heads. Anders throws up his arms as if signaling a touchdown. I don't know what they're trying to tell me, but I sense that this morning's exercise in social interaction has not gone well. And as soon as I step into the hallway I realize that the session will be extended. Damnation! I've left the meeting room too late. A woman in a wool jacket and knee-length leather boots stands in front of my office door. She has shoulder-length blonde hair, highlighted in the same way Mette had hers done, even after I told her that I thought she'd look better just letting it go gray.

"Daniel Peters?" the woman asks.

I nod.

"Ingrid Bendtner," she says, smiling. "I'm from the Copenhagen Police. I'd like to speak with you for a few minutes."

She has a pleasant face, round and full, and her smile is inviting. If it were 4:30 in the afternoon, I would be happy (or at least *happier*) to speak with her, but it's 8:30 in the morning, the half-hour chimes from the Town Hall clock have ended, and I have three pages from one of Kierkegaard's journals to translate before noon.

"May we speak in your office?" she asks.

She stands with her hands in her coat pockets. Her boot heels drip a tiny puddle of melted snow onto the floor. Most importantly, however, she's blocking the way into my office and the start of my day of work.

"No," I say.

She raises her eyebrows and juts her chin towards me, tilts her head slightly.

"Somewhere else, then?" she says. She looks both ways down the hall. "A meeting room, perhaps?"

"No, I don't want to talk to you. You can come back this afternoon. 4:30 would be convenient for me."

She raises her eyebrows again. They're like two lively caterpillars stretching their backs in tandem.

"I'm afraid that's not an option. I need to speak with you now. I understand that you were close to Mette Rasmussen, and her funeral was only yesterday. I appreciate that you may be grieving, but I have some questions that I need to ask you. I would appreciate your help."

I remain silent. There's a chance she'll leave. I look away from her and focus my attention on the framed drawing that hangs on the wall between my office and the one next door. It is a pen-and-ink caricature of Søren Kierkegaard that appeared in a Copenhagen magazine in the mid-1800s and shows the philosopher with his umbrella in hand and a top hat on his head. As in all the drawings of that period, Kierkegaard is dressed in trousers of uneven lengths and a short-tailed waistcoat that fits him poorly. He leans forward, as if his spine were severely curved, an artist's exaggeration, really. A wave of hair falls across his forehead, and his pinched face and beak nose make him look like some silly, exotic bird. I've looked at this picture a hundred times and always wondered how the artist could be so cruel. Kierkegaard, like me, just wanted to be left alone. When I turn back, Ingrid Bendtner is still standing in front of my door, her arms crossed, no smile on her face, and it dawns on me that I am not being given a choice in this matter. The sooner I answer her questions the sooner I can get on with my work. I brush past her and open my door. When I step inside, she follows me.

Whenever a new guest comes into my office, they always notice my Laurel and Hardy poster. Mette encouraged me to hang it on my wall, just inside the door, as a way to facilitate small talk, which I personally hate but which all sources agree is a necessary prelude to meaningful conversation.

"Are you a fan?" Ingrid asks and gestures to the poster where Stan and Ollie stand side by side in sailor suits looking quite ridiculous.

"Sure," I say. "Everybody loves a good laugh."

I sit at my desk and wait for her to have a seat, but she's still standing in front of the poster. She takes a step closer and studies it. This surprises me because I don't expect a police officer to appreciate the hidden meanings in that image. With visiting scholars I count on their intellectual curiosity, and I have a whole speech prepared for them. I wonder if she'll want to hear it, too.

"There are words here," she says, looking at me over her shoulder. "They're not English or Danish. What do they mean?"

I stand up and walk toward her.

"The word across their sailor hats is the Greek for utopia. Of course, utopia is a Greek word, in origin, the combination of *ou*, meaning not, and *topos*, meaning place. The word is meant to describe a perfect place with ideal conditions for its inhabitants, so there's a certain irony in calling it the 'not-place.'"

I wait a moment for her to take that in. Most people chuckle to themselves, but Ingrid Bendtner does not. I point to the top right corner of the picture.

"And there in the sky above the ship's mast," I say, "you have 'Thomas Morus,' which is Sir Thomas More's name rendered in Latin, New Latin to be specific. He published his *Libellus de optimo reipublicae statu, deque nova insula Utopia* in 1516. And here is where the picture gets really funny. In More's work, Utopia is an island, *insula*, and so that's where the two sailors, Laurel and Hardy, must be headed. Or maybe they've already landed there. The poster doesn't make it clear. Are we to fear that they will ruin the perfectly rational island of Utopia, or are they part of its welcoming committee? Has everything been turned on its head and the real rulers of Utopia are a couple of slapstick comedians? The poster raises questions instead of answering them. And one of the questions, of course, is whether the questions themselves should be taken seriously. I mean, you have Laurel and Hardy in the foreground staring you right in the face. You have to ask yourself, is this all a joke?"

I laugh, but Ingrid Bendtner does not.

"It just seems like an odd poster for a research center," she says and sits down in a chair.

"No," I say. "Not at all. Not at all. Not when the subject of research is Søren Kierkegaard. For over a century scholars have asked themselves how to read that man's work. When does he mean what he says? If that picture is hard to figure out, Kierkegaard is a hundred times more so. Do you know what the title of his dissertation was? It's called *On the Concept of Irony, with Continual Reference to Socrates*. And irony, in its simplest form, is saying one thing and meaning another. Of course, we know what Kierkegaard said, but it's hard to know how he meant it. Sometimes it's obviously meant ironically; other times it's not so clear. As his translator, I would seem to have the easiest job in this building. All I'm supposed to do is change the Danish into English. I can tell you, it's not that simple! One word in isolation might be easy to translate: *stol*, chair; *bord*, desk; *vindue*, window. But what if I say, 'Nice table and chair next to the window'? Maybe I don't mean it's a nice table and chair at all, but the exact opposite. And maybe the only clue is that I didn't start the sentence with the words 'It's a . . . ,' and their omission is a tacit sign of irony. But maybe not. Maybe I really mean that it's a nice table and chair, and if I'd wanted to be taken ironically I would have said, 'Nice table and chair over there by that window,' and the words 'over there by' and the somewhat derisive 'that' would tip the balance in favor of irony. It's a hard job, letting irony come into my translation when it belongs there and keeping it out when it doesn't. It's a hard job because I can't always tell how Kierkegaard wanted to be taken, and my colleagues don't always agree with one another. In fact, they seldom do. You know, even when I'm sure that Kierkegaard *was* being ironic, I still have the difficulty of conveying the right level of irony in my translation. I don't want to overdo it when he's being subtle. But what if I'm too subtle and my English audience doesn't catch on? That's a problem, too! Well, Kierkegaard—through one of his pseudonyms, of course—did say that it was his job to 'create difficulties everywhere,' so I suppose he wanted to give his translator a challenge or two. And he certainly has, I can tell you that."

I am standing and leaning over my guest's chair and she is looking up at me with a strange expression on her face when it suddenly occurs to me that I've probably done it again: said more than the other person cared to hear. Verbosity, especially on subjects of extreme personal interest, is common in people like me, but usually the guests who come in here share my interest in Kierkegaard. And they have something they can tell me to increase my knowledge. Ingrid Bendtner, I realize too late, is only interested in burglary and murder, subjects which I hope we'll get through quickly so I can return to my work. I have a seat and wait for her to ask me a question.

"Before we begin, I want to extend my condolences," she says. "I understand that you worked with Mette for eighteen years. . . ."

"Actually, I knew her longer than that. We met when I was an exchange student in Kolding, from 1985–1986. During most of that year, she was my girlfriend."

"I didn't know that."

"Yeah, we kept in touch afterwards. But then she met Peter and I was out of the picture!"

"I see. So this must be difficult for you, and I want you to know . . ."

"Actually, it hasn't been as difficult as I hoped it would be, in terms of grief and all that. I've tried grieving, but it just doesn't come. I'm not sure why. I've tried to bring it on, you know, but no dice."

"That's surprising," says Ingrid, whose eyebrows arch their backs again and seem to me the most surprising things in the room just now.

"You win some, you lose some," I say.

I believe that's the right expression for this context. But maybe not. Where do you find the script for talking to a police officer about your former girlfriend and your inability to grieve her death? It's so much easier translating Kierkegaard's words than coming up with my own. I check my watch and see that I've already lost five minutes of my workday.

"I'd like to ask you about your last encounter with Mette," says Ingrid. "When did you see her last?"

Now we're into that stuff. I sigh and look out the window. In the courtyard about a dozen children are bundled up in winter jackets and shuffling around in their snow boots. They must be from the day care in the building next door to ours. A few of them ride kiddy bikes up and down the stretch of cobblestone, and not one of them falls over, even though the stones are wet from this morning's snow. I wonder: if I'd been born in Denmark would I have inherited a bike-riding gene that would have counterbalanced my Asperger's and allowed me to join them? Two children are playing at a sword fight in front of the statue of N.F.S. Grundtvig. The old reformer and hymn writer wears the same costume as Jesper Olsen—long robe with fat buttons down the middle, the piped collar with its ridges jutting out around his neck. But unlike Jesper in his vestments, Grundtvig never makes me want to laugh. He is a serious, solid man carved in stone, unquestionably pious, presiding over this courtyard and the church that lines one side of it. It's actually referred to as "Grundtvig's Church," and the worshippers who meet there are called "Grundtvigians." In his lifetime, Kierkegaard despised the whole lot of them, most notably his own brother.

"Daniel?" Ingrid says, kindly I think. "I'm sorry, but I really do need you to answer my question. When was the last time you saw Mette?"

"After work last Thursday. We had dinner at her place. Pork with crackling, sugared potatoes, red cabbage, and asier pickles. That's my favorite! And Mette makes it the best. She was teaching me about the sugared potatoes, which I can never get right . . . ."

"Excuse me. Are you sure it was last Thursday, the night she was murdered?"

"Yes."

"What time did you leave?"

"Just before midnight. I wanted to hear the twelve o'clock chimes from Town Hall. I usually hear them from my apartment, but they sound different when you're outside on street level. And best when you're walking towards them."

"Did you see anyone on your walk home?"

"Yes. I walked partway up Strøget. Lots of people were coming out of bars. It wasn't real busy, though, not like in the summertime."

Ingrid nods her head. "Did you talk with anyone? Anyone who could verify that they saw you?"

"Well, I saw a guy named Mohammad. We talked for a while. He was looking for the bus station, but I couldn't help him. I never ride the bus."

"Could you get in touch with this Mohammad?"

What an odd question, I think. Why would I want to get in touch with someone I barely know? But to satisfy whatever it is that Ingrid Bendtner needs from me so she can go back to the police station and write her report and I can finally begin my work day, I answer her question as completely as possible.

"I don't know exactly how to contact Mohammad. He told me he's from Somalia, originally, but he's lived in Denmark for the last twenty years. He has Danish citizenship, he said."

"So, he lives here?"

"Yes. In Odense, with his wife and kids. When he told me that, I said, 'Oh, you live in Hans Christian Andersen's birthplace! Have you ever heard of his contemporary, Søren Kierkegaard?' He hadn't. And wouldn't you know, we were standing right in the middle of Nytorv, only a few steps from Danske Bank, which of course is where Kierkegaard lived with his family from 1813–1837, then again from 1844–1848. The original building has been torn down, but the one that was erected in its place has a plaque commemorating Kierkegaard. So Mohammad and I walked over to the plaque and I read it out loud to him. Mohammad didn't seem all that interested, even after I explained to him how important Kierkegaard had been to Danish culture and to intellectual history in general. He just walked away. I haven't seen him since."

Ingrid waits for me to finish, which may be a sign that she is interested in what I'm saying, or she may simply be a patient person. I have not learned how to distinguish between the two.

"We can check the CCTV cameras in Nytorv. There might be an image of you. If not, we'll ask help from the station in Odense. I doubt there are very many Somali families living there. If we need to, we can get in touch with Mohammad."

"Please give him my greetings," I say.

Ingrid smiles, which brightens her face and makes me like her more. She's not as pretty as Mette, I decide, but close. Although their hair is the same color and length, Mette wore hers down and constantly had to tuck loose strands of it behind her ear. The very movement of her hand reaching out and smoothing back her hair thrilled me more times than I can count. Ingrid, on the other hand, wears her hair in a ponytail, which is cute, but also a little girlish.

"Let me ask you something about the manuscript," Ingrid says. "We don't think that you took it because you left this building at 4:31 the day that Mette was murdered and you haven't returned until this morning. There's a CCTV camera above the door."

"There is?" I say.

"Yes. You pass in front of it every time you come into work."

"I had no idea."

"There is also a camera outside the vault where the manuscripts are kept."

"Oh," I say, laughing, "The vault! I've never seen the Center's vault. I'm not sure it really exists. I think it's a fable the philologists invented to make themselves feel more important."

"It really exists. I've been inside it. And it's where Mette returned the manuscript before she left at 5:15 on Thursday evening. As an additional precaution, she kept the manuscript inside a locked box, as you probably know."

"Yes," I say, looking directly into Ingrid's eyes and trying to force myself to sound interested. "She had the only key. She kept it in her briefcase and took it home with her every night. She was the only one who had access to the manuscript."

"That's right. We thought the key was still in her home, in her briefcase, after she was murdered. One of my colleagues described the key to the Center's secretary . . ."

"That would be Anders," I say.

"To Anders, and he confirmed that it was most likely the key to the box. So we assumed that the manuscript was safe. At the time, please understand, we thought we were looking for a vagabond thief, an opportunist who saw a wealthy woman entering the door to her home and took advantage of the situation. The entryway showed clear signs of a physical struggle between them."

"What kind of signs?" I ask. I feel excited because I know something about the state of Mette's entryway just before I left her for the last time. I think I might be able to help out Ingrid Bendtner and the Copenhagen Police.

"The railing leading up the stairs was broken off its bracket," says Ingrid. "Fresh scuff marks were found on the walls. A lab report identified the marks as coming from the soles of a pair of men's shoes, and considerable energy went into analyzing the tread pattern. The marks were the only physical evidence we had tying the perpetrator to the crime."

While Ingrid talks I begin unlacing my right shoe. Now that she's finished, I remove it and hand it to her with a smile. As she looks over my shoe, I roll up the sleeve of my jacket.

"I fell down Mette's stairs," I say. "Here's the bruise to prove it, although the scuff marks are probably even better."

"Thank you," she says and hands me back my shoe. She looks into my eyes for a few seconds before continuing. I try not to look away because I know that eye contact is an important part of communicating interest to another person.

"As I was going to say, we now have reason to believe that the forced entry may have been constructed."

"That was no construct," I say. "It was an accident and a painful one at that!"

"The reason we began to doubt the crime scene has to do with what I'll say next. When we returned the key to the Center yesterday morning, we discovered that it did not fit the box's lock. It appears that someone took the original key from Mette's briefcase and replaced it with a fake. This means the manuscript may have been taken from the vault anytime over the last five days. From viewing the CCTV tapes we know that only four people went in and out of the vault during that time period. I wonder—this might be awkward for you—but I'd like to ask you if you think any of these people would be more likely than the others to want to take the manuscript."

She passes me a sheet of paper with four names on it. I don't even have to look at it. The only staff members who know the code to open the vault are the philologists. But just to be sure, and in order to communicate my willingness to help, I glance down the list:

Lars Andersen
Lona Brøchner
Annette Rifbjerg
Per Aage Simonsen

"Well, it wouldn't be Lars!" I say.

"Really," says Ingrid. "How do you know that?"

"Lars wasn't interested in the new manuscript. He was one of only two staff members who declined the opportunity to see it when it was brought over from the Royal Library. The other person was me: I didn't care to strain my eyes on another Kierkegaard manuscript. Mette transcribed it for me."

"What about the next person on the list: Lona Brøchner?"

"Yeah, she might have taken it. She threw a fit when Mette wouldn't let her have access to the manuscript—except for the ten minutes everyone else got. Yeah, she probably took it. But I'm sure she'll give it back. Just ask her for it."

I return the list to Ingrid and smile. Now, I think, we must finally be finished. I have solved the mystery of the crime scene and uncovered the person who stole the manuscript. What more could the Police want from me? But for some reason Ingrid doesn't stand up to leave. She holds the list of names in her hands and studies it closely.

"What about the other two names?"

"Per Aage and Annette? No, they're too busy finishing their commentaries for the last volumes of *Søren Kierkegaard's Writings*. The Center is supposed to present the complete series to the University on Kierkegaard's 200th birthday, which is coming up on May 5th. Per Aage and Annette are taking microscopes to little scraps of paper where Kierkegaard jotted down notes that make no sense at all to anyone, but have to be studied and commented upon before we can say in all scholarly honesty that we've done our job. Those two don't have time for the new manuscript. They were happy to leave it to Mette."

"I see. But there might be other reasons for their wanting the manuscript."

"None that I can think of. It looks like Lona took it. All you have to do is ask her to give it back. She's nice, Lona is. I had coffee with her just this morning. Is there anything else you needed to ask me?"

"I'd really appreciate it if you gave the matter more thoughtful consideration," she says. "It would be helpful, for instance, to know about the interrelationships of the staff at the Center—and you've been here longer than anyone. Maybe someone with access to the vault took the manuscript for one of their colleagues. Or perhaps they had a pressing need for money and planned to sell the manuscript. We haven't received a ransom letter yet, but we are aware of that possibility."

"What? Someone stole the manuscript and is holding it hostage?" I say and laugh. "Some kind of literary terrorist organization!"

Ingrid Bendtner, I notice, is not laughing.

"Please give my questions some more thought," she says.

She reaches into her coat pocket and pulls out a business card, handing it to me as she stands up. When I read the card I see that Anders was right—she's from the Department of Personal and Violent Crime. Underneath the department heading there is a list of the crimes they're responsible for investigating: homicide, burglary, domestic violence, and child abuse.

"Which of the crimes do you specialize in?" I ask. This is Denmark, after all, and everyone has a specialty, usually a very specific one.

"Homicide," she says. "But don't worry, Daniel. I'm sure we'll find your image on one of the CCTV cameras in Nytorv. I'm not ready to take you down to the police station just yet."

"Of course not," I say. "Why would you?"

"Because, at least at this point, you don't have an alibi. You were the last person to see Mette Rasmussen alive—only an hour before she was murdered, according to what you've told me. And, as your shoes indicate, there is physical evidence tying you to the place of the crime. I won't ask you for them now, but you must not dispose of those shoes until the investigation is completed. We may need you to surrender them as evidence. I'll ask my Team Leader and let you know what he decides."

I nod my head, into which something important has just sunk: I'm a suspect in a murder case.

As Ingrid Bendtner is walking out of my office, I realize that in all the time we've talked, I never asked her if she wanted me to take her coat. In fact, I haven't taken my own coat off. It feels heavy and much too warm.

"If you think of something, anything, related to the list and what I've asked you about it," she says, "please call me."

"I will," I promise. As she leaves I watch her ponytail swing from one shoulder to the next. From where I'm sitting now, it doesn't look so girlish after all.

Chapter 3

I spend the morning in a way I had not expected to. On an ordinary weekday morning I would be engrossed in a translation problem requiring my full attention. Kierkegaard's original text would be placed to my right, propped up on my wooden book stand. To my left would be a volume or two of the *ODS, Ordbog over det danske sprog,* the Danish equivalent of the *OED,* with detailed etymologies, first-use histories, and exhaustive lists of variant meanings. A truly difficult word or phrase might occupy me for an hour, easily. Only after settling the matter without a single doubt in my mind would I lift my pencil and write my translation into one of the exercise booklets that I've used ever since my days as an exchange student. If I've done everything I can to penetrate the problem and still haven't found a solution, I would then mark the passage and add it to the list of questions to ask Mette at our regular weekly meeting. But Mette and I will no longer be having those meetings. Whatever problems I have from here on out I won't be bringing them to her, including the problem which her death (murder is the more accurate term) now poses.

And so I take the cloth-bound volume containing the Danish of Kierkegaard's *Journals AA-BB-CC-DD* and place it in a drawer. I fold up my book stand and place it in another. I leave the *ODS* on its shelf. And I start looking for a solution I'm not likely to find in books alone: who, among those people I work with on a daily basis, would want to steal a manuscript, and would want to do so so much as to kill another person? The question presents itself wrapped in a foreign language and written in an alphabet I don't know how to read. But I'm motivated to learn because self-interestedness is great in me, is hardwired into my brain as with few others. I don't want to go to jail. I don't want to get kicked out of Denmark.

The fear that my life might change radically is not only in my thoughts. It has gripped me in the belly, too, the place where one of my college professors said all existential questions announce themselves. I was only nineteen at the time and nodded my head as though I understood him. Now, only now, do I believe I get him, loud and clear. After two decades of translating the so-called "father of existentialism," finding the right language to convey his ironic or non-ironic writings about anxiety, despair, and passionate subjectivity, I suddenly feel all the analytical distance between us disappear. *Poof!* The safe fortress of dictionaries is blown to smithereens and I'm standing with a cannon aimed at my chest.

If I am to answer the question Ingrid Bendtner asked me—What are the interrelationships among the staff at the Center?—I'll have to do something I've never done in my life. I'll have to relate with others, and not only when I'm forced to or accidentally happen to, but on purpose, up-close and personal.

As a modest beginning to what may be a long and difficult process, I take out four exercise booklets and place them in a pile on the desk before me. Kierkegaard, when he began a new work, would take a small square card and snip the edges of all four corners. Then, in his neatest hand, he would write the work's title on the card and carefully glue it dead-center on the front cover. I don't have heavy card stock or scissors or glue in my desk, so I take my pencil and draw the shape on the front of each booklet. Inside these edge-clipped squares I write the names of four colleagues, one for each booklet. I spread them out on my desk, arranging them into a big square, then rest my eyes on one name at a time: Lars Andersen, Lona Brøchner, Annette Rifbjerg, Per Aage Simonsen.

I shake my head, which hasn't a single idea for how to begin. I don't know these people. I don't even know how to approach them. Why, I wonder, can't they be looked up in a book, as words can be looked up in a dictionary? It would be so much easier if they appeared on pages, arranged in columns, starting with their life histories and proceeding to their variant and associative meanings. If I could find them there, I could get down to work and finish in a timely manner; then I could return to Kierkegaard, translating what he says about existentialism rather than living it.

Truly, I don't know how to begin.

I stand up and take off my coat. As I walk over to my coat rack, my hat falls out of a pocket and lands on the floor behind me. When I reach down and snatch it up (or perhaps it is a second later, when

I shake it in my hand to dust it off) a thought occurs to me. When you lose something, my mother used to tell me, go back to the place where you remember having it last. Start your search from there. The advice has worked for me many times in the past with this very hat, my favorite one and hard to replace: red-and-black checkered, with a flannel lining, and with ear flaps that tie with a string, not the dreaded Velcro. I have lost then found this hat in the Reading Room of the Old Royal Library, in the Main Train Station, on three different water taxis, on a bench beside Pebbling Lake, at Mette's house, on the Metro between the city center and the airport, and in various rooms in my own apartment. It was a gift from my mother (now departed) and I have kept it for over half of my life. The truth is, if I really want something, I persist until I get it. Call it Asperger's-induced stubbornness. It keeps my head warm.

What I've lost now is my peaceful and stable life. Where was the last place I had it? I would have to go back further than this morning, just before my meeting with Ingrid Bendtner. I would have to go back further than Mette's funeral, further even than her murder. I would have to go back to the afternoon when I learned that a manuscript that no one in the Center believed could possibly exist did, according to Mette herself, in fact exist. That was the second Thursday of December, in Mette's office. And that is where I decide I have to go.

The first book I read by Kierkegaard was *Repetition*, written under the pseudonym of Constantin Constantius. I found the book in the Kolding Public Library, where Mette and I had gone together in direct disobedience of our Danish Literature teacher who told our class, "Whatever you do, don't start reading Kierkegaard! You'll only regret it." But I didn't regret reading *Repetition*; I loved it and I identified with its narrator, Constantin, who like me wants one simple thing: a life of predictable, repeated patterns. Everything in its place, each event according to a schedule. But then something happens to disturb Constantin's world. He comes home one day and finds that his house servant has moved all of the furniture outside in order to sweep the house. The sight of his front lawn looking like a living room is too much for Constantin, who flies into a rage. He wants to have the servant flogged, boiled in oil, hung up by his ears from Knippel's bridge, shot through by arrows of a hundred archers kneeling on the canal bank, then finished off with a cannonball or two. Although Constantin's reaction is somewhat exaggerated, I can't help taking his side. No one, it seems to me, should mess with another person's sense of order. Least of all mine. It makes me angry at whoever killed Mette and stole the new

Kierkegaard manuscript; but not, sadly, because I mourn the loss of a former girlfriend and a priceless manuscript. (I wish I could; I wish I did.) No, I miss the way life was for me just over a month ago, when I could count on the same schedule, every day, day after day.

Repetition. I never understand it when people talk about getting stuck in a rut as though that's a bad thing. Constantin Constantius wants, if anything, to extend the depth of his rut. He knows he can have his bookshelf returned to the library and the books put back on the exact same shelves in the exact same order—there's no problem duplicating the physical world. But what, he wonders, about the nonphysical world, such things as moods and feelings? He would like, of course, to have control over this area, too. Who wouldn't? So he decides on an experiment. He remembers an enjoyable stay he once had in Berlin, the fine hotel where he boarded and a theater nearby where a particularly entertaining farce was being played. Could he repeat this trip and thereby repeat the feelings he had? He tries. He rides the same carriage, books in at the same hotel, attends the same farce in the same theater. Much of the physical experience is unchanged—the same bumpy carriage ride, the same dining room with its chandelier over the table, the same actors playing their silly, silly roles on stage. But try as he might, Constantin cannot recapture what he remembers feeling—he can remember what he felt, but he can't re-feel it.

My experience in Mette's office is along these same lines. Some essence is missing—was here but is here no more. It doesn't help, of course, that to get inside I have to ask Anders for the key, something I've never had to do before. Nor can I look past the changes that greet me as I stand before her door, where someone has decided to make a shrine. Notes on colored paper, folded in half so you have to peek inside to read them, are taped to the door frame. I have never appreciated this custom. Why write notes to the dead only to have them read by the living? It doesn't make sense to me.

And now, standing inside Mette's office, I have the opposite problem. Nothing new has been added, but something very important has been subtracted: Mette. How can I bring her back? I can't, not even with my mind, which is poorer than most people's when it comes to visual memory. What was she wearing that day? No idea. What was the weather like outside her window? I'm clueless. Was the lamp on her desk lit or turned off? I simply don't remember. As I look around the room, I see what I've always seen in here: three full bookcases at each end of the room, reaching almost to the ceiling; her desk and chair, both antique; a long work table with separate piles of books and papers arranged in a particular order, known only to her, for writing her next book.

I walk over to the table and look down at the piles. Of course, I know what Mette was writing about; she didn't keep it a secret from me. She had even asked my permission, some years ago before she started, worried that I might take offense. It had come as a surprise to both of us that no one had yet written a book, not even a journal article, conjecturing that Søren Kierkegaard's chief mental abnormality might have been Asperger's. Plenty of authors had pegged him as Depressed—he referred to himself as a "Melancholic"—and others have insisted on Bipolar, Obsessive-Compulsive, or Anxiety Disorder. All had their reasons for seeing him so. But Mette was onto something different, and possibly truer. None of the other diagnoses could explain Kierkegaard's strange gait when walking, something many of his contemporaries commented on, noting how difficult it was to walk down the sidewalk with him without being bumped into or forced up against a building. There are also stories of his falling down unexpectedly. According to one of the more famous, Kierkegaard was at a party when he suddenly lost his balance and fell to the floor. He remained there looking up at the other guests and said, "Just leave the body where it is. The maid can sweep it up in the morning." Previous researchers had suggested that Kierkegaard might have had a mild form of epilepsy, but then again maybe he was clumsy, as I am. It fits with Mette's theory.

I would like to feel sorry that Mette never got the chance to complete her work, but I don't. I don't feel sorry. I don't feel much of anything. I suppose she had an interesting thesis, and given her position as the head of the world's premier center for Kierkegaard studies, she would have found a publisher for her work. Maybe it would have won a prize. I wouldn't have cared if it did, so I don't care that it didn't. She expressed frustration with me at times. How could I not care that Kierkegaard had the same condition that I have—how could I not be interested in that? I wasn't. I'm not. If he was like me, then Kierkegaard wouldn't have cared either—he would only have cared about his own work which, as it turns out, was a common complaint his contemporaries had against him.

More distracted than anything else, I rifle through the piles until I find something that truly does interest me. In the journal *Autism Outlook* Mette has placed a bookmark at the beginning of an article titled "Risk Factors Pointing to Violent Tendencies among People with Asperger's Syndrome, Concluding with a Proposed Predictive Scale: A Meta-Study." It makes me wonder: Did Mette think that I might be violent? To her?

By the second page, I see that she was in fact thinking of me. Who else could she be referring to in marginal notes about "D"? She has also made notes on "S," and that of course must be Søren Kierkeg-aard. The notes all follow the same pattern—beside each initial, every time it appears, Mette has written either a plus or a minus sign. When I look at the corresponding text, it always mentions a specific factor that, according to the author, would increase the likelihood of violence in a person with Asperger's. I get a minus for alcohol consumption; Søren gets a plus. We both get a plus for family history of mental ill-ness—my mother had Schizophrenia; Søren's father certainly had something wrong with him, probably Depression, and his brother spent the last years of his life in an asylum. As I flip through the pages and count up the plus signs, I feel strangely competitive with Søren Kierkegaard. Who will win this contest? And which score will deter-mine the winner, the lower or the higher tally?

It turns out to be not even close. Søren annihilates me, 12-3. Or I cream him. Take your pick. It doesn't seem to matter since Kierkegaard, who according to the predictive chart at the end of the article is at a high risk of violent behavior, never physically abused anyone in his life-time. What he did with his words was a different matter, and several of his contemporaries complained about Kierkegaard's verbal abuse, but there are no records of his taking a punch, swinging a club, or driving a knife into another person, even the ones he wrote about most savagely in his journals. And as for me, a score of 3 puts me in the company of pussycats. I didn't think I was violent, or prone to it, but would an article like this one have any bearing with Ingrid Bendt-ner and the Copenhagen Police? Probably not. To clear my name, I'll have to rely instead on a well-placed CCTV camera or an itinerant Somali Dane named Mohammad. Or else find out who really did kill Mette and steal the manuscript.

I put the journal back in its place, exactly where I found it—it's curious that I feel I have to do this, as if Mette would be coming into work again and might be upset at me for misplacing her things; but I respect order, even that of the dead.

As I am closing the door of Mette's office, I see Rebekah walking down the hallway toward me. She has her hand in the air, palm out, as if she were caught between waving to me or ordering me to stop. It's a confusing message. I wait to hear what she'll say.

"You have a phone call, Daniel. Anders asked me to tell you. He'll hold it for another minute."

"Okay," I say. I walk past her in the direction of the office. After a few steps, I notice that she's following me.

"You know, when you have some time I'd love to talk with you about the new manuscript. Lona told me there was an entire section devoted to the Religious stage, and that really interests me. Let me know when we can talk, okay?"

I nod my head and keep walking. Rebekah isn't on my list, so she's not a person of much interest to me. Unless she has some interrelationship with Lona. I stop and turn back.

"Are you and Lona friends?" I ask.

Rebekah smiles. "Yes. I really appreciate her. You know what they say about the Danes, that '*de er ikke så nem at kom i kontakt med*,' they're kind of clannish, you know. But Lona and Anders make me feel welcome. Not everyone around here does."

"I guess if you want to, you can find a clan to join."

"But you don't want to?"

I laugh. I'm not entirely sure why.

I step into the main office and find Anders standing behind a huge reception desk, wide in the middle and tapered at each end. It looks like an upturned Viking longship. Behind it are two smaller desks, each with a computer and telephone. One of the phones is off the hook, so I walk up to it and lift the receiver. I've taken my calls in the main office ever since I started working at the Center, and I wouldn't want it any other way. Mette thought I'd want more privacy, but I'd much rather have my own office free of a ringing telephone. Few noises are more irritating to me.

The person on the other end is Birgit Fisker-Steensen from the Copenhagen Museum. After scolding me in a playful tone about not returning her call for two days, she tells me what she wants.

"I've been so depressed ever since I learned that the manuscript was stolen, and the only thing that's given me any hope is knowing that you were working on a translation of it. Tell me, Daniel, how much of it did you finish?"

"All of it," I say.

"Oh, thank God! So at least we have the text in English. When can I have it? We are still planning on a one-week exhibit in February. Of course, I hope the Police have found the original by then, but we could get by with just the English."

"With just the English," I say.

"Sorry. When can you send it to me, Daniel? I'd like to get started as soon as possible."

"I'll tell Anders to send it to you today."

"That would be great."

After I hang up I walk over to Anders. He's sorting papers, pulling sheets from several piles stacked on the reception desk and making a new pile with the collated groupings. Anders' hands move quickly, without ever dropping a single page. It looks like sheer drudgery, and the job doesn't suit him, even if he is good at it. I've always thought that Anders looked more like a Norse god or a Viking warrior—he has a bodybuilder's physique, which he shows off by wearing short-sleeved shirts even in winter—and I could easily imagine him kicking over this desk and standing inside it at the prow, a shield in one hand and a sword in the other, off to raid another English monastery. He looks up at me and smiles.

"Can I help you?"

"Birgit Fisker-Steensen at the Copenhagen Museum wants the manuscript sent to her. Can you do that with the email?"

"What?"

"The email. The computer."

Anders puts down a stack of papers and looks at me closely.

"You have an email you want to send Birgit?"

"No! I'm not sending anyone an email. The manuscript—that's the thing to send with the email."

"Do you mean you want me to email her the manuscript?"

"Yes. Did I say something wrong?"

"It was a little confusing, but I think I understand what you mean. Now, which manuscript do you want me to email her?"

"The new one. My translation of it."

"The new Kierkegaard manuscript? The one that's stolen?"

"Well, Kierkegaard's manuscript was stolen, but my translation wasn't. You typed it up. In your computer. That's where you have the email, right?"

"I never typed your translation."

"Anders, you always type my translations! Don't kid with me."

"I'm not kidding. I never saw your translation. You never gave it to me."

"But I gave it to Mette. She was supposed to give it to you."

"She didn't."

"She didn't?"

"No, she didn't."

I am standing and staring at Anders, and he is standing and staring at me, when the sound of whispered voices reaches us from the hall. Two people walk into the office—Lona Brøchner and Carsten Rasmussen. They stand side by side and make an odd pair. Carsten is tall and slender and dresses stylishly. He's wearing a black sweater with a collar that looks like a turtleneck sliced down one side, folded over, and buttoned back together. His pants fit him snugly, even though they seem to be falling off his hips. I'm sure there are names for such clothes, but I don't have that particular vocabulary. All I know is that I routinely see the dummies in the display windows of the most expensive fashion stores wearing the clothes that Carsten wore a month or so earlier, as if they've been dressed in his hand-me-downs. Lona, on the other hand, is short and slightly overweight. She's let her hair, which is cut page-boy style, go gray. And she seems to have chosen her pantsuit to match the faded manuscripts she spends her days studying: she's dressed in what you might call "archive camouflage."

"Anders," says Lona, "I need the key to Mette's office."

"Daniel has it," he says.

Now Lona fixes her eyes on me and squints, as she did when I saw her in the line at Mette's funeral. I can never understand what her silent looks mean.

"What did you want in Mette's office?" she asks.

"Something I didn't find. But I'm going back there now. I'll leave the door open when I'm done."

I start to walk past them, but Lona reaches out and grabs my arm.

"Hold on," she says. "Just hold on. First of all, give me the key. It doesn't belong to you."

"It doesn't belong to you either," I say. I can feel the tips of my ears burning. There's a tightness in my chest.

Carsten starts to laugh. I look around and see him leaning against the reception desk with his hands in his pockets. Only the tips of his fingers can fit inside them. He looks ridiculous, I think, but I suppose this is what counts for cool today, or will tomorrow.

"Actually, Daniel, the key does belong to her. She's my mom's literary executor. That's what I came in today to tell her. We had an initial reading of the will last night."

"Literary executor?"

"Yes," says Lona. "You know what that means, don't you?"

"Of course I do. But she wouldn't have picked you."

Lona shakes her head. Why does Lona shake her head?

"I'm sorry, Daniel, but she did. And I am. May I please have the key?"

Lona holds out her hand. The other two stare at me and I feel like I'm burning up in their eyes. My throat has closed and tears are coming into my eyes. I feel the way I sometimes did in elementary school when other kids picked on me. There was never any winning, only the hope of retreat. I reach into my pocket and hand the key to Lona. As soon as she has it I start out the door.

"Wait," says Lona. "What were you looking for? If I find it, I'll bring it to you."

I shake my head and continue walking away. I have to get away from them. I have to. In my ears I hear a pounding, which may be my feet clomping up and down on the floor, or my blood pumping, or some drum beaten by a member of a clan I don't belong to, but with whom I am at war, for reasons I don't understand, so what can I do but flee?

After a lunch eaten outdoors in the courtyard, regardless of the cold and senseless of my surroundings, I now sit at my desk in a calmer state of mind. I am thinking of Søren Kierkegaard's work titled *The Concept of Anxiety* and remembering the distinction he makes there between fear (which has a well-defined object and will occur imminently) and anxiety (which remains mysterious both in what it is and when it will get you). With anxiety, all you know is that something has gone fatally wrong; all you have is a vague sense of a penalty you can't possibly pay. For Kierkegaard, the problem reaches back to the beginning of time, to the sin of Adam, which every human inherits as the common birthright and curse of existence. "To live is to suffer," he wrote, more than once. "The sufferer must assist in the cure of his own suffering," he told himself as much as his readers. As his translator, I have read these words more closely than anyone—I have had to in order to get the English just right—but until recently I have not applied what he wrote to my life. It is a small comfort to name what I am feeling now: anxiety. But still it is a comfort.

I have written a couple of sentences into the booklet with Lona's name on it when somebody knocks at my door.

"Daniel," says Lona from the other side, "Anders told me what you lost. I'm really sorry. May I talk with you for a minute?"

I slip the booklet into my desk drawer, then stand up and open the door. Lona is not alone. Carsten is with her. They both come in, but since there are only two chairs in my office and I've already taken the one at my desk, they have to decide which of them will get the other one. Carsten insists that Lona take it. Gallantry, I suppose. It allows him to stand with his arms folded over his chest and look down at us with a smirk on his face. It leaves him free to walk a few paces around my office, to stare briefly at the Laurel and Hardy poster, to laugh as though whatever the joke is, he gets it. He probably doesn't, but I've already given the speech once today, and I decide that even if he asks for it, I won't give it to him. This attitude, I believe, is called childishness. Kierkegaard often exhibited it, but he never accused himself of it. Maybe I'm one step ahead of him on that scale of emotional maturity.

"Carsten and I have spent the last two hours searching Mette's office," says Lona. "It's not there. And I know how you must be feeling. I lost the manuscript for my first book—five hundred typewritten pages—all because I didn't save it someplace other than my computer. The computer crashed, and I lost everything. It was months of work. I felt absolutely sick. I had to go back to my notes and start all over again."

"At least you had your notes," I say.

"Just as you have your drafts, right?"

I shake my head.

"You didn't save your drafts?"

"That's not how I work. I don't make drafts. Unlike Kierkegaard, I'm not interested in leaving behind a pile of waste."

"Well, I wouldn't call it waste," says Lona. "Each draft has its own claim to completeness and to superiority over the others, even subsequent ones. That's why Kierkegaard saved everything. He could never be entirely sure."

"No," I say, "he saved everything because he was a pack rat."

From a corner of the room Carsten chuckles.

"Seems like I've heard this argument before," he says.

When I look over at him, he's pulled a volume of the *ODS* off its shelf and is leafing through it. I've never thought of him as someone who's interested in words. Maybe he's just bored.

"You're right," Lona tells Carsten. "We don't need to rehearse that old thing." Then she addresses me, "But what about the transcription Mette made for you? Didn't she go through the manuscript and make a master version for your translation?"

"Yes," I say, "very 'old philology' of her, wasn't it? I gave her back the transcription with my manuscript." Suddenly I feel hopeful. "But she must have typed the transcription on her computer. Maybe it's still inside there."

Lona shakes her head. "We've already checked. I was hoping you'd have a copy."

From another corner of my office, Carsten chuckles. He's like some kind of witch doctor laughing a circle around me, casting a spell. I probably shouldn't be annoyed with him—he's lost his mother three years after losing his father; he's a twenty-one-year-old orphan, essentially—but I am annoyed at him, and at the way this whole day has gone. If I were Constantin Constantius, I'd want to have someone tied up and shot. Carsten would be my first victim.

"It's as if the thing never existed," he says. "No original. No translation. No drafts. Nothing."

Lona stands up from her chair. "It existed. I saw it all right. I was hoping to spend the next year working on that manuscript. Everyone in the Center had a plan for it." After a pause she says, "But it may not be lost forever. I think it will show up again."

"I hope you're right," Carsten says. He joins Lona at my door. "I know that's what my mother would have wanted—for the manuscript to be seen and used. And by the way, Daniel, she included you in her will. You'll hear more about it from her executor."

"From Lona?"

"No," says Carsten, "from the executor of the estate. My Uncle Erik. He told me to tell you he'd be in touch."

I nod to them as they leave.

Erik is the uncle who seemed poised to spring from his seat when Carsten spoke at the funeral. He's also the brother who made fun of his sister's American boyfriend some twenty-seven years ago, which is the last time I talked with him. Well, we won't be speaking in Daniel Danish, I can count on that much.

Chapter 4

I can't be sure that I'll live the rest of my life in Denmark, in freedom, and so there are certain pleasures I won't deny myself now. The pleasure of this moment involves a hot dog in my bare hands, cold rain coming down in Town Hall Square, my checkered hat placed firmly on my head with the ear flaps securely tied, neon lights on the tall buildings along Hans Christian Andersen Boulevard, and nameless people walking past me with umbrellas. Almost every part of my body is cold, especially my hands and feet, as I take a bite of the steaming hot dog, which is itself a complex pleasure of tastes I could never get back in the U.S. and which they probably do not serve in *Vestre* Prison: first there is the hot dog itself, Danish pork, the best in the world, from pigs that lived good lives as only Danish pigs and Danish people can; next, the bun, freshly baked and kept warm in an oven until just before being served; then the cucumbers (who would ever put cucumbers on a hot dog back in Buffalo, NY?), sliced thinly and bathed in a vinegar brine; and finally the French fried onions, a crunchy grand finale to it all, laced with a thin stream of strong mustard. I am getting absolutely soaked and chilled to the bone, people are passing me and cursing when their umbrellas get blown inside out by the wind, and yet I couldn't be happier. I couldn't possibly be happier than now.

As long as I live in this moment, as long as I still have a few bites left on my Danish hot dog, I will not complain about my day, the thought of complaining will not even occur to me, I'll only wish I had an endless appetite and an endless supply, I'll only wish that the kind woman with the curly gray hair who handed me my dinner through the little Plexiglas window had not shortly thereafter closed the aluminum shutters of *Morfar's Pølsevogn* and walked away, like a fairy godmother, off to do her good deeds elsewhere, leaving me with the last enchanted hot dog whose magic, inevitably, wears off when the clock strikes five and I swallow the final mouthful.

Then that's it. Now I stand with the rain-soggy, mustard-smeared paper wrapper in my hand and feel alone in the crowd. I look around. Everyone seems to have someplace to go, and somebody to go there with them. My apartment is a five-minute walk away and I feel too tired to budge. I am like the author of part one of *Either/Or*, the young man known as "A" or "The Aesthete," who sums up his life in the pithy *Diapsalmata*: "I don't want to walk because it takes too much effort. I don't want to lie down because then I'd either have to stay lying down, which I don't want to do, or stand back up, which I also don't want to do."

I let the rain fall on me. The sky is dark and has been for over an hour now. All these electric lights illuminating the square, the boulevard, and the buildings were not here in Kierkegaard's lifetime. In his day, this part of the city would have been pitch black, or perhaps dimly lit by gas lamps. Town Hall hadn't been built on this spot yet; it was still housed in Nytorv Square, in the neighborhood where Kierkegaard spent his childhood. I don't know what he would have made of the present structure. He probably would have thought it gaudy, at least I do. The golden statue of Bishop Absalon dressed in his medieval vestments, wearing a mitre and carrying a crosier, looks tacky in its covered alcove between the two towers. I can't take seriously the brass griffins that guard the front steps—they look like famished dogs with bats' ears. In fact the only thing that I like about Town Hall is its clock tower, and not the sight of it, but its sound. After living in Copenhagen for less than a year I became used to its quarter, half-hour, and full-hour chimes; now that I've lived here for close to twenty, I miss those sounds like dear friends whenever I go away.

My pants are so wet they cling to my legs, and water has started to seep into my shoes. Registering these facts triggers a thought: how pleasant a hot shower would be! And so I begin the march home, passing construction sites where idle machinery is parked among mounds of dirt and piles of broken stone. I walk on the left side of Vester Voldgade, in the direction of the harbor, on a newly completed stretch of sidewalk made out of large tiles and strewn with fresh sand. I wonder if the sand will work its way into the tread of my shoes and render invalid the only evidence that ties me to the scene of the crime. At present they make suspicious squishing sounds as I plod my way home, moving slowly and desultorily though Copenhagen's rain-gloomy early evening hush.

"I don't want to walk . . . I don't want to lie down . . . I don't want to do anything."

My apartment is the entire fourth floor of a nineteenth-century building with a mansard roof. From my three dormer windows I can look out across the city and see the spires of several churches, including the famous Baroque spire on the Church of Our Savior, all the way across the inner harbor in Christianshavn. It was Mette's idea that I live here. Her husband, Peter, owned the building. At first he was my landlord, then Mette. It didn't seem to matter since I never paid a kroner for rent. But now I suppose Carsten is my new landlord and I worry that my days of rent-free living may be coming to an end. If they do, I may have to move up north where rent is cheaper and live in one of the refugee communities. I would not welcome the change—not because I have anything against refugees, but because I dislike change, period.

I didn't grow up rich, like Søren Kierkegaard, or like him inherit a fortune in my early twenties. My parents were working class. The things in this apartment are of far greater value than anything we ever had in our home. The designer furniture, the Bang & Olufsen TV and stereo, the original artwork on the walls—all of it was in the apartment when I moved in. I've tried to leave things exactly as I found them and live among them as a guest. Whenever I've burned up one of the candles that I found left behind in a cupboard, I've made sure to replace it with one of the exact same kind. I've never touched a bottle in the wine rack, nor have I kept track of the value they've gained over the eighteen years since I moved in. Once I accidentally broke a Royal Danish serving bowl. I immediately swept the shards into a paper bag and brought them to the flagship store on Strøget, where I learned that the bowl was over a hundred years old and only a few of its kind could be found. The storekeeper would have to make inquiries. That is, if I was still interested. Which meant, I knew, if I still thought I could afford it. I handed him my credit card and took three months to pay it off.

I will always be "incommensurable" (to use a good Kierkegaardian term) with this lavish apartment. Here I am, after a hot shower using Neutrogena body products (the kinds that were here when I moved in, and will be well stocked whenever the time comes for me to move out), dressed in frayed flannel pajamas and walking barefoot on the smoothly sanded hardwood floors. It's just after 6:00 p.m., about the time the proper owner of such a place would welcome dinner guests, motioning them toward a buffet of caviar and cheeses, but I'm thinking I want a handful of licorice from the plastic bag of Matador Mix that I keep on the kitchen counter (Italian marble) next to the stainless steel coffee maker (Krups). I am heading in that direction when my doorbell rings.

The noise is so shocking I literally jump. I can't remember the last time I heard it. I've never invited anyone up here, not even Mette, who knew that I valued this apartment for its seclusion on the top floor, for the absence of any neighbors. I walk over to the door and try to peek through the little round peephole, but I can't figure out how the thing works. I'm so disoriented, I'm not sure what I see: a shape, some colors, the rounded walls of a tunnel. Before I've made any sense of the situation, the doorbell buzzes again. I open the door quickly and find a fiftyish man dressed in a suit and an unbuttoned overcoat. He's wearing strong cologne. I have to look up to see his face: ruddy cheeks, fat lips, a receding hairline.

"Daniel, I'm sorry. I tried calling first. You never answered. I even called from my car just outside." He laughs. "It looks like you're ready to go to bed. Do you know it's only six o'clock?"

Erik Thorvaldsen, Mette's oldest brother, stands on my doorstep and smiles at me the way I remember him doing when he teased me years ago. I feel a cool breeze from the hallway, and when I look past Erik I see that someone else is standing and holding the elevator door open. It's Carsten. Have they come to evict me?, I wonder. Already?

"Look," says Erik, "I have to drive my mom back to Kolding tonight, and then I'm off on a trip for at least a week. There's something I'd like to settle about my sister's will. It involves you. Daniel, she left you this." He holds up a key, but doesn't give it to me. After a second, he puts it back in his pocket.

"What's it to?" I ask.

"A safety deposit box. I'll tell you—it was a big surprise to us when we reviewed her will. No one knew about it. I've talked with lawyers and the Police, and the best we can determine is that, although the contents of the box belong to you, you can't take possession of them until the estate is settled, which will be months from now. Technically, you're not even supposed to get the key. But the Police are interested in knowing what's inside the box. In case there may be a clue to my sister's death. So I've made arrangements with the branch manager (he's an old friend of mine) and we're to meet him at Danske Bank in ten minutes. I'm sorry I didn't get in touch with you earlier. You're not an easy person to reach. Why didn't you answer your phone?"

"I don't have it plugged in," I say. "I keep it in a drawer."

"Oh, well that explains it." He shakes his head. "Anyway, we should get going. You'll come, right?"

I am still holding the doorknob in my hand and blocking the way into the apartment. For most people, I suppose, there'd be no problem in getting dressed and going down to Danske Bank with Erik and Carsten, but I really don't want to disrupt my evening. I already have my pajamas on; it would be going backwards to take them off. And it would be too far of a jump forward to dress in clean clothes before tomorrow morning—and I certainly couldn't wear those wet things I peeled off my body an hour ago. My coat is drip-drying from a hanger above the shower drain, and my shoes are placed on a mat beside a heater so they'll dry by tomorrow. There has to be a way out of this. When it occurs to me, I blurt it out.

"You have my permission to check the box. There's no need for me to go. I hope you have a good evening."

I start to close the door, but Erik puts his hand flat against the frame. In any contest of strength, he would surely win.

"Hold on! I'm sorry I disturbed you. I really am. I know you're sensitive about this stuff. But we need you to be there when we open the box. Technically, you own the key, or will own it. It's complicated. But as long as you're with us, we can look. And it won't take long. I promise. You'll still get to bed by seven o'clock."

I am about to suggest that we wait until tomorrow, but then I remember what Erik said about going away on a trip.

"Give me a couple minutes," I say. "I'll get dressed."

I start to shut the door, but Erik is still leaning against it.

"Do you mind if we wait inside? It's cold out here."

He and Carsten step into my apartment, which is not really my apartment, and start looking around. I head back to the bedroom to change. It's occurred to me that I can pull a sweat suit over my pajamas and wear my slippers, which look a lot like the shoes some of the youth wear these days. What do I care, really? The more I try to fit in, the less I do. When I come out of the bedroom, I notice that one leg of my pajama bottoms is sticking out from my sweatpants. I don't even bother tucking it in.

"I'm ready to go," I say.

Erik and Carsten look up from the wine rack, where they've been studying the labels.

As we leave the apartment, Erik holds his phone in one hand and presses buttons with his thumb. I have never in my life sent a text message, but I see Danes doing it every day. It's another secret handshake I'll never learn, so why try? Erik finishes his rapid thumb movements and slips his phone into a pocket, but it rings before we even reach the elevator.

"Morten's waiting for us," says Erik. "We should hurry."

On the ride down the elevator, Carsten comments on my fine collection of vintage wines.

"They were there when I moved in," I say. "They're not mine. They're yours, I guess."

"Or will be, one day," says Erik.

"Well," says Carsten, "I'd be happy to take early possession of that 1986 Château Margaux."

"There's a bottle of Château Margaux?" I say.

"Oh," says Erik, "now all of a sudden he doesn't want to share."

"You can have it. I don't drink wine," I say.

"But you've heard of Château Margaux?" asks Carsten.

"Yes. Of course. It's the wine served at the banquet called "*In Vino Veritas*" in the first part of Kierkegaard's *Stages on Life's Way*."

The two of them laugh together.

"Kierkegaard," says Erik. "Why does there always have to be a connection to Kierkegaard?"

Morten Nielsen holds open the door to Danske Bank as an odd trio passes through: a well-dressed businessman, a young and fashionable male model, and a bum who's dressed in two layers of clothes and wearing slippers without socks. Or at least that's how we must appear to the bank's security cameras. It's quiet inside here. Advertisements for banking services pass silently on large flat screen TVs mounted to the wall, and two empty chairs stand behind the front desk. All of the cubicles in the back of the lobby are vacant, computers turned off, chairs pushed in. Tall arched windows surround the outer walls, and the whole place has an on-hold feel to it, as if it were being kept under a glass dish, preserved in pristine order until tomorrow morning when another banking day begins.

Erik hadn't told me which Danske Bank branch we were going to, but I should have guessed it would be Nytorv. Where else would Mette have left my mysterious inheritance but at the site of Kierkegaard's childhood home? Over two hundred years ago Kierkegaard's father bought a home on this very spot, and for years the young Søren passed in and out of its doorways. He read his Latin lessons and wrote his Danish exercises here before walking off each morning to The School of Civic Virtue. Here he listened to his father argue calmly and intelligently with guests, getting his first taste of dialectic. Here he dressed for church each Sunday morning and walked across the square to Our

Lady's Church, where he heard Bishop Mynster preach sermons that didn't agree with his own growing sense of Christianity, but out of respect for his father he kept his thoughts to himself. It was here that his brothers and sisters nicknamed him "The Fork" because he liked to stab food at the table and to stick people with his witty comments. Here, in the parlor, wherever that was located, they held his mother's viewing. Here he experienced early bouts with melancholia, living with his father and brother as the sole survivors of a family reduced from nine members to three. From here, in 1837, he left to live on his own, first on Løvstræde, then Kultorvet, returning again in 1844, after his father had died, and sharing the oversized home with his older brother, Peter, whom he disliked more and more and could tolerate less and less. In April of 1848, Søren left for good; the home was sold. He found other places to live, always alone, throughout the city.

All of this information I have stored in my head, but I resist the temptation to share it with the others. What would they care? The most important lesson I have learned over the last several years is this: outside of the Center, most people don't care about the things I care about. And an ancillary lesson to it is this: I don't care about the things most other people care about. What's happening now is a good example. While Morten Nielsen leads the way across the lobby's floor, through a glass door, and down a flight of stairs, he speaks the entire time, and with great animation, about the chances of the Danish men's handball team defeating Poland tonight and moving closer to becoming European Champions. It's surprising how worked up Morten gets. He flails his arms in the air, mimicking what one of the star players will do when he gets the ball in front of Poland's goal. In the process, Morten's shirt comes untucked from his trousers and reveals a white fold of fatty skin hanging over his belt. Not only is his speech uninteresting, but it turns him into a clown. Am I that way to others?

We reach the basement where the security boxes are kept. The room is brightly lit and meticulously organized: evenly spaced rows of identical steel cabinets rise from a thin blue carpet. A wide aisle runs down the middle of the room, and at both ends there is a table and chair, presumably for private viewing. Morten stops in front of Box 1242, and Erik hands him the key. Until this moment I have not imagined what might be waiting for me inside that box. My mind has been preoccupied with the irritation of having my evening interrupted by an unexpected demand. But now it occurs to me that Mette has left something specifically for me—she thought of me—she thought to leave something for me. Morten starts to fit the key into a brass keyhole, then stops.

"Actually, Daniel, I think you should do this."

I take the key from him and place it in the keyhole. As soon as I turn the key, the door opens smoothly and I pull out a metal container somewhat larger than a shoebox.

"You can sit over there and look through it," says Morten. "When you're finished, I'll need to make a list of the contents."

As I walk away I hear the others begin to speak in Danish, again about tonight's handball match. The table is about thirty feet away, and when I reach it I set down the container and pull back the chair. "Well," I say to myself as I sit down, "what did you leave me, Mette?"

I lift the hinged lid and look inside.

"The manuscript!" I shout. At the same moment, I push back my chair. I stand up and reach inside to pull out the booklets. I have them in my hands when the others have rushed over to me.

"She saved it," I say shaking the booklets in my hand. "It's here! It's not lost!"

On the faces of the other three I notice something. And it is not excitement. Not like what I'm feeling.

"That's not Kierkegaard's," says Carsten. "That's not the original manuscript."

"No," I say. "It's my translation. I wonder why she put it in here. I know someone at the Copenhagen Museum who'll be very happy to know it's not lost!"

I turn and face Morten Nielsen.

"It's okay for me to take these, right? I mean, I wrote them. These are mine."

Morten shakes his head.

"No, you can't take them. You can't take anything from the box. Erik, I thought you explained that to him."

"I did," says Erik. "Daniel, those have to stay here."

"But," I say. "But couldn't I copy them down? Couldn't you Xerox them for me? Birgit Fisker-Steensen wants to use them in a display at the Copenhagen Museum. It's very important. She needs my translations. I told her she could use them."

Morten takes off his glasses and rubs the bridge of his nose.

"I'll have to look into that possibility. Copyright laws can be very complicated."

"Copyright laws!" I shout. "Copyright laws! I wrote these. They're *my* translations. They're *my* words."

Behind me I hear Carsten laughing; I think I could strangle him.

"You wouldn't have a translation without the original. So, really, they're Kierkegaard's words, right? That'll be something trying to get his permission."

The other two laugh at what is not a funny joke. Not funny at all.

"Daniel," says Erik. "Was there anything else in the box?"

"I don't know," I say. I shrug my shoulders.

Erik takes this as permission to search the box, and I move aside as he steps up to the table. He leans over the container, then reaches inside.

"Is this what I think it is?" he asks and holds out an amber necklace I haven't seen in over a quarter of a century. Not since the day I gave it to Mette. I didn't think she'd saved it.

I nod.

"Whatever it is, whatever personal value it holds for you, it will have to remain in the box until the estate is settled," says Morten. "I'm sorry, but I'm afraid those are the rules." He looks down at his watch. "Now, we really should be going."

"Could I have a few more minutes to look this over?" I ask.

"A few, yes," says Morten. "And then I have a form I'll need you to sign."

He and the others back away and leave me some private space.

I sit down and turn the pages of the new manuscript. Or, rather, my translation of the new manuscript. Carsten was right about that. Still, a translation is a new work, and this is my work. Hours of pondering, hours of difficult choices. I remember going back and forth on the title—should it be *The Poems of S. Kierkegaard* or should it be *Poems by S. Kierkegaard*? I settled on the former, and I still like it better. Every page in these booklets represents doubts I had then finally conquered. The right words in the right order, one poem at a time, one poem after another. Mette and I agreed that, as a translator, this was to be my magnum opus. And now it will sit here in a metal container inside a steel cabinet in the basement of Danske Bank. Kierkegaard trapped in the dungeon of his childhood home. And not a thing I can do to get him out.

I gather the booklets and place them back inside the container. The necklace catches my eye, so I pick it up and hold it. The amber is clear orange, shaped like a tear, with dark specks trapped inside it. In my palm it feels warm, but cheaply made, like plastic. Twenty-seven years ago it cost me more than I'd ever spent on anything in my life. Not only did I pick what I thought was the best piece of amber in the store, but I also ordered a special clasp to attach the amber to its silver chain. The clasp was hollow inside and just wide enough to hold a small rolled-up piece of paper. And on that piece of paper, at the tender age of eighteen, I wrote my marriage proposal to Mette Thorvaldsen, which she accepted, but which her parents and older brothers did not.

Our engagement lasted just two days. According to her family, it never even happened.

I unscrew the clasp from the chain and look to see if, after all these years, the note is still there. It is. With the fingernail of my pinky I drag it out and let it fall onto the desk, still coiled up around itself. I'm about to unroll it when I hear Morten's voice.

"We really should be going, Daniel."

With my back to him, I nod my head.

It takes me a few seconds to screw the clasp back on. Leaning over, as if I might be crying, I slip the paper into a zippered pocket of my sweat suit top. Then I stand up, lift the box, and join the others. After a brief inspection, Morten places the container back into its slot and shuts the door. He hands the key to Erik, who pockets it.

"I need you to sign this," says Morten, holding out a metal clipboard and a pen. "It witnesses that you have viewed the contents of the safety deposit box and that you swear you haven't removed any of the items."

I sign the form quickly, and why not? Who could possibly miss a scrap of paper with the words "Will you marry me?" carefully written in pencil by a romantic youth over a quarter of a century ago? And who would blame a middle-aged man for wanting to relive the moment when someone promised to spend the rest of her life with him? Like Constantin Constantius, I might not be able to re-feel what I felt when Mette said, "Yes." What happiness that was! But I can try. And after the day I've had today, I think I deserve the opportunity.

Back in my apartment with no one to disturb me, I place a chair in front of the middle dormer window. I sit down, stand up, re-adjust the chair, and sit back down. With the angle just right, I can look out over the inner harbor and see the corkscrew spire of Our Savior's Church. On the very top there is a gold ball, which you can reach only if you climb four hundred wooden stairs winding their way up the spire, the staircase growing narrower as you ascend, and then climb another external staircase to reach the "tippy top." On May 5, 1986—Kierkegaard's 172nd birthday—Mette and I stood together on the very top step.

I have to struggle to see us there now, but I push against the intervening years and the difference of season and time of day, and then as if I've shoved open a door, I do see us. We stand above the city, its red tile roofs and slow-moving canals far below us, a gold ball over our heads but close enough to reach out and touch. The wind blows Mette's hair into her face; she pulls strands out of her mouth, but they blow right back in again. She is wearing a multicolored scarf with bright silver sparkles sewn into it. We are both smiling. It is sunny. I hand her the amber necklace, still in its cushioned box from the jeweler's store, and she hugs me before she even opens it. Then she looks inside. She smiles. She kisses me. But she doesn't yet know about the secret note. I show her how the clasp works. She watches me closely. She sees what I'm getting at and wants to do it herself. I'm glad to let her. There is a moment when I stop breathing, and then a moment when she touches my hand and nods her head and I breathe again. Remembering it now, I can almost feel the skin of her hand on mine.

If I could, I would stop the memory there. Daniel and Mette three hundred feet above Copenhagen, engaged to be married. But what followed, had to follow. The call that Mette made from a phone booth to tell her mother the happy news. The wet rags of reality that the adults (especially her brother Erik, who was hosting our visit to the capital) casually threw on our youthful exuberance. Re-thinking, re-calibrating, un-deciding, un-engaging. I never had time to tell my own family, and then I was glad I didn't. The only proof that I was ever someone's fiancé is this piece of paper in my pocket. I unzip it now and take out the note. With the spire of Our Savior's still in my line of vision, I turn my chair just enough to get light on the page. I unroll the paper and look for the words I wrote there.

But they're not there. Something else is there, written in pencil, but not what I wrote.

Even before I switch on the light over the dining room table and hold the paper in place with a salt shaker on one edge and a pepper mill on the other, I know it's Mette's handwriting. On paper smudged by erasures she has written this:

"KBHA SKA D Pk 4   KBHA NkS 3883,4"

To anyone in the field of Søren Kierkegaard research, that jumble of letters and numbers is immediately decipherable. "KBHA" stands for *Kongelige Bibliotek Håndskrift Afdelingen*—the Royal Library's Manuscript Department. "SKA" stands for Søren Kierkegaard Archives. I don't know why, but Mette has left me the call numbers for two manuscripts, and to access them, I'll have to visit the new addition to the Royal Library. The thought does not excite me. In fact, I feel duped. I propose marriage to her; twenty-seven years later, she counters with a proposal for research.

What is Mette up to? I don't know, and there's nothing I can do until the morning.

I leave the scrap of paper spread out on the table, turn off the light, and head into the bedroom. I'm in bed with the duvet pulled up to my chin before it dawns on me that I've forgotten to take off my sweat suit.

God, what kind of a husband would I have made?

Chapter 5

I'm not sure what time the Manuscripts Department of the Royal Library opens, but I know that there's a coffee shop in the lobby, and that they have delicious pastries, so I stuff some bills and coins in my pocket. My coat, which is made of a lightweight waterproof fabric, has completely dried out, and my shoes have if anything gotten too dry and feel stiff. Only my checkered hat remains slightly damp—but I wear it anyway, with the flaps tied over my ears. In fall and winter, I never leave the apartment without it.

By the time I reach the street, the 8:00 a.m. chimes from Town Hall have already begun and the morning commute proceeds in its usual orderly fashion, with a lane for cars, a lane for bikes, and a sidewalk for pedestrians. Except for the noise of the ubiquitous construction workers—which is more than enough noise for me, thank you—the road is relatively quiet. Unlike in cities in the U.S., drivers in Copenhagen never blow their horns, unless there really is an emergency or the Danish National Team has just won the European Championship— neither of which is the case this morning. At the light on Tietgensgade, cyclists stand three in a row and five or more rows deep, waiting for the light to change. Most of them are dressed for work, some of them quite nicely. After all these years, it still strikes me as odd to see a woman in a fancy woolen coat and high heel boots straddling her bicycle in the middle of a busy intersection, or to watch a man in a business suit take out his cell phone and prop it on his handlebars, dragging his thumb down the tiny screen.

When the light changes, I turn onto Stormgade and enter one of the busiest parts of the city. Ahead of me is Christiansborg Palace, where the Parliament meets, and beyond it I can see the twisted spire of the Old

Stock Exchange. Politics and money—two things that I neither understand nor care to understand. In the congested traffic I feel my nerves
bunching up inside of me and wait for the right moment to dart across
the cobblestone and through the gate to the Library Gardens.

Once inside, the street noise dies away and I find myself in an en-
closed space. Here, everything is arranged for contemplation and peace.
Ivy grows along brick walls. Tall beech trees stand on both sides of a
sandy path. Benches with plenty of space between them line the pe-
rimeter, and everything is kept neat and tidy: even the trash cans for
disposing cigarette butts are encircled with picket fences.

In the center of the garden there is a pool where a pair of ducks
swims around. Someone, I see, has built them a nesting box and placed
it in the water—it looks like a miniature cottage, complete with a
thatched roof and painted beams. Small windows let you look inside
and see the nesting material. Maybe in spring you can observe hatch-
lings. The only eyesore in this entire place is a sculpture the locals call
"The Shower Nozzle," which juts up some thirty feet from the same
pool where the ducks paddle around contentedly, poking their bills at
old pieces of bread or diving for weeds. It's hard to tell what they think
of the artwork looming over them.

Of course, the library garden is prettier in spring when the flowers
are in bloom, but then it's also crowded. This morning I'm the only
person here, which is the way I like it. Maybe it's selfish of me to
want the whole place to myself, but I get annoyed with the tourists
who only come for a quick look at the Søren Kierkegaard statue, just
long enough to say they've seen it. They check off a box on their "Copenhagen Landmarks" brochure, then stride through the rest of the
garden on their way to see the Queen's Riding Circle or the City Arse-
nal. There's no slowing them down for a closer look. I tried once, and
regretted it. It happened a few years ago, in springtime, when I was
sitting on a bench near the statue and heard two Americans trying to
say the name "Søren Kierkegaard." I thought I'd be helpful.

"Say the 'S' like the 'Z' in 'Zurich.' Don't pronounce the final 'd.'
'Kyerk-ah-gore.' "

It turned out to be a father and his teenage daughter, from Cincin-
nati, Ohio. They walked up to my bench and introduced themselves.

"Sounds like you're an American, too," said the father. "Where you
from?"

Small talk. For me, that's where everything starts to go wrong. Ten-
sion fills me from head to foot, even when I know what's expected of me.
I know, for instance, that the question "Where are you from?" is meant
as a catalyst for conversation, a polite way of showing interest in

someone else, but I've never understood how the answer to that question could possibly matter or why I should want to talk about a place I've decided to move away from. If I was interested in talking about Buffalo, NY, I'd be living in Buffalo, NY, but I'm in Copenhagen because it's more interesting and it's where Søren Kierkegaard lived an interesting life.

"The statue," I said, keeping my head down and holding my lunch on my lap, "is based on a much smaller model that used to sit on Harald Høffding's desk. The model is on display at the Copenhagen Museum."

"Really?" the father said. "That's interesting."

"Høffding taught philosophy at the University of Copenhagen. He was influenced by Kierkegaard. And naturally he passed on his interest to his students, including Niels Bohr."

"You don't say. Hey, what about the green stuff on the statue? We've seen it on spires and roofs all over the city. Do you know what it's called?"

Verdigris? Was this man actually more interested in the oxidization of copper than about the story behind Kierkegaard's statue?

"The statue isn't one hundred percent accurate," I said, still looking down at my open-faced sandwich. "For instance, the sculptor has depicted Kierkegaard holding a quill pen, but he actually used a steel pen for most of his writing. When he edited one of his manuscripts, he often used a pencil, especially for crossing out passages that he no longer wanted to use. Another error—at least I would call it an error—is the careless pile of books strewn beneath the chair that Kierkegaard's sitting on. Kierkegaard was if nothing a careful person—'persnickety' might not be a bad word to describe him—and so it's hard to imagine him having such a messy study."

When I looked up, the father and his daughter had quietly walked away and left me all alone talking to myself—like an idiot. They were already several paces off when I saw them glance back over their shoulders, which were shaking with laughter. Another group of people stood nearby and seemed to be in on the joke. I returned to my sandwich and cursed the Tourist Office for adding the Søren Kierkegaard statue to its list of city landmarks, but then I remembered that Mette had lobbied for the statue to be put on that list and my anger subsided. I couldn't be mad at her. I could only sit there on my bench and feel like a fool.

Today I pause in front of the statue just long enough to remember the sting of being ridiculed. It's a feeling Kierkegaard understood all too well, having been teased throughout his life. As a child, his schoolmates made fun of him for dressing like a choir boy. When he became an adult, a satirical magazine called *The Corsair* allowed its cartoonists to depict him so unflatteringly that Kierkegaard became the biggest joke on the street—to the point that, for a while, he had to give up his much-loved walks through the city. "I feel like I'm being trampled to death by geese," he said of the relentless mockery. Wit was always his way of getting back at detractors. How else to overcome suffering but with a joke?

In front of me now is the Old Royal Library, a brick building in the grand style, with trimmed hedges around its base and ivy growing up its front entrance. Each floor has a row of tall arched windows, and behind them are stacks of books as far as the eye can see. During my first two years in Copenhagen, I spent hours inside this library, mostly in the Reading Room, seated at a wooden desk with a shaded lamp spilling light across one of Kierkegaard's manuscripts. Those were glorious days! A librarian would bring me a wheeled cart with boxes of manuscripts, which I could handle right there in the open, surrounded by university students and other scholars, each of us in that quiet, private space of word-study. When my eyes felt strained from trying to read Kierkegaard's handwriting, I could relieve them by looking up at the bookshelves that encircled the room with virtually all of world literature and feel that here, at least, I was part of something vast and important. It didn't last long. As the Center grew, it employed specialists for reading the manuscripts—philologists, usually young and very bright graduates from the University of Copenhagen trained in the newest techniques of manuscript analysis. They took my place in the Reading Room and then, after time, the Center installed its own vault and transported most of the Kierkegaard manuscripts across town, within easy access of those who needed them the most. I started spending all my time translating Kierkegaard's texts and scholarly commentaries, which only made sense because I'm the best translator the Center has ever had. (That's what Mette told me, and a reviewer of my work went even further to say that I'm the best Kierkegaard translator ever, a conclusion he reached by comparing my work with that of others.) When the time came for me to stop reading the original manuscripts, I didn't complain, nor did I miss the headache of trying to decipher Kierkegaard's handwriting, which has that nineteenth-century quality of being amazingly neat and at the same time practically unreadable. On the other hand, I did miss spending my early mornings in the Reading Room—in fact, I miss them now. As I pass by the main doors to the Old Royal, I feel a longing to sit quietly in that spacious room ringed with books, filled with light.

Another feeling comes over me, and I try to name it. Naming my feelings is something I try to do occasionally since it's part of the "treatment" Mette and I developed, years ago, for addressing my Asperger's and overcoming certain limits. According to her, I showed better progress in emotional awareness than in social interaction—but how could she say that? How is it possible to know when someone's named a feeling correctly, especially when feelings can be so complicated? The feeling I am having now is, I think, a mixture of sadness and fear—sadness that something has passed and won't return, and fear that harm will come to something I care about. At the same time, I feel the exact opposite: I feel that I want to, and that I could, do something courageous, right now, in connection to the library. I feel as if I could be its hero—the savior of bookshelves, and books, and the words inside them.

It's a silly and melodramatic feeling, and I catch myself just in time to realize that the mood would not have lasted anyway. As soon as I come around the side of the Old Royal, I face the new addition, what's called "The Black Diamond." In its presence, feelings freeze. What could I possibly *feel* for this imposing structure? It's like some gargantuan, black-paneled, steel-girdered, intergalactic spaceship that's landed on a concrete slab beside the bank of the inner harbor. I can't fathom it, let alone have feelings for it. I don't even understand why it's called a diamond. It looks more like a cube to me—like a gigantic Rubik's Cube with all its squares painted black.

I wait to cross the street. To my left, cars pass under a sky bridge that connects the Old Royal with the New. I can see people up there walking between the two buildings, caught in the air above Christians Brygge, midway between two very different architectural languages—on the one side, brick and ivy; on the other, glass and steel. It makes me wonder about my translation of the new Kierkegaard manuscript. Did my English do his Danish justice? Or do the two versions stand as opposed and incompatible as these two buildings? Now that his manuscript is stolen and mine is locked away in a safety deposit box, when will anyone be able to make a comparison?

The light changes and I cross over to the only street in Copenhagen named after Søren Kierkegaard. Mette had wanted something longer and more centrally located, but getting even this small section named after Kierkegaard took many years and caused her plenty of grief. She had to work with city officials and library administration staff and go to I don't know how many meetings. I remember her complaints, but I don't remember doing anything to help her. And when "Søren Kierkegaard Plads" officially opened, I didn't go to the ceremony with her and the others from the Center. Besides the crowd that was expected, I didn't want to stand so close to the Black Diamond. As my excuse, I said that I was afraid the building might still have traces of radioactivity from its years of space travel. No one laughed at my joke. Mette told me it didn't actually make sense.

For years I never went inside the Black Diamond, and I tried to avoid even looking at it. For me, it conjured up memories of high school geometry class, where my balding math teacher, Mr. Mann, lost patience with me for, as he put it, not trying. He couldn't understand how I could be so bright in my other classes and a total failure in his. I must not be trying hard enough, he told me. In truth, I didn't care, and I didn't want to care. Geometric shapes with their dangerously sharp angles seemed the mortal enemies of words, and formulas were written in a hostage-taking language that made me despair of ever freeing the words from their captors. The best I could do was to avoid the enemy and save myself. In a similar way, the Black Diamond represented to me the victory of glass and steel over brick and wood, sharply defined scientific truths over the mysteries of the human condition. I feared that if I stepped inside its doors, I would be swallowed up like an insect in a terrarium; and there'd be no way out. Best then to keep my distance.

Over the years I turned down several invitations to dine at the library's restaurant, "Søren K.," even though it serves the city's best plaice and other local seafood, always on fine porcelain at linen-covered tables topped with vases of colorful irises. I was not enticed either by fancy dining or by the restaurant's name. If I wanted to be close to the spirit of Søren K., I reasoned, I could do better by eating a falafel sandwich in the middle of Strøget and reciting a line of text I'd translated that day. But then, just when I thought I'd escaped the shadow of the Black Diamond, a café named "*Øieblikket*" opened up in its lobby. It was named after a series of pamphlets Kierkegaard published during the last year of his life, at a time when he launched a direct and merciless attack on the established church and took a few good shots against university professors as well. It was an unusual name for a café—I liked that—and it was also a word that English translators of Kierkegaard had argued over. Should it be translated as "The Moment" or "The Instant"? I hadn't made up my own mind, but would have to eventually if my publisher continued to print the complete new edition of Kierkegaard.

It must have been a Wednesday morning when a colleague from the Center brought in pastries from *Øieblikket* and I cautiously accepted one. It was delicious. I less cautiously accepted a second, and then, with complete abandon, I took a third. Before morning coffee was over and we dispersed to our separate offices, I had lost my resistance to the

Black Diamond the way a boy loses a molar to tooth decay. That week-end, without anyone prompting me, I visited the new addition to the Royal Library, overcoming my fear of sharp-edged geometric shapes and my disdain for a library that looks like a laboratory. Once inside, I felt like I'd entered a hotel lobby or the waiting area in a large inter-national airport. Steel beams and glass partitions overhead, potted plants on the Information Desk, acres of uncluttered tile floor, and the smell of strong coffee wafting in the air. I gladly handed over the equivalent of twelve dollars for two pastries, then sat on a stool at a bistro table. Looking around at the other people enjoying their coffee and pastries, I noticed that no one was reading a book. I kept my own hidden inside my jacket in case books were forbidden in here. Who knows? If I'd taken mine out, a laser beam might have struck from the ceiling and zapped me dead. Eventually, I figured out that all the books and periodicals were kept on the upper levels, and to get there you have to go up an escalator. Preferring the creaky stairs of old libraries to something that looks like it belongs in a shopping mall, I stayed put in the lobby. Even after my visits to the Black Diamond became weekly occurrences (good pastries are addictive) I didn't ride the escalator. But I will today. It's the only way I'll be able to view the material that Mette thought I should see, and getting to the Manuscripts Reading Room (which one of my colleagues described as "antiseptic" and "sta-tioned with a guard") is the first order of business. After I have my pastries, of course.

I stand at the Information Desk with my hands in my pockets and grit my teeth. I have not called ahead to make an appointment, and so I won't be able to view the materials this morning. That is what the young woman on duty tells me. I insist that she call up to the Manuscripts Department. Reluctantly, she does so and learns that, even though they don't open until 10:00, someone will see me right away. It helps to be from the Center. It helps to have the right credentials.

I start to walk toward the escalator, but I don't get far before the attendant calls after me.

"Sir," she says, "you'll have to put your jacket in a locker."

This annoys me and I groan audibly. In the Reading Room of the Old Royal, they never had such rules.

"What's next?" I grumble. "A strip search?"

She smiles at me from her side of the desk, and I realize that she's just another sweet Danish girl doing her job. I'm the one being difficult.

"No strip search," she says. "You can even wear your Elmer Fudd hat if you like. I think it's cute. But you might be a little warm."

I reach up and touch the top of my hat. I'd forgotten I still had it on. When I try to untie the strings and walk toward the lockers at the same time, I stumble and bump into a wall. At least I don't fall down. It takes me a couple of minutes to read the directions printed on the inside door of the locker (I have to insert a 20 kroner coin, which will be returned to me upon emptying my belongings) and a few more minutes to come up with a strategy for recalling which locker is mine. Random numbers are the hardest things for me to remember especially when, like this one, they begin with a zero. But I'm pleased with my solution: 0612 can be translated to June 12th, which is the date in 1842 when Kierkegaard published his "Public Confession" in the Copenhagen newspaper *Fædrelandet*, stating quite emphatically that he was not the author of a number of witty articles that had been attributed to him. Of course, he *was* the author of those articles. He'd published them under false names, and when his contemporaries tried to unmask him, Kierkegaard simply tied his masks on tighter. "I confess my weakness," he said with a wink, "I played no part in that entire affair, nor even a partial part—no part whatsoever" and begged his readers to "never consider me the author of any work that does not bear my name." Over the next several years he went on to create enough pseudonyms to populate an entire masquerade ball. But the intricate game of charades—pretending to be someone else, then pretending not to be pretending to be someone else—started with his public disavowal on June the 12th: 06/12. How could I possibly forget such an important date?

I ride the escalator to the next floor, and when I reach the top I am immediately faced with a problem. The woman at the Information Desk had told me that an escort would meet me at the top of the escalator, but I don't see anyone. I stand in a wide open space with a colorful abstract painting on the ceiling, a few cushioned seats to my left, and a Reception Desk ahead to my right. Nothing here helps me. I am struck with complete confusion. At banks and bakeries there is a machine that produces a ticket with a number on it. You take the ticket and wait for someone to call your number. But there's no machine like that here. I don't know what this escort looks like, and he or she doesn't know what I look like, so how are we going to find each other? When I look around I see a young woman who is probably a university student (she's dressed all in black—black T-shirt, skirt, leotards, and boots) sitting cross-legged on one of the seats. She has her head down and appears to be sleeping. The man at the Reception Desk is on the telephone, but I walk up to him anyway and tell him my problem.

"I'm sure someone will be with you shortly," he says, holding his hand over the receiver.

"But how will they know I'm the one they're supposed to escort to the Manuscripts Department?"

"Usually, they do," he says. "Just look like you're waiting. The person will come from that elevator." He points across the floor to the far wall where, in fact, I do see an elevator. I walk over there and stand with my arms crossed. That's what people do when they're waiting. I wait for five minutes and the door never opens. When I am about to leave, the black-clad university student gets up from her seat and walks to the elevator. She inserts a key and the door opens.

"Hey," I say, "if you know any of the escorts from the Manuscripts Department, will you send one down here?"

She leaves her key in the slot and walks up to within a few inches of me. Then she stops and stands there looking down at her boots, which are shiny black and have squared-off steel toes. On the surface of each boot I see a bright orb: reflections from the overhead lights.

"Are you Daniel Peters?" she asks. "From the Søren Kierkegaard Research Center?"

"Yes." I hold out my hand, but she doesn't reach out to take it.

"So what the hell took you so long? The escalator's not broken. It doesn't take fifteen minutes to ride up one floor."

"I had to put my coat away. It took a while. And you didn't look like you were waiting for me. You looked like you were sleeping."

"I was waiting for you." She glances up at me. "What am I supposed to look like? I was sitting right over there waiting for you. Well, let's go."

She walks into the elevator and I follow behind her. Once we're inside, she leans against the far corner and keeps her head down.

"Push the button for the fifth floor," she says.

I follow her order and we ride up in silence. When the door opens, she brushes past me and starts leading the way down a narrow hall.

"So who am I going to see?" I ask.

She stops and looks back at me. The expression on her face is either a smirk or a grimace—I'm not sure which, and I'm not sure what it means.

"Me. You're seeing me. Who else would you see?"

"I thought you were the escort."

"No. I'm nobody's escort. My name is Susannah Lindegaard. I'm a research librarian in the Manuscripts Department of Denmark's finest library. I've worked here for the past four years. My specialty is in forgery detection. If they'd had me on staff at the University of Oslo's library, they would never have wasted their money on that fake Knut Hamsun manuscript. That was ridiculous. To mistake the handwriting of a Nobel Laureate when you have so many examples in your own collection. It's really inexcusable. I'm the person who worked with Mette on evaluating the new Kierkegaard manuscript. I'll show you my report."

We step into Susannah's dimly lit, cluttered office. Pushed against one wall is a table piled with books, journals, and file folders. The different-sized, disorganized piles lean into each other and form a sort of precarious support system. I am reminded of the arcade game where quarters are strewn along a ledge inside a glass box, and every time another quarter is inserted, a mechanical arm pushes the whole stack closer to the edge. It would take just one more piece of paper placed in the right spot and this entire table would collapse under the weight and spill onto the floor. Underneath the table there are cloth tote bags bulging with who knows what. I think I see an empty wine bottle protruding from one of them. Would drinking be allowed in the Royal Library? Cardboard file boxes are placed randomly on the floor, and I have to pick my way around them to join Susannah at her desk. There is only one chair in the office, and she is sitting in it. I stand and look over her shoulders as she performs the mysteries of operating a computer. From her necklace she takes a short plastic stick with a metal tip and puts it into a slot on the side of her computer. In a moment, graphs and numbers appear on the screen.

"I began with a basic physical inspection of the manuscript. I didn't think we'd have to involve ourselves with carbon dating since I expected to find the telltale signs of forgery rather quickly. You realize, I suppose, that no one's found any new material by Søren Kierkegaard in over a hundred and fifty years. He left all of his papers neatly organized in his apartment before he died. Everything was arranged systematically, tied with string into neat bundles. It made things pretty easy for his editors. Of course, he left a lot behind. Stacks and stacks. Something might have gone missing when the papers were shipped from Copenhagen to Kierkegaard's brother in Aalborg, then back to Copenhagen again. But care was taken with the material, especially after the University got involved. An inventory was made—and that list exists. There certainly wasn't anything on that list that was at all like this new manuscript. To tell you the truth, when I got the call from the Copenhagen Museum saying they'd discovered what appeared to be a manuscript by Kierkegaard, I almost told them not to waste their time. Someone was pulling their leg. You know what convinced me that I should have a look?"

"The fact that it was hidden inside Kierkegaard's desk."

"Exactly."

"At the Center, that was a reason many of us had for doubting the manuscript's authenticity."

Susannah turns her head around and looks at me. I notice that she's put on a pair of glasses. They look like the kind my mother wore in the 1950s, called kitty-cat glasses, I think. I suppose anything can come back in style.

"No," she says, "the desk is the only place the manuscript could have gone overlooked for all this time. And, of course, it was in a secret compartment."

"It wasn't a question of whether a manuscript could go unnoticed, but whether Kierkegaard would stoop to hiding it there. The 'found manuscript' is such an old and tired device. I know: Kierkegaard used that gimmick in his own books—there's a manuscript discovered in an antique secretary, another left behind at a book bindery; there's even one fished up from the bottom of a lake. But would Kierkegaard hide his own work in hopes that it would be discovered later? It just seems too cliché a thing for him to do."

"Cliché or not," Susannah says and shrugs her shoulders.

I shrug mine, too. "If the manuscript is by Kierkegaard, it doesn't matter who put it there."

"Exactly. So, I decided to give the manuscript a close comparison to other Kierkegaard manuscripts—of which we have many examples. They haven't all gone over to the Center, you know. There were no dates on the pages of the new manuscript, so for comparison I selected a range of time periods, starting from when Kierkegaard was in his early twenties and ending a few months before he died at forty-two. I also varied the examples in terms of his perceived writer's purpose— journal entries, draft pages, letters, random notes, and fair copy. I made sure to touch on a little of everything. I guarantee you, not since 1977 when Annelise Garde published her article "Graphological Investigation of Søren Kierkegaard's Handwriting in the Period 1831– 1855" has anyone made anything like the comparison I made between the new manuscript and the known examples of Søren Kierkegaard's handwriting. I will confess—the similarities I found stunned me. After a few hours I concluded that I was either looking at a very high-order forgery—the work of an artist on the level of the Spanish Forger—or I really was looking at an authentic manuscript that had escaped detection. These first four graphs represent the occurrences of exact or near-exact duplications of Kierkegaard's most characteristic features: his famous hooked "S," the relatively under-expressed middle zone letters, the decidedly overexpressed lower and higher zone letters, and his peculiar habits of crossing out or deleting unwanted text. Unlike Annelise Garde, I wasn't interested in making any psychological con- clusions about Kierkegaard based on his handwriting, but I did sense something kind of spooky after I finished my comparison. It seemed as though the same spirit rose from this new manuscript as from the old. I wasn't sure what to call this freaky thing I felt, but then I came up with a really clever phrase for it."

Susannah pauses and looks off to one side, past her computer screen.

"What?" I ask. "What's the clever phrase?"

"I forgot it. Shit. It was really clever, too. Let me think."

"It doesn't matter. Anyway, you decided the manuscript was by Kierkegaard and . . ."

"Stop it! I'm thinking here. And, no, I didn't decide so soon that the manuscript was authentic. In fact, I still have my doubts. Ah! Now I remember. 'Literary resurrection from the dead.' That's the phrase, and it really captures what I was feeling. But to go on—a comparison of handwriting is only the beginning, and I wasn't ready to stake my reputation on this new manuscript without a thorough, scientific in- vestigation. All right, I told myself, on the surface this thing looks genuine. I get a tingly feeling just sitting in its presence. But what does that count for? Not much, I'll tell you."

Susannah scrolls down the screen to show me another set of graphs. Some are pie charts, some are blocks, but all are multicolored and contain not only regular-looking numbers, but all sorts of squiggly math symbols. Looking at them, I find it difficult to breathe. It's as though the room has been emptied of words, and so I have to struggle to get air into my lungs.

"You're probably familiar with the September, 1999 article in *Danish Chemistry*."

"No," I say. "I don't read that stuff."

"Too bad for you. It was one of the most interesting articles ever printed on the subject of ink analysis in nineteenth-century manu- scripts and concerned a study of Kierkegaard."

"Oh, I did hear about that. Yes. For a while that was a big deal at the Center. The philologists were going nuts trying to read what was underneath Kierkegaard's deletions. And they were unsure about some marginalia—whether the writing was Kierkegaard's or that idiot editor of his—what's his name?"

"His name's H.P. Barfod. And he wasn't an idiot. Which you'll see before I finish. The study wasn't conclusive in the way your colleagues hoped it would be. They learned that even with an electron microscope you couldn't peek-a-boo under the ink. And they also learned that Kierkegaard used several different kinds of ink, so you couldn't say which of the marks were made by Kierkegaard, and which came later by Barfod. But the article did present a chemical analysis of several different kinds of ink, some of them quite rare because Kierkegaard used only the very best, and there was less of that sort made. When I ran a lab report on the new manuscript, using the same microscopy techniques as the previous study used back in 1999, I found exact matches of two inks. That's what these charts illustrate. Naturally, the likelihood of matching the exact chemical composition of ink from the mid-1800s with something found on the market today is, well, miniscule. But I still wasn't convinced that the new manuscript was definitely authentic."

"Seems like you had plenty there to convince you," I say and hope that she doesn't have another set of graphs to show me. Naturally, she does.

"Almost. I'd say I was 85% certain by this point. But then I narrowed down my examples to only those written in the same inks as appear in the *Danish Chemistry* study and were also found by the new analysis. That's when I discovered something interesting." Susannah pulls out a drawer in her desk and reaches inside. She hands me an antique leather notebook—very ornate, with gold stenciling on the front cover, and a brass clasp for keeping the pages closed. When I try to open it and look inside, I can't get the clasp to budge. She laughs, but for some reason I know she's not laughing at me. I like the sound of her laughter and I find her, momentarily, charming.

"Try this," she says and hands me a pencil. "It works like a key."

I place the tip of the pencil inside a tiny hole beside the clasp and immediately the notebook springs open.

"That thing's almost two hundred years old and the mechanism still works," says Susannah.

She shakes her head in wonder. I bet she's opened and closed this notebook a hundred time, sitting here in her dark office, laughing each time it works.

"But look inside," she says. "What do you notice?"

"Barfod the Butcher's been here," I say.

"Huh?"

"That's what the philologists back at the Center call him. Barfod was more of a butcher than an editor, they say. He'd cut passages out of Kierkegaard's manuscripts and send them to the printer, then never bother to retrieve them. We lost a lot of Kierkegaard's originals thanks to the Butcher."

I hold up the nearly empty notebook.

"The pages that were in here are probably lost forever," I say.

"Maybe they're not lost," says Susannah. "Maybe they were stolen."

"Stolen," I echo. "You think the pages in the new manuscript came from this notebook? But how would you know that?"

"Macrophotography. When I had the manuscript—and oh how I wish I still had it!—I compared it with the tears from the binding of this notebook. They matched. Exactly."

"Photography? So you have pictures of the new manuscript?"

"Well, sort of. I have enlarged images of the torn edges. No words. I was only trying to see if pages might have been torn out from one of Kierkegaard's notebooks—which, of course, have been in our vault for decades now. These charts give the torn angle dimensions of the pages in the new manuscript and match them to tears in the notebook. It's nearly conclusive."

"How could you possibly have any doubts after that!"

"It's still theoretically possible that we're dealing with a forgery. I want to be honest about that. It would be very difficult—I wouldn't even know how to do it myself—but someone might get hold of the right paper and ink, and that person might have the necessary skills to imitate Kierkegaard's handwriting. In theory, it's possible."

"Not if you're right about the torn pages. No one could fake that."

"Let's say I'm 95% certain. I won't go any higher than that."

"How can you still have doubts?"

Susannah looks past me across her office. "Close that door, will you?"

I walk across her office and close the door. To do so I have to bend over and move a heavy box overflowing with books. Susannah had placed it there as a door stop. Even with the door closed, she speaks in a whisper.

"I don't trust all of my colleagues. And there's no way for me to test their truthfulness. They're not like manuscripts. I can't put them under an electron microscope. What if one of them forged the new manuscript, even replaced some of the notebooks in the archive with fakes? It's possible that someone is trying to trip me up. I've never been wrong about a manuscript before, and I guess you can say I'm a little proud of that fact. Why shouldn't I be? Maybe someone is jealous of me. Maybe someone would just love to say, 'Gotcha, Susannah!'"

"Well, one thing's for sure."

"What?"

"No one could have done a more thorough job than you've done.

I respect your care. I really do. I try to pay close attention to details in my own work, and I hate it when people are sloppy." I look around the office and ignore the obvious comment. "But I still don't understand something. Who put the manuscript in the desk? Are you saying Barfod did that?"

"Possibly. If he did, he saved a manuscript so we'd have something of Kierkegaard's to enjoy later. Or else Kierkegaard put it there, which means he sometimes tore pages out of his notebooks. And if he was in the habit of tearing pages out of his notebooks, it doesn't seem fair to criticize Barfod for doing the same thing later. I think the people at the Center owe him an apology, one way or the other. Calling him a butcher is just mean."

"I'll let them know."

"So. Should I email the document to you? What's your address?"

"I don't have email. I don't have a computer."

Susannah turns her head and looks at me. Her mouth is open, like a fish starved for air, and her glasses have slid down the bridge of her nose and sit cockeyed.

"You're kidding?"

When Mette started thinking I had Asperger's, she couldn't understand this part about me either. She thought everyone with the diagnosis was supposed to love computers and do math in their heads. But I was off the charts in so many other ways—a real Asperger's overachiever.

"Sorry. I don't even know how to use a computer."

"All right," Susannah says, recovering. "Then I'll print off my report. I'm sure you'll be needing it."

"No. Don't. I don't need it. I don't know what I'd do with it. Don't waste your time."

"Of course you need it. You have to show it to whoever's going to pay the ransom and get the manuscript back. They'll want proof that the manuscript is for real."

Susannah pushes some keys, and a printer underneath her desk starts to produce pages. She reaches under her chair and retrieves them as they come out.

"Really," I say. "I don't have anything to do with that. I wouldn't know who to show your report to. I wouldn't know what to do with it."

"But you're the new director. You took Mette's place, right?"

I laugh.

"Oh, no. They'd never make me the director!"

"I checked the Center's website. You've been there the longest. I just assumed they'd put you in charge. And here you show up before hours to talk with me. I don't get it. If you're not here as the director, what are you doing here?"

"I came to see some manuscripts," I say. I reach into my pocket and take out a slip of paper with the two reference numbers on it—but not the paper in Mette's handwriting. That's too valuable to me. I left it back in my apartment.

Susannah looks at the paper and shakes her head.

"These aren't even Kierkegaard manuscripts. They're related to him, but they're from sometime after he died. They're probably letters by one of his contemporaries writing about him to another contemporary. God! Why would you want to see these?"

"I have my reasons," I say.

She hands back the paper.

"I just wasted an hour of my morning talking to the wrong person. You're not who I thought you were at all. If you're not the director, you can't help me."

She takes the printout and flings the pages across her desk. Then she stares into her computer screen, intent on something. Whatever it is, I don't think it has to do with helping me. Still, I try.

"Will you get the manuscripts for me?" I ask.

"No. Ask someone else. I'm busy. Good-bye."

"Who? Who do I ask?"

Susannah says nothing.

After a few seconds of silence, I leave. I walk down the hallway until I see a light under a door. When I knock on it, a middle-aged man opens almost immediately and greets me with a smile. It's clear that he's just arrived to work. Even so, he invites me, a complete stranger, into his office. While he removes the bike clips from his trouser legs and hangs up his jacket, I tell him who I am and what I've come for.

"But how did you get up here?" he asks. "Who brought you?"

"Susannah," I say. "But she decided she didn't want to get the manuscripts for me after all."

The man gives a weak laugh. "Ah, you met Susannah. I'm sure she meant well. But it's no problem. I'll get the manuscripts for you and bring them to the Reading Room. Do you know where that is?"

I shake my head.

"Not a problem. I'll show you."

Chapter 6

The Manuscripts Reading Room is self-contained, about the size of a typical living room, with a circulation desk, several rows of steel bookcases, and two wooden tables with white enamel tops. The doors on each end, locked and protected by an alarm system, are made out of glass. The walls are glass, too. I can look out into the library and see people walking together in groups, as if they are being led on tours. Around them there are yet more glass walls. I feel like I'm trapped inside an aquarium, which itself is placed inside a larger aquarium, and I want so much to fall to my knees and hug a wooden leg of one of the tables just for the sense of security it would give me. But then anyone out there could see me in here, and who knows what they'd make of my behavior. So, instead I browse the bookshelves.

It doesn't surprise me when I find two entire shelves lined with the work of the Søren Kierkegaard Research Center. Over the last two decades, the Center has produced one new volume after another in a series titled, in good Danish simplicity, *Søren Kierkegaard's Writings*, and neatly divided between works published in his lifetime and works left unpublished at the time of his death. They are serious-looking books of the highest order of scholarship—thick, cloth-bound volumes, each with the same logo on the spine, numbered according to a system that Mette's husband, Peter, worked out with infinite care. I can remember the meticulously handwritten chart he kept on the wall of his office, back when he and Mette shared an office, back when both of them were alive, and how pleased he was whenever one of the volumes arrived newly printed from the publisher. He would assemble the staff in his office, and we'd watch as he drew a much-satisfied check mark next to *Volume VII: Concluding Unscientific Postscript* or *Volume XIX:*

Notebooks 1–15. After Peter died, Mette took down the chart, rolled it up, and put it I don't know where. But the series continued to be produced. Here it is in front of me—twenty-five volumes of Kierkegaard and twenty-four volumes of commentary. Only a few more left to go and the set will be complete. I am looking through Volume *XXVII: Loose Papers* when the man who led me to the Reading Room returns with the manuscripts I requested.

"It's unprecedented in the whole history of scholarship," he says. "What Peter and Mette were able to do is just amazing. We have researchers from around the world who absolutely rave about the thoroughness of this series. They've never seen anything like it because there is nothing like it. To think that you could document a writer's career as closely as they've done with Kierkegaard—down to the tiniest scraps of paper—and use the most up-to-date theories in philology so that the writing is not manipulated by the editors, but revealed, displayed. They show you Kierkegaard as if he stood behind polished glass—so clear you could bump your head against the window thinking it was pure air. I know that's what they dreamed of. Those two. There will never be another pair like them."

"I notice you only have the Danish here," I say. "Some of the volumes have been translated into English, you know."

"Yes. I know that. Of course, the library owns them—multiple copies. But we don't keep them here. They're in general circulation, and I can tell you they get used."

"They do?"

"Quite a lot. Would you like to sit down over here? The circulation assistant should be here soon. I'll just wait with you until he comes."

He leads me to one of the tables and we sit down.

"I hope this is what you were looking for," he says and passes me two thin bundles in standard archival wrap, each with the Royal Library's seal stamped on the outside. "I haven't been back in the vault in years. But I can still find my way around."

Once I have the manuscript pages in front of me and my pencil and exercise booklet off to one side, I vanish to the world, and I am gone I don't know how long. My concentration, when I'm really working, can be like a trance, and I am perhaps more deeply swallowed now because so many days have gone by without my having had any chance to do the work I love to do—pay attention to words, hear what they say and say back what they mean, what they could mean or most likely would mean in English rather than Danish; what the words mean, in some sense, beyond both languages, in another more essential language, which is like a sea I cast into and draw out words—some I throw back, others I keep; and I do this over and over again in my mind, until whole sentences of the right words are strung together with a rhythm that holds them like a taut wire—and these word-strung wires I place carefully on the lines of my exercise booklet, one after another, down the page and onto the next. When I am about halfway finished with the first manuscript, I have this:

November 1, 1898

Dear Fru Schlegel,
Since everything has already been given to me "as my rightful possession," as people say, it will not surprise you if I now remind you of the pledges you made when we parted earlier today: 1) that you shall not withdraw any of the material upon which I, in good trust, built my presentation; and 2) that the packet will be sealed in your presence and stored in the library. As number 3, I wish to ask if you would agree to add the condition that the packet shall remain unopened until ten years after your death? That was my intention, and I have a strong wish to arrange it accordingly. When it comes right down to it, everything that people may wish to know something about is set forth in my presentation. But even though I painstakingly and conscientiously held myself to the truth, a certain guarantee was nevertheless necessary . . .

When I look up from my writing, the man is still there, sitting quietly with one leg crossed over the other, a pleased expression on his face.

"You love your work, don't you?" he asks.

"I guess so. I'm good at it. It's easy to enjoy something you're good at."

"That's probably true most of the time. As long as the work is also meaningful to you."

"Translating Kierkegaard is not only meaningful, it's meta-meaningful. The work itself is meaningful, and the words I translate are often about finding meaning. I have no scarcity of meaning in my life."

"That must be nice. You know, Peter and Mette helped me get my job. And then they did the Library an even greater favor by convincing us to hire Susannah. They sold us on doing our civic duty, but she's been amazing for us. Susannah has saved us several million kroner by detecting forgeries. She is a little unusual, as you probably noticed."

"I thought I noticed something. What's wrong with her?"

"Nothing's wrong, really. She's different." He pauses a moment.

"Oh, I'm sure she wouldn't mind my telling you. She's actually proud of the fact that she has Asperger's. Some days she wears a T-shirt to work that says . . ." He laughs to himself. "It's a little crude, to tell you the truth. She got it in America. It says, 'I'm an Aspie, So Stick It Up Yours!' "

"Stick it up your what?" I ask.

"Ass, I presume. Like I said, she's a little different, including her humor."

"She told me a funny joke," I say. "She actually thought I was the next director of the Kierkegaard Center. Imagine that!"

"Why not? Why couldn't you be? I mean, if that's something you wanted."

It is always hard for me to know when someone is teasing me, and naturally I am inclined to think I'm being teased now. Daniel Peters, Director of the Søren Kierkegaard Research Center: Ha! But when I take a closer look at my conversant, I don't see any signs of his joking. His half-smile seems a hundred percent genuine, and he looks so solid and self-assured. He is a man whose picture could be placed in a dictionary's margin right next to the word "confident." It's not only that he wears a starched white shirt and a crisp blue blazer, but it's also the way he exists inside his clothes, completely at ease. People like him and Jesper Olsen and N.F.S. Grundtvig amaze me. They're what people call "a man's man."

"I don't know," I say. "Maybe I would like being the director."

He nods his head. "Have you applied? Have you seen the protocol?"

"No. What protocol?"

I like that word "protocol." It makes me think that a set of clearly defined rules has been established, is printed in dark ink on extra-heavy typing paper, and all I have to do is request a copy.

"When there's a vacancy in a position as important as this one, the Board usually meets right away and agrees on the sort of person they'd like to fill the vacancy and how they will proceed in generating candidates. That's called the 'protocol,' and it's usually posted on the official website. Often times, they look for someone within the institution, usually someone with many years of experience. In some cases, they'll simply pick an internal candidate without extending the search to outsiders. How long have you been with the Center?"

"Almost twenty years," I say. I feel a flush spreading up my neck. It's as though I've already begun my interview process.

"That's a long time. Someone like you would be highly valued because you know the history of the institution, of the Center, and not merely by reading about it, but by living through the experience. You would know who gets along with whom, what crazy ideas have been tried in the past and failed, which donors are most likely to give money for particular projects—and a whole host of other things. Experience counts tremendously."

I nod my head and try to control my breathing. If I were the director, I wouldn't have to ask Anders for any of the keys. I'd have my own set. And when it comes time for that annual letter to Danish Immigration, which Peter wrote for me for fifteen years in a row and Mette for the last three, I'd write it myself stating that I hereby affirm that I am uniquely qualified for the job that I hold and which I attest to with my signature provided below.

"Where did you say they keep the protocol?" I ask, holding my pencil against the page.

"It's probably on the Center's website."

While I write down that valuable piece of information—"Center's website"—the door closer to where we are sitting opens and a young man in blue jeans and a knit sweater walks in.

"*God morgen*," he says. Good morning. He walks around the desk and turns on a computer.

"Karl's here," my companion and job coach tells me. "You'll be in good hands." He stands up. "I'll be interested to know if you apply for the job, and I wish you all the best luck if you do."

We shake hands and he leaves. A moment later, just as I'm getting back to my translation work, Karl walks over to my table. He's holding a clipboard in his hand.

"I see the Director's broken his own rule," he says, smiling. "Everyone is supposed to sign in and sign out. I'm afraid you need to sign your name here. Even if you are a friend of Thor's."

I take the clipboard and write my name on one of the blanks.

"Thor?" I ask.

"Yes. Thorkild Grønkjær. The Director of the Royal Library."

I nod my head. So that wasn't just anyone who thought I could be the next director of the Søren Kierkegaard Research Center. That was a director himself. And maybe, as the expression goes, it takes one to know one.

When I finish my translations and leave the Black Diamond, it is already past two in the afternoon. I take a series of narrow side streets, through a part of medieval Copenhagen, and wend my way onto Strøget, where it's easy to find lunch to go. Today I decide on a big slice of ham and cheese pizza from a shop I often go to. The owner is Italian and he keeps a tidy storefront with all his choices displayed under a clear plastic cover. He uses a wooden paddle to slide my slice into the oven directly behind him, and while it warms up he takes my 25 kroner and drops it in a till. We've never introduced ourselves, but he knows what my favorite kinds of pizza are and apologizes profusely whenever he's out of one; and I know that his favorite soccer team is Juventus, though we have agreed not to talk about sports because the topic doesn't interest me.

"*Værsgo*," he says with an accent even I can tell is foreign. Then he hands me my pizza wrapped in paper.

"*Tak*," I say.

That's it: two words and 25 kroner and I have my lunch.

I eat while I walk through the crowds of tourists and city dwellers. I doubt Kierkegaard ever ate while he was walking this street, but he surely did walk this street, sometimes for hours, to the point that he ran up quite a bill at the cobbler's having new soles put on his shoes. Like many philosophers, Kierkegaard was peripatetic, and the habit of daily walks helped him with his writing in at least two ways. First, he often had new thoughts that occurred to him while walking, the motion of the body stimulating the firing of synapses, and he would return to his apartment with hours-worth of material all prepared in his head and ready to be transcribed onto the page. And second, he needed something to break up the monotony of his strenuous, even if pleasurable, work. He often referred to his walks as taking a "people bath," and there are hundreds of accounts of Copenhageners who met Magister Kierkegaard on the street and walked along with him in intense conversation. After Kierkegaard died, one of his biographers published a request for anecdotes about him, and the most common setting was the street I'm walking on now. There's a good reason for it: this street was practically the only place where people could see and interact with Kierkegaard, who spent most of his day hidden away at his writing. Except for his secretary, his house servant, and his one close friend, Kierkegaard never allowed anyone to visit him in his apartment. Visitors to his door were turned away with the report that Magister Kierkegaard was not at home—even though many of these disappointed visitors reported that they saw a light in his study window, along with the figure of a man hunched over a desk. One person said he exchanged a look with Kierkegaard, who spied out his window at just the wrong time and had to give an embarrassed smile for being caught "at home" when his servant had said he wasn't.

As I walk and chew, enjoying the warm, lightly seasoned red sauce mixing with an aged mozzarella, salty ham slices, and a thin crust coated on the bottom with cornmeal, I am aware of my own thoughts, which are divided between two subjects. Although I translated the complete texts of the two manuscripts Mette directed me to in her hidden note, and I had no difficulty whatsoever with understanding the meaning of the texts, both of them being fairly straightforward letters, still I have no idea why she wanted me to read those particular manuscripts. I can't translate my translations. They make sense, but they make no sense to me, personally. "Why are you showing me this?" I would ask Mette, if she were alive to answer me. And I don't know how much time to spend trying to solve her riddle—especially since I have this other thought, the thought of applying for the position of Center Director. I am thinking about that now as I stand in front of the glass window of an expensive men's fashion store. Stenciled in different fonts across the top of the window are the names of famous designers, some of whom Carsten probably knows personally, or at least keeps in business. I lick the last of the red sauce off of my fingers and crumple up the paper. If I am to become the next director, shouldn't I dress like it? I toss the paper into a waste basket and walk into a store I've never before dreamed of entering.

Lights encased in cylinders hang down from the ceiling and illuminate the fine merchandise, some of which is tucked into wooden cubbies, and some of which is neatly arranged on hangers placed in a staggered fashion on stainless steel rods that jut out from the wall. This is not the JCPenney's of my youth. I can remember going back-to-school shopping with my mother, pulling shirts and pants from the racks and going into the dressing room with my arms loaded. Back in the '70s, a brand called Garanimals was popular, and all you had to do to create a perfect outfit was to make sure both top and bottom had the same animal decal on it, say a zebra or a monkey. You would never mix the two. Even I understood that to wear a zebra with a monkey was to commit treason in fashion sense, and I genuinely appreciated the help of this ingenious line of children's clothing. I only wish they had a line for adults. How to do without Garanimals, or some similar sartorial aid, is the first problem that strikes me as I pass through the door and step across a shiny marble floor.

"May I help you?" a thin, gray-haired man asks me. He is dressed in a pinstriped suit with a red silk tie, and across his shoulders a yellow tape measure with large black numbers dangles down the front of his suit coat. Immediately I know I am in way over my head. Not only do these clothes not have animal decals on them, they don't even have sizes. This is one of those places where a tailor—apparently they still exist— walks around you while you hold your arms in the air and he measures your waist, your inseam, your arms, and neck. Then he takes pins with colored beads on them and sticks them here, there, and everywhere. This is the sort of place I need to leave. Quickly.

"Ah," I say. "Actually. Actually, I was looking for something different . . ."

"What were you looking for?" he asks, smiling. "We have many choices here, as you can see." He waves his arm across the store. "Some of the designs were shipped from Milan just this week. If you're looking for something different, we're likely to have it."

"I was looking for a suit," I say.

"Yes?"

"But I needed it today, and I see . . ."

"Not a problem. We have finished suits here, or if you need an alteration done, I'm not that busy. I could have you ready to go in an hour."

"Really?"

"Really."

He is such a nice man, an old tailor out of a Hans Christian Andersen story, and I don't want to disappoint him.

"I'd like to look more professional," I say. "More like a director of an institution. An important one."

"Financial or cultural?"

"Oh, cultural. Definitely cultural."

My tailor nods his head sagely.

"I have just the thing for you," he says. "Follow me."

Less than half an hour later I step back onto Strøget looking considerably different. In the store's bag I have my waterproof jacket, my checkered hat, my flannel shirt, my corduroy pants, and my Denmark's Most-Wanted Ecco shoes with the tread pattern that matches the scuff marks on Mette's wall. And on my person I have a silk-blended suit, blue to bring out my eyes, a bright-white shirt with an open collar, and brand new leather shoes made in Italy and costing more than six times the airfare from Copenhagen to Florence. I look, I think, the part. Now as I walk to the Center I rehearse in my head the words I will say to Anders:

"I'd like a copy of the protocol for the director position. I believe you will find it on the Center's website. Please put it in my mailbox before the end of the day."

I have said these three sentences to myself about fifty times before I walk through the gate of Vartov. The cobblestone path feels different to me—smoother, more evened out, less bumpy under the heels of my new shoes. I take out my key and wave it in front of the sensor. The lock clicks open and I push the door forward, stepping inside not as Daniel Peters the translator, but as Daniel Peters the future director. It feels, I have to confess, really good.

At the top of the stairs I pass the plaster bust of Søren Kierkegaard, which is mounted on a pedestal so it stands a little taller than most people, although Kierkegaard himself stood a good deal shorter than most. It is based on a composite of artist sketches, of which there are many, although only one was drawn from direct observation of Kierkegaard, who did not want to sit for a portrait. The artist who drew him from life did the work surreptitiously. Unknowingly, Kierkegaard walked underneath the window of the artist's studio, and always at the same time of day, so the artist had a few seconds to peek at the famous man and make adjustments to his sketch. In this bust, Kierkegaard's hair is a main feature. It is full and wavy, reminiscent of a Romantic composer. His forehead is wide, but his cheeks are gaunt, almost sunken-in. There is a pensive quality to the way he holds his thin lips closed. Everything, it seems, is going on inside his head, inside that very big brain of his.

What strikes me about the bust today is that someone has tied a red scarf around its neck. And the person who tied it knew what she was doing. I am pretty sure it is Rebekah's scarf, the same one I saw her wearing yesterday. As director, will I allow pranks like this to go on? Mette tolerated them. Peter didn't. I'll have to make my choice, eventually. But for now, I just need to remember the words I'll speak to Anders. The most important ones are "protocol" and "website." What if he doesn't know those words in English? Then, I tell myself, I'll calmly look them up in a dictionary. That's what a confident, self-assured director-to-be would do. When I reach the main office, I set my bag down in the hallway and tug on the lapels of my suit jacket. Here, with this next step, my new life begins.

I enter the office but no one is there. The big, Viking-ship-sized reception desk is clear of all paperwork. The two computers are on, but no one is working at them. What is going on, I wonder. Where is everyone? And then, from down the hall, I hear a sound like the shot of a gun, followed by screams. For an instant, I panic and believe that someone has broken into the Center and corralled all the staff into one of the back offices, and is now shooting them. But then I hear laughter. I hear hoorays, followed by more gunshot noises.

The sounds, I discover as I walk down the hallway, are coming from Mette's old office. As I reach the door, I notice that the shrine has been removed, and more importantly a new nameplate has been installed:

"Lona Brøchner, Director." I step just inside the doorway and feel a press of bodies. Near me, too close to me, my colleagues open bottles of champagne and pour glasses. They are smiling and moving about with a loose joy in their limbs, tipping back their glasses of champagne, laughing. Among them I see Anders and Rebekah, all of the philologists, most of the scholars, and a few of the staff from events planning. Lona is in the middle of the throng. She is wearing the same drab brown pantsuit she wore yesterday, but she has a flower corsage over her left breast, and draped over her shoulder is a gold sash that reads "*Dronning*." "Queen." The three other philologists are standing together close to the door and see me when I come in.

"Hey, Daniel, you made it," says Per Aage.

He offers me a glass of champagne, but I shake my head.

"Nice suit, Daniel!" says Annette.

"Yes," says Lars with a smirk. "I believe the line is from *A Midsummer Night's Dream*: 'Bless thee, Bottom! bless thee! Thou art translated!' "

"What the hell's going on?" I ask and look at them looking back at me.

"It's a party to celebrate Lona's success," says Annette. "She's the new director. It was just announced this morning. You look angry. Don't be. You should go congratulate her."

"What for?" I ask. "For dancing on Mette's grave?"

"Tsk, tsk," says Lars, who may be drunk but never passes up an opportunity for irony. "We bowed most cordially to your king and queen, but you will not stoop to honor ours? 'He's mad, 'tis true, 'tis true 'tis pity. And pity 'tis, 'tis true.' "

Annette gives Lars a shove and he almost topples over.

"It's not like that, Daniel. It's not supposed to be like that. We all loved Mette, but we have to move on. She died almost a week ago, and the Center has to have a new director."

"Oh, oh," says Lars. "I've got one for that. Same play, earlier scene, but this would be your line, Daniel: 'Thrift, thrift, Horatio. The funeral baked meats did coldly furnish forth the marriage tables.' We'd only have to change 'marriage' to 'coronation,' and instead of 'baked meats,' " he says and raises his glass, "we'd substitute 'champagne.' " Which, believe it or not, came from the son of the deceased. With all his blessings. Unlike some ingrates."

"Cut it out, Lars," says Per Aage. "Leave him alone."

I look past them and see Lona, dressed up as Queen of the Center. She is standing holding one hand in another, massaging her knuckles.

She shakes her head at me. I can't read the expression on her face, and I can't stand being here for another second.

I leave and walk down the hall toward my office. When I arrive at my door, I stand in front of it, not sure why I would want to go in there. But I don't know what else to do with myself, either. Out of habit I open my door and walk inside. For several seconds I stand in front of the Laurel and Hardy poster. Each comedian has a tight-lipped grin on his face, almost a pucker. Their eyes are open wide. Either *they* have arrived in Utopia, come to spoil it, or *I* have arrived in Utopia, with them to greet me. It doesn't matter to me now. If Utopia is an island, I want it to be a deserted one. Otherwise, it's hell for me.

"Daniel? I'm so, so sorry. May I please come in?"

I hear Lona's voice, but I don't answer right away. She continues to speak from behind my door.

"I meant to tell you the news. I thought for sure you'd be here this morning for pastries. You always are. And that party in there was not my idea. I fought against it, but they insisted. If I thought you were going to be here, I wouldn't have let them do it. I shouldn't have let them. It was a stupid idea. I think you're right. It was like dancing on Mette's grave. Please, may I come in? I feel silly talking to you from behind your door."

I open the door and let her in. Lona is still wearing her corsage, but she's removed the gold sash. We sit down, and I wait for her to start.

"I know you had a special relationship with Mette, and so I realize this transition must be difficult for you. I'd like to do whatever I can to make it easier. You're a very important part of our staff, Daniel."

"It's not just Mette," I say. "It's Mette, and something else."

"What?"

"I know it's ridiculous now. And it no longer matters."

"What is it?"

"I was going to apply for the job."

"For what job?"

"To be the director."

Lona puts her hand over her mouth to cover it, but she can't help it—a sudden burst of laughter escapes her.

"I know," I say. "Funny. Ha. Ha."

"No, Daniel. Look. I'm sorry. I just don't think you would like this job."

"How do you know? I might."

"Really? Would you like to go to functions three or four nights a week? You didn't even go to the grand openings at the Black Diamond, for all the things they named after Kierkegaard. How would you like formal dinners with the Board of the Carlsberg Foundation or the Augustinus Foundaton?"

"Maybe I wouldn't like that so much," I say.

Lona nods her head.

"You'd hate it. And do you think you'd like being available twenty-four hours a day? That would mean getting a computer, an email address, a smartphone. You'd have to be on Facebook. You'd probably need a Twitter account."

"What's a Twitter account?" I ask.

"Exactly my point. You don't want to know. Believe me: you don't want to know. Come on, Daniel. You're not meant to be the director. You're the best English-language translator we have, and I don't want to lose you."

"I guess you're right."

"Thank you." Lona adjusts her corsage and breathes quietly. After a few seconds she continues. "Now, can I discuss a couple of things with you? One of them is good, and the other is potentially not so good."

"Go ahead."

"Carsten told me about the safety deposit box. I've talked with Erik Thorvaldsen. He's willing to let us access your translation of the new Kierkegaard manuscript. I'd like to make it a central feature in SK 2013, whether we are able to retrieve Kierkegaard's original or not. We'd like to use some quotes from your translation for posters, and I'd also like to arrange a panel discussion at the scholarly conference in May. Would you be in favor of this?"

I nod my head. Of course, Lona is right. I'm a translator. I'm a very good one. Let her be the director. What was I thinking?!

"What about Birgit Fisker-Steensen?" I ask.

"Oh, no! I was supposed to call her, but I got caught up with the party. Let me text her while I'm thinking about it."

Lona takes out her phone and does that thing with her thumbs that people do when they send text messages, but I will not have to do because (thank God!) I am not the next director of the Kierkegaard Center. She pauses and looks up at me.

"Are you free tomorrow at 10:00? I'm meeting Birgit at the Copenhagen Museum. I'd like you to come, too."

"Sure," I say. It's easy to follow; too much work to lead.

Lona finishes with her phone and puts it away.

"Now for the potentially not so good. Ingrid Bendtner of the Copenhagen Police came by to see you again this morning. She left you this."

Lona hands me a note.

"I couldn't help reading it. She didn't fold it up or anything. Daniel, can you tell me what's going on? Are you in trouble? Do they honestly think you had something to do with stealing the manuscript?"

"No," I say, "I don't think they'd consider me a suspect in the burglary."

"Well, that's good to hear!"

"But they think I may have killed Mette."

"What? No!"

I tell Lona about the shoes, the scuff marks, being the last one to see Mette alive, and not having an alibi.

"Here in the note," I say, "Ingrid says they couldn't find my image on the CCTV camera. And there's no Somali named Mohammad living in Odense."

"Right. But that doesn't prove anything."

"'Guilty? Not Guilty?'" I say, alluding to a famous section in Kierkegaard's *Stages on Life's Way*.

"Kierkegaard was never accused of murder, only of being a cad. Daniel, you're neither. Would you like me to get you a lawyer?"

I laugh.

"Oh, I'm not guilty, but I need a lawyer?"

"Lawyers are for the innocent, too. I don't want you to take this too lightly. She's asked you to report to *Politigård*. That's potentially serious. What are you going to do?"

"I'm going to go there now. I won't turn myself in, but I'll hand over my shoes. I've got new ones, as you can see."

I lift my feet in the air so Lona can have a good look at my brand-new Italian fashion shoes.

"They're nice," she says and stands up to go. "The whole ensemble is nice. I hope you'll keep it. Maybe you'll have another occasion to wear it."

I watch her go down the hall, back to the party that hasn't abated. Music and laughter pour out of Peter and Mette's old office. That's something I can't remember ever happening before.

STAGE II:

The Crimes

Chapter 1

Politigård. Literally: "Police Yard," which calls to mind "Scotland Yard" and shares with it the primary meaning of "Police Headquarters," while also retaining the more pleasant agricultural and domestic associations of "yard"—such as barnyard, backyard, and courtyard. In Danish, "*gård*" is the modern spelling of "*gaard*," and the name Kierkegaard means "churchyard" or "cemetery." Thus, to bring Kierkegaard into *Politigård* is to bring "the place where bodies are buried" into "the place where crimes are dug up."

I entertain these thoughts while walking down Niels Brock's Street, still wearing my designer suit and these remarkably comfortable and stabilizing Italian shoes. For practical purposes, *i.e.* it's cold out, I wear my hat with the ear flaps down, the string tied into a bow under my chin. In my hand I carry the bag from the men's fashion store, and inside of it are the shoes I wore the last time I saw Mette Rasmussen alive, only an hour or so before she was murdered. Evidently, the Police have no better leads than my size-11 Ecco Walkers—and if that's the case, then there's little hope of their discovering Mette's murderer, or the thief who stole the new Kierkegaard manuscript. But I want to help in whatever way I can, and so I am willing to surrender the evidence available to me. For as long as it is possible, I want to be a cooperative member of Danish society—a status I much prefer to being, say, a prisoner at *Vestre Fængsel* or an American citizen deported back to Buffalo.

I cross the street and walk beside the towering walls of *Politigård*. The building is triangular shaped and takes up about half of city block. From the outside, it is massive and looks like a fortress—but not like the Pentagon with its drably repeated square windows and overall

Industrial look. Passing by *Politigård*, as I do now, as I have on many occasions, I notice features that humanize the building without weakening its overall impression: the side along Otto Mønsted's Street, for instance, has a row of archways that lead into a marble-floored vestibule. I once sought refuge there during a downpour and found myself, along with a few other damp Copenhageners, grateful for the shelter this portion of the police headquarters provided. For close to twenty minutes I milled around with the others and admired the tasteful architecture and the interesting details on the walls, including a pair of sconces in the form of iron stars that held white-frosted glass lamps. From them a gentle light spilled at our feet. Walking around in this area, I felt like I was in a monastery's cloister, not a police station, and I still remember the experience as one of my favorite rainy days in the capital.

Soldered to the bars of the window I am passing now is the figure of a gold sunburst. The bright color and the sheer imagination to put it there remind you that a person and not a machine designed this building. It goes along with the philosophy of the Copenhagen Police—to always have a human face, to be "the people's police force." With the exception of a small minority, Danes respect and appreciate their police officers, who are not on the power trips of their counterparts in other countries. And so I know that I shouldn't feel nervous about going inside this building, where Ingrid Bendtner will welcome me into her office, most likely with far greater grace than I showed her in mine, but if I were to name my feeling at this moment, the word for it would have to be "nervous." For although I kid myself about getting locked away in prison or banished from my adopted homeland, still on some level of my being I remain jittery. And I remember what Lona said: being called to *Politigård* is "potentially serious." Maybe I should have brought a lawyer. But it's too late now, I decide, as I read a sign directing all visitors to the guard's station.

I walk around a corner and find a uniformed officer seated inside a glass booth. He is dressed in a light blue shirt and a dark blue sweater and looks to be near the age for retirement. A silver badge above his shirt pocket reads "A. Hansen."

"I would like to see Ingrid Bendtner," I say, speaking into a circular hole in the glass. "My name is Daniel Peters. She asked me to come."

He nods and picks up a telephone. After a few seconds he puts it down again.

"She will come and she will take you to her," he says with a thick accent.

"That's okay," I say. "She doesn't have to bother. If you tell me where her office is, I can find it myself."

The guard smiles.

"You have never been inside *Politigård*?"

I shake my head.

"Let me tell you a little story. When they finished building *Politigård*, the architect went inside for a final inspection. And do you know what happened to him? He got lost. He got lost inside his own design. It is like a labyrinth in there. We are still looking for the last visitor who said he wanted to find his own way around."

"How long has he been missing?" I ask.

"Quite some time. Twenty or thirty years now."

"Really?"

"No, no," laughs A. Hansen. He smiles and crows-feet appear beside his blue eyes. "It is a joke," he says. "But you would better wait for Ingrid. You are welcome to walk around the courtyard. She should only be a few minutes."

In front of me is a large circular courtyard surrounded by pillars. The pillars go all the way around the courtyard and form a covered colonnade, which I can walk underneath or step away from and stand in the open air. It is beginning to snow. The flakes are big and wispy and float down onto the marble tile, melting almost immediately. I drop my bag beside the wall and walk out into the center of the courtyard, where I can stand and look up through the round opening. I watch the snow as it comes down, trying to follow the path of a certain flake, losing it in a crowd of others, then picking out another and following it for as long as I can. I don't know how long I play this game. When I become self-conscious and look up at the rows of windows in the two floors above, a glare prevents me from seeing inside. People in those offices might be gazing down and laughing at me, but I wouldn't know about it.

"Welcome to *Politigård*," says a voice I recognize.

I turn and see Ingrid Bendtner smiling at me. She looks more like Mette than when I saw her the other day, in part because she is wearing her hair down, the way Mette always did, and also because she is dressed extra-casually in a puffy down vest, blue jeans, and running shoes. Mette, too, preferred to wear relaxed clothes whenever she could, which wasn't as often as she'd have liked. When I saw her dressed up for one of her evening functions, I always felt sad for her knowing she'd rather be in a sweatshirt than an evening gown. But she belonged to a wealthy world I didn't understand, and I suppose it had its obligations.

"It's quite a remarkable courtyard, isn't it?" says Ingrid.

I nod and walk over to retrieve my bag.

"Did you notice the stars in the tiles?"

"No," I say. But when I look down, my eyes pick out a few tiles with raised stars imprinted on them. "Oh," I say, "Now I see them. Leave it to the Danes. Who else would think to make a police station so *hyggelig*."

"It's not exactly that. Of course we want our station to have warmth. But the stars are a symbol of our history. The first police officers came from regular citizens who patrolled the streets and tended the gas lamps. They carried long poles with iron stars on the ends of them, and if they spotted a fire, they could use the star end to put it out before it spread. The city, you know, has burned down more than once, but not for over a century now. Eventually, the street patrol became responsible for putting out other kinds of fire. Crimes. The poles with the stars on them became their first weapons. As a police force, we date our existence back to this citizen patrol."

"I brought my shoes," I say and hold up my bag.

Ingrid laughs. "Not too interested in police history, are you?"

"No," I say. "Not much at all. But I think the wall sconces are pretty. I've seen them in the vestibule, and now I see they're all around this colonnade, too."

"And inside the building, along the corridors. It's a repeating pattern. Let's go inside. My office is on the second floor, which means we can take the circular staircase. Most visitors are impressed with that."

I stand with Ingrid Bendtner at the bottom of a circular staircase and look up. Immediately I feel dizzy, as if I'm peering through a kaleidoscope with its shifting pattern of circles and rays. The impression comes from looking past a spiral railing, following it up to the focal point in the ceiling: a round window with a small circle in its center and iron bars radiating from the hub. Seen from below, the window looks like a glass wheel with black spokes, and between the spokes are impossible triangles of sky. Snow falls on the window, and the wheel seems to spin. I lose my balance for a moment and bump shoulders with Ingrid.

"It's a little disorienting, isn't it?" she says.

"Yes," I say and follow her up the wide marble stairs. In one hand I clutch the bag with my shoes in it, and with the other I hold onto the thin but surprisingly sturdy iron railing.

"The architects designed it this way on purpose," says Ingrid. "When suspects come into the station they're meant to feel overwhelmed and confused."

The stairs wind upwards past beige walls that echo our steps. No one else is coming up or going down. When we reach the second floor, Ingrid leads me through a door and into a curved hallway that seems to go on forever. Except for the sconces, which provide the only light, the walls are entirely blank. Ingrid stops beside one of the lamps and shows me how a switch in the form of a small iron star moves up or down to control the light. She smiles. I nod. We pass one tall office door after another, each one exactly alike and none of them bearing a nameplate.

"How do you know which office is yours?" I ask.

"It took me a while. The first year I worked here, I wasn't always sure I was on the right floor. The hallways all look the same. I've missed more than one appointment by going too far around the circle and getting lost. Again, it's part of the architects' design: you're meant to feel helpless."

She stops in front of what seems a completely random door and holds it open. I step inside expecting an office with four walls, maybe a window, a desk, and a couple of chairs, but instead I find myself in another hallway. I don't know whether to go forward, where there appears to be yet another hallway, or to my left or right. I feel Ingrid's hand on the small of my back.

"Straight ahead," she says. "I want to introduce you to my Team Leader, Rolf Poulsen."

We walk through a passageway and Ingrid steers me in the direction of a particular desk. As we approach it, a man seated behind the desk stands up and offers me his hand.

"I'm glad to meet you, Daniel," he says with a smile. "We've been hearing a lot about you around here."

The man who addresses me is probably in his early fifties. Deep wrinkles are scored into his forehead, and his hair is beginning to turn gray, but he looks to be in great shape. He wears a tight-fitting ribbed sweater with nylon patches on the shoulders and elbows, the kind that serious outdoorsmen wear when they ski down mountainsides or go out hunting. I'm aware that, of the three of us, I'm the only one dressed up for work, and I feel ridiculous. I untie the strings of my hat and stuff it in the pocket of my suit coat.

"We can sit together over here," says Rolf and points to a round table with three chairs pulled up to it. "I started some coffee when I heard you arrived. Do you drink coffee, Daniel?"

I nod.

"Excellent. I'll be right back."

I sit down with Ingrid and try to get my bearings. I am in a room that has three walls. Where the fourth wall and a door would be, there is a straight hallway, and when I look down it in either direction I see similar three-walled rooms. Overall, this place, Rolf's office, is extraordinarily neat. Paperwork on the desk is minimal, and what there is of it has been arranged in tidy piles. On the walls, spaced evenly apart, are several framed black-and-white photographs. Two of the shots depict winter scenes with long expanses of snow-covered fields, several others show close-ups of dogs with snow in their fur, and one features a man in a hooded parka with icicles in his beard and moustache. I believe I see a pattern. A little over a month ago I watched a show on TV2 about the elite police force that patrols remote parts of Greenland. They travel on dogsleds and sleep in tents during the harshest parts of winter. I felt chilled just watching the program.

"Was Rolf in Sirius?" I ask.

Ingrid nods. "Yes, but don't ask him about it unless you're ready for a two-hour story, at least. He's pretty proud of having been a member, and he should be. Only the best are chosen. But it's an honor I can live without. Too cold for me."

"Why did he say that he'd heard a lot about me?"

"Oh, I mentioned you in our group meeting. Everyone in this hall meets together in the morning, and we give updates on our cases. You're known around here as 'The Guy with the Shoes.' "

I lift my bag and hand it to Ingrid.

"Not any more. They're all yours."

She takes the bag from me and sets it down beside her chair.

"Thank you. I hope it's not too much of an inconvenience. They'll be sent to the lab, then kept with evidence until the case is settled. It may be a while before you have them back again."

I shrug my shoulders.

"I have others," I say.

Rolf returns pushing a small cart with our coffee things. As he passes around the white porcelain cups and saucers with tiny Danish flags emblazoned on them, I think to myself how glad I am that I live in Denmark. As a boy I grew up watching *Starsky and Hutch* and *S.W.A.T.* on TV, and whenever the police weren't in hot pursuit of a criminal or scaling the walls of a tall building, they'd congregate in crowded offices and drink rancid coffee out of paper cups. If I have to be the suspect in a murder case, let it be Copenhagen where a senior officer brews fresh strong coffee and offers you sugar from a crystal bowl. I spoon the sugar into my cup, filling it about a quarter of the way, then slowly pour steaming coffee over top, watching closely while the sugar dissolves in the liquid.

"I've never seen anyone use so much sugar," says Rolf, laughing.

"I learned it from Kierkegaard," I say. "He used twice as much sugar as I just did, and he usually drank a whole pot of coffee before he started writing. Some of the philologists at the Center swear they can detect certain moments in his manuscripts when Kierkegaard's caffeine buzz was at its strongest. They call it 'The Trembling Hand.' "

"That's interesting," says Rolf.

"Yes, there have even been papers written speculating about how Kierkegaard's caffeine and sugar use affected his mental state. One scholar equates the practice to self-medication. I can't remember the exact title, but it was something like 'Søren Kierkegaard and the Prozac Sugar Pill.' It was published about a decade ago. I could have the secretary send you a copy."

"No need to trouble yourself," says Rolf. "The questions we want your help with are a little more ordinary."

I sip my coffee as Rolf elaborates.

"For instance," says Rolf, "I was just wondering where you were this morning. Ingrid tried to reach you both at work and at your apartment, but you weren't there."

"Oh," I say, "I was at the Royal Library doing research." The words are out before I realize I may be incriminating myself. I take a quick sip of coffee and almost burn myself.

"It's hot. Be careful," says Rolf. He hands me a napkin.

"Is that something you normally do?" asks Ingrid. "At the Center, they were surprised at your absence. They didn't seem to know that you were at the library."

"No, as a translator I don't often go to the Royal. But I had some, you could call it independent research."

"Would this research have anything to do with Mette Rasmussen?" asks Rolf.

"Sort of," I say and realize immediately how lame that answer is. I stare down into my coffee cup, which is not, I know, the proper attitude for indicating interest to my fellow coffee drinkers. But when I raise my head and try to look at Ingrid or Rolf, I can't manage it. I end up looking away and staring at the photographs on the wall, where the sled dogs have started to look more wolf-like than canine, and the younger, bearded Rolf Poulsen eyes me with infinite, arctic patience. I hear the sound of a coffee cup being placed on a saucer then pushed across the table. After silence comes the slow, calm voice of Ingrid Bendtner.

"Daniel, we'd really appreciate your cooperation. If you know something that may help us solve these crimes, please tell us. It's not fair, is it, for Mette's murderer to walk free? Wouldn't you like to see Kierkegaard's manuscript returned?"

I nod my head but don't say anything. I stare at the wall where the frozen, hairy face of Rolf Poulsen eyes me. From the opposite direction, on other side of the table, his voice addresses me.

"The safety deposit box," he says, "did you have any idea that Mette had left you something?"

I shake my head.

"It's unusual, maybe the most unusual fact in this case so far," Rolf continues. "You didn't know about the box. MP Thorvaldsen had no idea either."

"Who's MP Thorvaldsen?" I ask.

"Mette's brother," says Rolf. "You've met him. He said he drove you to the bank last night to view the contents in the box."

"Oh, Erik. He's a Member of Parliament?"

"He's a rather prominent member," says Ingrid. "He speaks for the Conservative Party."

"Danish politics," I say, "I don't even try to understand it. Too many parties! Too confusing!"

"If you can understand Søren Kierkegaard," says Rolf, "you can understand Danish politics."

I am beginning to say something about Kierkegaard's apolitical tendencies, but from the corner of my eye I see Rolf raise his hand, halting me as if I were one of his sled dogs about to step into a crevice.

"The box. The safety deposit box. Let's focus on that. You say you didn't know about it until last night, and I believe you. Still, it's curious. According to the bank, Mette opened the box in 1986. Her lawyer has you listed as the inheritor in the earliest version of her will, which she made at around the same time."

"She was only eighteen years old then," I say. "That's pretty young to have a will."

"Not in her case," says Ingrid. "Her father was dying, and she was about to inherit a fortune. You knew about that, didn't you?"

"No," I say. "I guess I didn't pay attention."

Rolf laughs. "You didn't know that her father owned the largest shipping company on Jutland?"

I shake my head.

"I met him once," I say. "He told me he owned some boats. But when he started to tell me about them, I told him to save his breath. Boats bore me."

"You said that to Herr Thorvaldsen?" Ingrid asks, grinning as though I'd just told a joke.

"There's something else about the safety deposit box, and I wonder if you can help us," says Rolf. "Of course, we don't know what Mette put into or took out of the box over the course of twenty-six years, but we do have a record of when she visited the box. The bank supplied us with a list of dates. Her most recent visit was the afternoon before she was murdered. It was one of the last things she is known to have done that day. Naturally, this raises our suspicions. It seems possible that she knew her life was in danger and she wanted to leave behind some kind of clue."

"There was nothing like that," I say. "Only my translation of the Kierkegaard manuscript and an amber necklace I gave her a long time ago."

"Nothing else?" asks Rolf.

"Nothing else."

Rolf nods to Ingrid and she reaches into the pocket of her vest. Slowly she takes out the amber necklace and places it on the table, with the silver chain laid out in the form of a "C" and the amber stone protruding from the bottom like a bright cedilla.

"There's something very unusual about this necklace," says Rolf, "and since you are the one who gave it to Mette I suppose you know what that special feature is."

I nod, and Rolf nods back to me. He picks up the necklace and unscrews the clasp, rotating the threads slowly and gently. When he finishes, he holds up the hollow compartment and blinks his eyes. How many times, I wonder, has this man stared into a tunnel of snow, seeing nothing but a white blur but knowing for certain that his dogs were on the right track?

"If she had wanted to," says Rolf, "Mette might have put a very small note inside here. Would anyone besides you know to look there?"

"No," I say.

"Did you look inside?"

"Yes."

"And did you find anything?"

I am about to answer when Ingrid breaks in.

"Before you answer that . . ." she says, but Rolf interrupts her.

"Yes, before you answer that question, Daniel, you should know you have the right to a lawyer. Do you wish to have a lawyer?" He speaks calmly, not rushing me, but I've already made up my mind.

"No," I say. "I'd rather just tell you."

"Are you sure?" asks Ingrid. "It's not a problem finding you a lawyer, if you don't already have one. We can call down to the Court and have one here in fifteen minutes."

"Don't bother," I say. "I'm guilty. I took the note. And I signed my name swearing that I didn't. Does this mean I'm going to jail?"

Rolf and Ingrid look at each other.

"Not necessarily," says Ingrid.

"Right," says Rolf. "It depends. We would prefer to have your full cooperation. Why don't you start by telling us what the note said?"

Chapter 2

By the time I finish telling them about the note Mette left for me and the rather uninformative manuscripts it directed me to, my coffee has grown cold and tastes like syrup. I drink it anyway, in order to have something to do while Rolf and Ingrid confer with each other. They speak in Danish, but I don't think they're trying to hide anything from me. They must know that I understand them. Probably, under the circumstances, they're simply not paying attention to me. I've brought them a clue and they're eager to examine it. I've seen the same thing happen with Kierkegaard scholars: tell them something they didn't know before and they can't wait to incorporate the new knowledge into their theoretical framework. They'll mumble to themselves like idiots, right in the middle of a conference hall full of distinguished colleagues.

"We don't know when she put the note there," says Ingrid. "It might have been years ago, or it might have been the day she was murdered."

"That's true. But we'll have to begin by assuming it was recent and meant to communicate specific information about her killer. Otherwise the note is meaningless to us."

"Why didn't she just write the name of the person she was afraid of? Why this riddle?"

"Yes, why? And why hide the riddle where only one person was likely to find it?"

"Who was she hiding it from?"

"That's a very good question," says Rolf. He switches into English and addresses me. "I assume you haven't told anyone about the note?"

"No," I say.

I've come to the end of my cold coffee. At the bottom of the cup there is a mound of sugary sludge I'm interested in. I lean over the table and take one of the stirring spoons, and with it I begin to scrape out as much as I can. It would be a shame to let that super-sweetness go to waste. And now that it doesn't look like I'm headed for jail, why not have a little celebration? When I swallow a spoonful, a jolt goes through me as if I've just plugged myself into an outlet.

"Please don't tell any of your colleagues at the Center about this," says Rolf.

I nod.

"Or," he continues, "Erik Thorvaldsen, if he happens to contact you."

"Why would Erik contact me?" I ask. "We're not friends, not even close."

Rolf and Ingrid look at each other and without saying a word they seem to agree on something. It's amazing this telepathy people sometimes have. I've never had it with anyone, not even Mette.

"Erik Thorvaldsen," says Ingrid, "felt that it was necessary to make a private inspection of the safety deposit box. He spent over an hour viewing it this morning. When we spoke to him this afternoon, he told us that he thought you might have taken something out of the box."

"But an hour is a long time to search a box with only two items," says Rolf. "When we pressed him, he admitted that he was worried that his sister might have written a note to you on the pages of your translation. At first, he looked for a torn page. But there was none. Then he decided he'd have to read through the manuscript to see if Mette had embedded a note somewhere in your text."

"He read the entire manuscript?" I ask.

"Yes," says Rolf, "I believe so."

"Did he tell you what he thought of it? Did he like it?"

"I don't think he was concerning himself with literary quality," says Ingrid, who's grinning again. "It's more likely that he was hoping to protect his family name. From what, of course, he didn't say. He's satisfied that the contents of the box have not been disturbed. At this point, only the three of us know otherwise."

"Yes," says Rolf, "and I'd like to keep it that way. About the manuscripts: you say they're letters and you've translated them both. Do they mean anything to you?"

"No," I say, "not really. They're letters from Henriette Lund, one of Kierkegaard's nieces. She wrote a book about her uncle, a long time after Kierkegaard died. The letters must have been written just as her book was about to be published. They had to do with the book's primary sources and making sure they were properly cared for at the Royal Library—which, of course, they were."

"What kind of book did she write?" asks Ingrid. "A biography?"

"Yes," I say. "It was a narrowly focused biography about Kierkegaard's broken engagement to Regine Olsen. Everyone in Copenhagen was curious about that part of his life, because it had been such a scandal. Kierkegaard himself wrote about the engagement, in thinly veiled fiction, in many of his works, but primarily in *Either/Or*, *Repetition*, and *Stages on Life's Way*. Some think he was just trying to justify his behavior—he really did treat Regine poorly—but others regard him more favorably as a pioneer in personalized philosophy, turning over the events of his life in order to examine broader questions of ethics and aesthetics."

While I talk I glance over at Rolf and Ingrid, looking for signs that I may be saying more than they wish to hear. Often, one can determine another person's interest by what's called "body language," and though I'm still a poor student in this subject, I have made progress over the last few years. One of the exercises Mette devised for me involved looking at photographs she'd cut out from the newspaper and trying to guess what the people in them were feeling. She was amazed at my wrong guesses, and I was amazed at my right ones. As I got better at the game and started to get more of the answers correct, I felt like half foreign language student and half mind reader. But there's a big difference between still shots in a photograph and the ever-changing positions of living people. Rolf, for instance, leans forward and holds his coffee cup in both hands, but then he sets down his cup and starts pinching his upper lip. Does this mean he's growing more or becoming less interested in what I'm saying? And Ingrid keeps nodding her head like one of those bobble-head dolls. Do her nods mean, "Yes, I believe what you're saying," or "I agree with you," or "Keep talking because what you're saying interests me"? Or is the meaning mixed up somewhere in these three possibilities, or somewhere in others?

"It's interesting that Mette chose letters from Kierkegaard's niece," says Rolf. "Why do you think she picked those?"

"That's the part I can't figure out. They didn't tell me anything I don't already know. And Henriette Lund is not a major figure in Kierkegaard scholarship. Really, she's just one of the early gossip mongers cashing in on Kierkegaard's famous name and the interest the public had in knowing every little tidbit about him."

"The letters must mean something," Ingrid says. "Mette went to the trouble to ensure that you, and only you, found her note, and then those two letters. They might not tell us who killed Mette, but we won't know until we understand how she meant for you to take the letters, how she hoped you'd read them."

"I'd appreciate it if you would read the letters again," says Rolf. "Give them some thought, and let us know if you find any significance in them. And, as I said, please don't mention them to your colleagues."

"I won't," I say.

I think we must be finished now, and I'm eager to leave. I can tell by the growing dark at the windows and the growing empty of my stomach that it must be near 4:30, my usual quitting time. Coming to *Politigård* has taken me an extra five-minutes' walk from Town Hall Square and my favorite hot dog vendor, who closes her shutters at 5:00 p.m. sharp. I stand up from my chair and smile at Ingrid and Rolf.

"I can see you're anxious to go," says Rolf, "and I don't want to keep you any longer than necessary. You've been very cooperative, and I'd like you to know how much I appreciate that. This has not been an easy case for us—what with all the media attention and the false trail we followed at the beginning. When someone as prominent as Mette Rasmussen is murdered in her home in the middle of the city, and the Police are without a suspect for over a week, naturally the public is outraged. Rightly so. But I feel that we're getting closer now. Sometimes you don't know it but the answer is standing in front of you, staring you right in the eyes."

While he addresses me, I make sure to maintain good eye contact with Rolf, in order to be polite, but also to speed things along. There's no way I could find my way out of this building alone, and it's obvious that no one's going anywhere until Rolf releases us from his "Stay!" command.

Finally, Rolf stands up, reaches across the table, and shakes my hand.

"Ingrid," he says, "can show you out of the building. On your way out, however, I wonder if you'd do us a small favor. As our investigation continues, it will be important for us to rule you out as a suspect. The lab can take a DNA sample from you in a matter of a few minutes. It's just a quick swab of your mouth, nothing very invasive. Would you consent to this?"

I look down at my watch. It's 4:35. I try to calculate the minutes it will take to walk to the lab, give the sample, exit the building, and walk to Town Hall Square.

"No," I say. "I don't have time for it."

Ingrid stands up from her chair.

"I think, Daniel, you need to make time for this."

Beside her Rolf nods his head.

"Oh," I say. "Okay. I see. I think I see now."

"It's a formality," says Rolf. "But a necessary one."

That word, *formality*, reminds me of something I should say. In America you can get away with a simple good-bye after having coffee with someone, but in Denmark there's a regular ritual for ending a coffee table.

"*Tak for kaffen,*" I say. Thanks for the coffee.

"*Velbekomme,*" replies Rolf. You're welcome—or, literally, "may it do you well."

Then Ingrid leads the way out of Rolf's office and back into the maze-like hallways and hidden passageways of *Politigård*. I follow closely behind her, feeling exactly what the architects wanted me to feel: helpless and disoriented.

And now, after watching an officer drop a Q-tip with traces of my DNA on it into a bag, seal the bag, and place it in a metal drawer, I feel something else: guilty. Giving up my shoes was one thing—a voluntary act of good citizenship—but letting the Copenhagen Police subject my spittle to advanced scientific analysis, under which they will learn things about me that even I don't know, is something else entirely. Maybe I did kill Mette. Maybe I took the key to the box that held Kierkegaard's manuscript and slipped it to one of the philologists, who has hidden the manuscript someplace no one would ever think to look. Maybe even now we are plotting together for how best to write our ransom note and to make sure the money is available to us when we reach our undisclosed location. Maybe this whole last week I've walked around in a daydream, believing myself innocent when I'm a terrible criminal, so terrible I've blocked the truth from myself and only intensive psychotherapy or DNA analysis will uncover it. Daniel Peters: murderer, thief, liar.

"Daniel," says Ingrid as she leads me out of the lab and into another hallway, exactly like the one in front of Rolf Poulsen's office and exactly like others we passed down on our way through *Politigård*, "I'm sorry if that experience made you feel uncomfortable. Until we settle this case, there are certain protocols we must follow. I hope you understand."

I don't say anything. I'm a silent prisoner being led around by my benevolent jailor. Might as well get used to it. Soon, they'll take away my designer suit and Italian shoes and dress me in whatever inmates in Danish jails wear. Dungarees? Striped pajamas? An orange jumpsuit?

"We aren't saying that you committed these crimes—I'd actually find that hard to believe—but we do need your help. The information you brought us today may be the breakthrough we've been looking for. It's possible that Mette trusted you, and only you, with everything that's needed to solve this case. It's a lot of responsibility, I know, but it also says something about how much she trusted you. If I thought my life was in danger, and I could only tell one person, I'm not sure who I'd tell. We've conducted over a hundred interviews with people who knew Mette. None of them had any idea that her life was in danger. If she left behind a clue, it was that note she wrote you."

It's after 5:00 p.m. I've missed dinner, but I don't care. Once Ingrid shows me the way out of here, I'll walk to my apartment. I might not eat anything. Or I might take a whole bag of Matador Mix with me to bed and see what an overdose of licorice will do to my dream-state. "Awake, Sleeper!" Kierkegaard's married man tells the young aesthete, and it's impossible to know which character Kierkegaard identified with more. The life of responsibility, the one the married man represented, was that the life that Kierkegaard believed in? Or did he prefer a life of pleasure, leisure, and adventure, like the young aesthete? "Existence spheres," he called them. "Life stages." The Aesthetic or the Ethical. It's impossible not to act out of one or the other. But I feel like I'm trapped between them. I want to help Ingrid Bendtner find Mette's murderer and discover where the manuscript has gone to, but I also want to turn off all the lights and stuff my face with candy.

I have not been paying close attention to where Ingrid has led me—we went through two or three passageways, I know that much, and we went down some stairs, but not the circular staircase, a different one, I believe—and now I find myself on the ground floor, in the open air. A cool breeze blows on my face and neck.

"This is the Memorial Garden," says Ingrid. "I know you're not interested in police history, but whenever a guest comes to *Politigård* I like to show them this statue. It was on your way out anyway."

We stand in front of a tiled alcove. In the center of it, mounted to the floor, is a bronze statue of a nude male holding a club over his head. His feet are set at shoulder length, and under his right foot there is the coiled, bulging form of a snake. The boy's weight presses down on the snake's body and makes its head rear up.

"In Danish," says Ingrid, "it's called *Slangedræberen.* 'The Snake Killer.' "

"Or," I say, shifting instantly into translator mode, "you could call it 'The Snake Slayer.' "

"Yes, maybe. Actually, that does sound better."

"It's the alliteration that does it—the s's and the long a's. Even if it's not the same in Danish, why not choose the best possibility English has to offer? And the two k's in 'Snake Killer' are too close together. They'd make it hard to pronounce the title."

"I hadn't really thought of that. What strikes me about the statue is how vulnerable the boy is. Here he is, without any clothes on, standing barefoot on a snake! I think it depicts bravery."

"Or," says a voice that suddenly rises from somewhere behind us, "he may just be stupid."

Ingrid and I turn at the same time and watch a figure emerge from behind one of the pillars, half-hidden in shadow. He approaches us slowly, holding a lit cigarette in his hand. As he gets closer and steps into the light, I see that he has dull red hair and is probably about my age. Something about the way he walks, that swagger, or how he's dressed, blue jeans and a blue jean jacket, reminds me of someone else I've seen before. But I can't place the person.

Ingrid shakes her head. "Daniel," she says, "I'd like you to meet Sven Carlsen. He's also a member of my Team."

I reach out my hand, but Sven ignores it.

"*Hold kæft!*" he says to Ingrid. "*Er det ham med skoerne?*"

"Yes," I say. "I'm the guy with the shoes."

"I'm sorry," Sven says, smiling. "I didn't know you spoke Danish. I didn't mean any offense. I know that Ingrid was quite eager to see you again. Welcome to *Politigård*."

We shake hands.

"Actually," says Ingrid, "he's on his way out. We had a meeting with Rolf."

"Hmm," says Sven, taking a drag of his cigarette. "Anything come of it?"

"Yes. Maybe. We hope so. You'll hear all about it in tomorrow morning's meeting."

"Or you could tell me over a beer. I'm finished for the day. You must be, too."

"I'm having dinner with my daughter. Sorry."

Sven turns to me.

"Ingrid is our local historian. She's writing a book on *Politigård*."

"Don't believe him," says Ingrid. But she's smiling, for some reason.

"It's true," insists Sven. "She knows everything about this place. All its architecture and artwork."

"I think we're lucky to work here," says Ingrid. "This place has a soul. So many workplaces are lifeless."

"Right!" says Sven. "*Politigård* is full of stories. Were you going to show him, you know?" He gestures toward the statue, then looks into Ingrid's face.

"No," she says. "Daniel was just leaving. I don't want to keep him any longer."

"Show me what?" I ask.

Sven takes the cigarette out of his mouth and holds it between two fingers. He wraps his other arm around my shoulder.

"I'll show you," he says.

I don't like being touched by him, by anybody really, but it happens so quickly that I'm taken off guard. We walk together for three brisk steps then stop close enough to the statue to reach out and touch it.

"You see that?" he says. With the glowing tip of his cigarette he indicates the boy's penis. When I look closely, I see that something has been carved into it.

"Is that," I ask, looking into Sven's face, "what I think it is?"

"A swastika," says Ingrid, who has joined us. "During the Occupation, the Nazis took over *Politigård*. In 1944, they sent all of the Danish officers to concentration camps because none of them would cooperate. A hundred and fifty-nine of them lost their lives as part of the Resistance. Those are their names etched in the wall."

"What gets me," says Sven in a less reverent tone, "is imagining the Nazi who must have bent down here with a chisel and a hammer in his hands. How long did the work take him? And what did he look like kneeling in front of the boy?"

Ingrid turns her head and frowns at Sven.

"Why doesn't it get erased?" I ask.

"It's part of our history. Part of our story," says Ingrid. "The Danish Police didn't do anything wrong. And after the Occupation, we took back our station. They were difficult times, but nothing for us to be ashamed of."

"Yes," says Sven, "she's absolutely right. The Police acted valiantly. We usually do. It's not often that we're asked to sacrifice our lives, but we're always ready to. When the occasion presents itself."

"Which is not that often," says Ingrid. "We have violent crimes in Denmark, but not on the scale of what you have in the U.S."

"But the worst crimes we have," says Sven, "are imported from the U.S. Ten or fifteen years after your police had problems with biker gangs, they showed up here in Denmark. The members were Danes and Danish immigrants, but they took all their cues from America. They even held their pistols sideways, the way they see it done in American movies."

Sven makes his hand into a pistol and pretends to blow my head off.

"Daniel is an important aid to us in the Rasmussen case," says Ingrid. "We're very grateful for his help."

"Of course," says Sven.

"I've given you my shoes and my saliva, and I've pointed you to a couple of confusing letters. It's hard to imagine that'll be much help."

"So how well did you know Mette Rasmussen?" asks Sven.

"She was my girlfriend for a year," I say.

"Oh?" says Sven. "Then you knew her *really* well. Was that before or after her husband died?"

Ingrid pinches her lips closed and glares at her colleague.

"What?" asks Sven. "Sexual relationships aren't relevant to this case?"

"We were only in high school. In Kolding."

"This is a difficult time for Daniel," says Ingrid. "Someone important in his life has died, and under complicating circumstances."

"I'm not grieving for her," I say. "I wish I were."

"Now that's interesting," says Sven. "When someone dies like she did most people feel sorry for her."

"Sven has studied the coroner's report closely," says Ingrid. "He knows more details than we care to hear."

"It's my job," Sven says and lights another cigarette. "From my analysis I can give you a reasonably good profile of the killer. About your height and weight, Daniel. And not very skilled with a knife."

"I read the papers," I say. "I know she was stabbed to death."

"I can show you where and how, if you'd like to know," says Sven.

Ingrid looks at him, unkindly I think.

"Maybe it would help me grieve," I say. "Nothing else has. It seems like I ought to feel something for Mette."

Sven turns to Ingrid.

"It's up to Daniel," she says.

I nod my head.

"Okay," says Sven. He pinches the end of his cigarette then stuffs it in his breast pocket. "Let's say I'm the killer. And Ingrid, you're Mette. I might not have the sequence exactly right, but I think this is pretty close to how it happened."

In the Memorial Garden, evening darkens; shadows pool around the pillars and spill across the tile floor. The best light is directly under a lamp, another sconce in the shape of an iron star. We stand a few yards from "The Snake Slayer" as Sven begins his demonstration. He raises an imaginary knife and plunges it into Ingrid's back.

"The first stab was here, between the shoulder blades," he says. "It was the least lethal. The blade sank in less than three inches, which tells me the killer either lacked the strength for a proper stabbing or may have been off balance when he struck."

Sven lowers his arm and steps away from Ingrid, who stays rooted to her place. The scene has the look of a magician putting space between himself and his assistant in order to address the audience, who in this case happens to be me.

"Now at first we thought the killer met Mette at her door, and the attack began there. The entryway and the staircase showed signs of a struggle. But Ingrid informed us that you, Daniel, actually fell down those stairs and broke the railing off its hinges, and that this happened just before the killer arrived. I'll tell you, hearing that news made a lot of sense to me. You see, there wasn't any blood in the entryway and the body was found upstairs in the living room. I couldn't understand how someone with a knife in her back would make it up the stairs—or why she would want to. To call for help? But it would make more sense for her to run into the street. Thanks to you, we know the attack began and ended inside the home. The killer either had a key to the front door, and let himself in, or Mette opened the door for him. Either way, Mette probably knew and trusted her killer."

Sven returns to Ingrid's side and continues. He places his hand on the back of her neck, but Ingrid shivers and turns her head.

"Watch it," she says. "Your hands are cold."

He laughs, and the way he laughs reveals to me the person from my past that Sven reminds me of: Jørgen. That was his name, Jørgen. He had been Mette's boyfriend before I came along, and he kept showing up at the worst times, when Mette and I were in a park together or sitting on a bench beside a lake. He usually arrived on a scooter with a loud, whining motor and he always wore a Levi's jean jacket, which he thought was really cool and really American. Jørgen was a sarcastic snot and loved to tease me. I haven't seen him in over twenty-five years, but my hatred for him has never gone away.

"All right," says Sven. "I won't touch you, I'll just point. Here, just below the right ear, is where the second blow landed, too far from a major artery to cause instant death, but close enough to start some serious bleeding. Mette's hand was caked with her own blood, so it's possible that she reached behind her head and tried to stanch the flow. Ingrid, can you do that for me?"

Ingrid obliges.

"The killer, by this point, is probably frustrated with his own ineptness, and maybe scared that someone will come along and hear the victim's screams. With one arm behind her head, Mette has left her midsection wide open, and that's where the killer goes next. A little better study of anatomy would have told him to aim for the heart, but he doesn't. He stabs her in the stomach. Not once, but three times."

Sven stands in front of Ingrid and taps her puffy vest with his fist. Stab. Stab. Stab.

"Finally," he says and walks around Ingrid to stand behind her, "the killer gets smart." Sven wraps his arm around Ingrid's neck and holds the knife to her throat. He places one hand on her forehead and pulls back her head. Under the light, Ingrid's hair looks golden and it reaches halfway down her back. She holds her lips together, sweetly I think, and closes her eyes anticipating what is to come.

As Sven begins to make the motion of slitting Ingrid's throat, something strange comes over me, a kind of blurring. I am aware of my body in motion, my arms flailing, the knuckles of my right hand striking something soft, and the sensation of warm liquid running down my wrist. For a while, I don't know how long, I exist inside a soundless vortex, and I can't tell if I am rising upwards or plummeting downwards. Finally, I feel a wall run into my face, against my right cheek, and soon afterwards something stabs me in the small of my back. My hands are bound at the wrists and my arms are being pulled out of my body, broken off like the wings of an overcooked turkey.

When I open my eyes (if they were ever closed) I see two figures before me: the naked boy standing with his arms over his head, still holding onto the club for slaying the snake at his feet; and in front of him, with his head bowed and his hands covering his face, Sven Carlsen.

In Danish he says, "He broke my nose. He broke my fucking nose."

When I try to move, I can't. There is a weight holding me down. I can't even turn my head, which is pressed into the tile floor.

"Daniel," I hear Ingrid say from somewhere above, but close to me, "if you promise to stop swinging your arms, I will let you up."

"I promise," I say.

Instantly, my hands are released and whatever was stabbing me in the back is removed. I sit up and lean against the wall.

"Where did Sven go?" I ask.

"He went to his locker to get a towel. I don't think you broke his nose, just bloodied it. Either way, whatever happens next is up to him. If he wants to press charges for assault, you'll be spending tonight in jail."

I nod my head.

"What came over you?"

"I don't know. It brought something back. You kind of remind me of Mette."

For a moment, Ingrid doesn't speak.

"I'm sure it's been an emotional day for you," she says. "And it couldn't have helped that we acted out that scene in front of you."

"It's my fault. I can't believe what I just did, but I did it. I've never hit anyone before in my life. When I was a kid, I was always the one getting beat up. And you know what? I've never been in trouble with the Police, not once."

"I know that. I've checked your record. You've been a model guest in our country for almost two decades."

"But this kind of ruins it, doesn't it?"

Before she has time to answer, Sven returns. He stops a short distance away from us and crosses his arms over his chest. A white wad of toilet paper protrudes from his nostril. Ingrid walks over to him and they stand together for a while discussing, I can only imagine, me and where I'll be sleeping tonight. I feel a throbbing pain in my back and shoulders. My wrists feel like they've been rope burned. When I look down at the sleeves of my suit jacket, I see dark stains of blood. I touch them. They're still moist.

After a few minutes, Sven turns and leaves. Ingrid walks up to me and holds out her hand.

"Let me help you up," she says.

I give her my hand and she pulls me to my feet.

"He's agreed not to press charges. I'm a little surprised. But it means you can go home now. I'm sorry you haven't had a better experience at *Politigård*. It's not usually like this, I can tell you that."

"Thank you," I say.

I follow Ingrid past the statue of "The Snake Slayer," out of the Memorial Garden, and through the front entrance where I began my afternoon visit to the Copenhagen Police. A. Hansen, I notice, is still sitting inside his glass booth, and he smiles to me as I walk past. Would he, if he knew I'd just assaulted a fellow officer?

"Daniel," Ingrid says, "I need a way to get in touch with you without your colleagues at the Center knowing about it. I know you don't have a cell phone, and I noticed you don't have a phone in your office. When I've called your home phone, it only rings. There's not even an answering machine."

"I'll plug it in," I say.

"Thank you. And you have my number?"

I nod.

Before I leave, Ingrid has a few more words for me, but she speaks them stiffly, in the tone of a formal statement. It's as if she were addressing a complete stranger, which is perhaps how she regards me after the way I've behaved.

"If you have any insight about the letters Mette directed you to," she says, "please get in touch with me immediately. We want you to continue to be our partner in this investigation. We're the Police and we'll do the heavy work, but we can't do it without the assistance of the people we serve."

"Okay, Mette, I will. I promise."

"Good-night," says Ingrid.

"Good-night," I say.

I am two blocks from *Politigård* before I realize that I just called Ingrid Bendtner "Mette."

And three blocks before I realize she didn't correct me.

Chapter 3

Lona Brøchner, my new boss, has asked me to meet her at the Copenhagen Museum at 10 a.m. sharp, but I'm here early because I overestimated how long the walk from my apartment would take. The museum hasn't opened yet, so I walk around the grounds. I stop in front of a clay model of medieval Copenhagen, which is spread out across the front lawn: tiny houses and churches, the old city walls, ramparts, and gates, the original harbor as it looked before the city filled in the area that is now the Library Gardens (until that happened, ships moored at a bank near Christiansborg Palace; you can still see the iron rings there today), and many other interesting details. I study the display with my hands cupped over my ears—but not to block out construction noise. This part of the city is blissfully free of that racket. No, I cover my ears because it has turned earlobe-pinching cold today and I am without my first line of defense: my faithful hat with its flannel lining and the supremely well designed ear flaps that fold around my cheeks like a baby's blanket. It must have fallen out of my pocket when I was slugging a police officer who had done nothing to provoke me. I still can't believe what happened last night. But it happened. And now what? Maybe the loss of my favorite hat is the penalty I'll have to pay. In my head I've already drafted several versions of an apology letter to Sven Carlsen, but as yet I have not lifted a pencil. I'd like to get the wording just right. And I hope it'll be the last time I'll ever have to say I'm sorry for hitting someone.

According to numerous reports, Kierkegaard surprised and confused many of his acquaintances by saying to them, usually right out of the blue, "Of course, I am a penitent!" Theories abound as to what he meant by that. A penitent for what? The way he treated Regine Olsen?

His sarcastic wit? The loathing he felt for his own brother? The philosopher never elaborated, although clearly he judged himself guilty for something. Maybe he had a run in with a police officer, someone from that early force who patrolled the streets with an iron star attached to the end of a long pole. Or maybe, like me, he failed to grieve as he knew he should. (He'd lost, in fairly quick succession, his mother, his father, and five siblings.) But how do you bring on a grief that refuses to come? And if you can't force it, is it enough to remain a penitent?

With my hands protecting my ears from the cold and looking like that ghostly figure in Edvard Munch's *Scream*, I glance across the scale-model of old Copenhagen and search the bike lanes on both sides of Vesterbrogade. Lona, I'm pretty sure, will arrive on her bike, but from which direction I don't know because I don't know where she lives, even though I have worked with her for over twelve years. Last night as I lay in bed unable to sleep because of my aching body and (perhaps) a twinge of conscience, I decided it's time for me to get curious about other people. Ask some questions. Perhaps I will uncover clues that will help Ingrid Bendtner do her job. I am, after all, a man with blood on my hands. Would the price of my flannel hat and the solving of two crimes pay the debt I owe? I could at least give it a try.

Lona, it turns out, must live to the west of the city, probably somewhere in Frederiksberg. She arrives on the east-bound side of the street and coasts to the sidewalk. I watch her dismount, rather awkwardly but better than I'd manage, and lift her front tire over the curb. *Bumpety-bump* goes her bike, and *clickety-clunk* go the heels of her shoes. This is not the scene you would see depicted in a Danish Tourism poster. For starters, Lona's bike looks like a wreck. There's paint chipped off the body where she's leaned it against fences and buildings, and the plastic child carrier mounted on the back is askew, as if it dumped out its last passenger and hasn't been righted for the next one. And Lona, although she's dressed neatly and professionally in dress shoes, slacks, and a beige cape, looks a little lumpy, as if she really ought to cut back on the butter in her diet. She takes off her helmet, which resembles a hollowed out bowling ball, and musses her hair, what little there is of it, gray and cut unevenly across the bangs.

"I'm not late, am I?" she says and finds a space for her bike, against the wall, alongside about a dozen others. She reaches around her rear tire to set the lock.

"I don't think so," I say.

This far from Town Hall it's impossible to hear the clock chime, but when I check my watch I see that it's precisely 10:00 a.m. The punctuality of the Danish people continues to amaze me. Never late, but never early either. The Danes must have a special gene that keeps them running exactly on time.

I follow Lona through the front door of a sprawling two-story brick building, probably from the mid-1800s, maybe a former warehouse. At the front desk a young woman sits beside a cash register and looks up at us as we enter. Lona speaks to her in Danish and asks for directions to Birgit Fisker-Steensen's office. It is on the ground floor, we're told, but to get there we will have to pass through one of the museum's installations.

We make our way through a gift store with books and postcards and enter a large room, sectioned off in many places with glass display cases. On the wall to my right I see the exhibit's title: "Danish Immigrant Stories." We pass by areas devoted to Dutch immigrants, Romas, Germans, Jews, and Arabs. In one corner a film is being played about the Palestinian community in Copenhagen. I hear Arabic spoken and see Danish subtitles on the screen.

"What about the American immigrants?" I ask Lona.

"I think you're the only one, Daniel. Traffic usually flows in the other direction, doesn't it? And anyway, after talking with Birgit last night, I have the sense she wants to make you your own display. She thinks the poems are amazing."

Warm tributaries flow up the sides of my neck; my jawline and the tips of my ears feel as if they've suddenly been set ablaze. Finally, someone has judged my work! And she loves it!

"Mette and I were pretty happy with the results," I say.

"Humble, humble," says a melodic voice that greets us from around a corner. When we get closer, we see Birgit standing in a doorway. She is tall and slender, probably in her early sixties, with long gray hair arranged in a loose bun that's held together by nothing more than a curved wooden barrette with a pin through it. Mette, I think, would have looked nice with her hair this way, if she had reached such a mature age and given up on hair coloring.

"Please," says Birgit, "come in and sit down. I'm sorry I didn't make coffee for us. I was in such a rush this morning. I'd forgotten it was my turn to take my grandson to daycare. I only just got here."

"I didn't know you had grandchildren," says Lona.

And so the small talk begins.

"Just one," says Birgit. "You?"

"Three. But they're all grown. No more little ones for me to pedal around the city. That stage of my life is over. I've tried removing the child seat from my bike, but I can't seem to get it to come off. It's been stuck there for years."

"How about you, Daniel? Do you have any grandkids yet?"

"Ha!" I say. "I guess I nipped that one in the bud."

"Excuse me?"

"Daniel doesn't have children," Lona explains.

"I'm like Kierkegaard," I say. "A celibate bachelor living alone in the city. So no, no grandchildren for me. No pets, either."

"Must be lonely," says Birgit. "But I guess it gives you more time to do your work. And it's excellent work. Even without the Danish originals, I can tell that you've more than done justice to Kierkegaard."

"He's the best translator around," says Lona.

"Yes," I say, "I am."

Birgit laughs. "Watch it. Or I may have to take back my comment about your humility."

"I'm not humble," I say. "Or proud."

Birgit pours water into glasses and passes them to us. We are sitting at one end of a conference table, with Birgit at the head and Lona and me across from each other. The room is filled with natural light, which pours in from tall windows and from a skylight in the ceiling. On one of the walls is a whiteboard with hastily written words above imperfectly drawn circles, all of it in red dry-erase. This must be the room where Birgit meets with her staff and plans the museum's exhibits.

"Well, let me start off by telling you what we have in mind for the display," says Birgit. "We are still hoping that the Police will recover Kierkegaard's originals, but even if they don't we'd like to go ahead with Daniel's translations—which we all agree are extremely well done. Essentially, we are looking for a way to tell the story of the manuscript's discovery and, in the process, incorporate as many items as possible from the museum's Kierkegaard collection. Naturally, we'll showcase Kierkegaard's desk and detail its provenance, from when it was first sold at auction, to its change of ownership, and how it finally came into the possession of the Copenhagen Museum. People will want to know that history. I also hope to have a video interview with the carpenter who was in the process of restoring the desk when he discovered the manuscript—but he hasn't been easy to get ahold of. Susannah Lindegaard from the Royal Library, the woman who authenticated the manuscript, has agreed to let us use her analysis of the originals. She has some amazingly detailed charts that most people won't understand, but they'll show how rigorously the work was tested."

"Susannah Lindegaard?" says Lona. "I got a text from her this morning. She's sending me her report. She seemed to think I'd need it for some reason."

"Probably in case the thief asks for a ransom," says Birgit. "Do you know yet who'd be willing to pay it?"

Lona shakes her head. "I've been in this position for less than a day, but I've already been asked that question a dozen times. Everyone seems to think the manuscript was stolen for its monetary value. But that's not my theory. I think it was pure scholarly interest, and I'm waiting for the scholar to return the work, no questions asked. I won't be surprised if I have it in my hands by this afternoon."

"Really? Well, that would be great! You'll let me know immediately, won't you?"

"Of course."

"Now," says Birgit, "since we've mentioned the Police and the theft, we should also mention the murder."

"You're going to include all that in your display?" asks Lona.

"No, that's just my point. I wanted to mention those things to assure you we are not including them. We've considered the entire crime element of this story as beyond our scope of concern. We've agreed that it would be excessive prurience to repeat what has already been reported, *ad nauseam* to tell you the truth, in the media. We want to focus on the manuscript and its relationship with artifacts in our collection. Of course we want to make the display interesting, but we don't have to stoop to titillation. We're perfectly happy to leave that job to *Ekstra Bladet*."

"That's a relief," says Lona.

"But I hope you won't mind if we take some liberties. The manuscript was discovered in the desk, as we all know, altogether in one envelope. The obvious, the most faithful, but also the most boring display, would be a single glass case with Daniel's translations in it and next to the case, Kierkegaard's desk."

"Two seconds ago," I say, "you called my translations 'excellent.' And now they're 'boring'?"

"I didn't mean it that way," says Birgit and reaches her hand behind her head to adjust her hair. "I wouldn't want to change a thing about your translations. But I would like to spread them out over a larger area than just one display case. We're thinking about taking down the installation you just passed through and filling the room with Kierkegaard objects highlighted by the texts of the poems. If you look here, you'll get an idea of what I mean."

Birgit stands up and walks to the whiteboard.

"Each of these circles would be a separate display. And each display would represent a different form of love—romantic love, family love, the love of work, the love of food, self-love, friendship love, the love of

God, and so on. We would pair, for instance, our portrait of Kierkegaard's mother with the elegy he wrote for her. I thought that was a very moving poem. Naturally, we'd have a large display for Kierkegaard's relationship with Regine Olsen."

"You'd use the cupboard, wouldn't you?" I ask, referring to the mahogany cabinet that Kierkegaard had specially made after his breakup with Regine. She had once told him that she would be glad to live with him in a cupboard, if only he would go through with the marriage. He insisted on ending the engagement, but for the rest of his life he saved reminders of her in his "cupboard without shelves," as he called it.

"Yes," says Birgit, "we were thinking of that. There are so many poems to Regine, though, that we'll have to spread them out. The one—oh, I love the one set in the coffee shop while he's waiting for her to pass by. But that one will probably go with 'love of food' next to one of Kierkegaard's china cups. And we don't have many objects that represent 'love of God' all that well. I mean, how do you represent 'love of God'? But there's the poem that begins, 'This ring, the ring I gave to you,' another wonderful poem. It's about having the stones in Regine's engagement ring re-set in the shape of a cross."

"I know the poem," I say. "I translated it."

"Well," says Birgit, "I think that one would go well with the actual engagement ring, which we have. But I'd like to place it in the 'love of God' section since both the ring and the poem represent Kierkegaard's decision to, so to speak, marry God instead of Regine."

"That sounds perfect," says Lona.

I nod. I couldn't agree more.

"You don't mind," says Birgit, "that we're changing the structure of the manuscript? Kierkegaard had the poems divided into his famous categories of existence: the Aesthetic, the Ethical, and the Religious. We tried following those, but they just wouldn't work for our purposes."

"I don't mind. Do you, Daniel?"

I shake my head.

"Mette told me she had to make some inferences when she transcribed the manuscript," I say. "In one place, Kierkegaard wrote a note to himself about how he wanted to arrange the manuscript according to the 'life stages,' but then in another place he indicates a different structure. That's typical Kierkegaard—he could never make up his mind. So Mette made it up for him."

"I didn't know that," says Lona.

"It's not your idea of sound philology, I know."

"It's hardly anybody's idea of sound philology these days," Lona says in a tone that doesn't quite mask her righteous, scholarly indignation. She collects herself and continues more calmly. "But you two were trying to create art, not recreate a manuscript, and I can understand that. Once we have the originals, we can study them and let Kierkegaard speak for himself. In any case, I don't think this matter should affect your work, Birgit. I'm happy the museum's bringing attention to the manuscript, and to Kierkegaard. It can only help us as we plan for his bicentenary. We want people to be interested. And I know that's what Mette would have wanted, too. She and I didn't always agree on scholarly approaches, but when it comes to making Kierkegaard more accessible . . . well, I'll gladly carry her torch."

Birgit comes back to the table and sits down.

"Then we'll move ahead with our plans," she says. "One other thing I wanted to ask. The evening before the exhibit opens to the public, we'll have a special preview for our Friends of the Museum. You know, wine and cheese, a few celebrities on hand. I was hoping you'd both attend. And, Daniel, I wondered if you might say a few words to the guests. Maybe something about how you translated the poems. Perhaps you would read one or two of them to us?"

I shift in my chair.

"How many people?" I ask.

"A few hundred."

"Oh, I don't know. I'm not very good with a crowd."

Lona reaches across the table and squeezes my shoulder.

"I think you would do a great job," she says. "And I know you have the perfect outfit for the occasion."

I shake my head and stare down at the table.

"Well, think about it and let me know," says Birgit. "Whatever you're able to do, I appreciate it."

"It's always best when we can cooperate," says Lona.

I hear her chair scrape against the floor, and from the corner of my eye I see Birgit Fisker-Steensen rise from her seat. Our meeting, I gather, is over, and I am glad to stand up and follow Lona out the door.

"I thought that went well," she says as we make our way through the building.

"Mostly," I say. "Until the end. I don't want to stand up in front of three hundred people and talk about the mysteries of translating poetry."

"You don't have to," says Lona. "But if you were the Director, you wouldn't have a choice. Now aren't you glad you're not the Director?"

"Yes. Mightily."

"Oh," she says, "I'd really like to hear how it went at *Politigård*, but I'm meeting someone for coffee in a few minutes." While she's talking to me, Lona has her cell phone out and stares down at it. She starts pushing some buttons. "You'd be welcome to join us."

"Okay," I say.

"What? Really?"

Lona looks up at me with a look I can confidently identify as surprise.

"Unless you don't want me to," I say.

We exit the front door and start walking towards Lona's bike.

"No, please. You're welcome to. It's just, I've invited you out to coffee maybe five hundred times since I met you and this is the first time you've accepted."

"I was hoping to hear all about your grandchildren," I say.

Lona leans over to release her bike lock.

"Right," she says. "I'm sure. But I'll spare you that." She puts on her bowling ball helmet and cinches the strap. "Since you're on foot, it'll take you a little longer to get to the café. It's *Den Sorte Hest*, just up Vesterbrogade. Do you know it?"

"Yes."

Lona mounts her bike and shoves off into traffic. She waves to me over her shoulder.

"Meet you there," she says.

I turn and start walking down the sidewalk. It's a relief to know we won't have to talk about Lona's grandchildren. I wouldn't have known what to ask her. And I wouldn't have been interested in what she said. On the other hand, I know exactly what I do want to ask her, and I'm interested in the answer. The only problem is, I'm not sure how to ask the question without letting on that I think she took the manuscript.

Den Sorte Hest, or The Black Horse, has been one of my favorite cafés ever since I moved to Copenhagen. They have a single-portion layer cake called "The Mozart" that may be my all-time favorite: it's a four-inch-high square of sugary decadence featuring almond cream and three kinds of chocolate, and they serve it to you with slices of glazed kiwi and strawberries piled on top and some kind of mint-colored confectionary paste drizzled in each corner of the plate. As soon as you set your fork into the cake, one or more of the layers slides out of place and creates a sad, sweet wreckage that encourages you to eat faster, to gobble it down now that it's lost its outer beauty but promises oh such goodness once it reaches your mouth and fulfills its true purpose in life. It's a shame that The Black Horse lies so far from the center of town, but even so I make it a regular stop on my pastry-eating circuit.

Outside the café I find Lona's bike standing in a rack with several others, and parked nearby in a gravel driveway is a shiny, sporty Jaguar that used to have a permanent spot at Vartov. That was when Peter Rasmussen drove it to work every day—and I mean every day, including Saturdays and Sundays—for over fifteen years. Somehow the car always looked new. Who knows, maybe Peter bought new ones and I didn't notice. Cars, in general, don't interest me. But I know from seeing this one here today that Carsten Rasmussen is the person Lona is meeting for coffee.

I find the two of them in the back, seated at a table next to a wall with a saxophone mounted on it. Other jazz instruments hang from the ceiling, old retired trumpets mostly, and I am reminded of the only time I did not enjoy my visit to The Black Horse. It happened in July, around the time of the Copenhagen Jazz Festival, and I'd walked the nearly two miles on a Saturday afternoon sweating my head off but dreaming of an air-conditioned room and my first bite of cake. But as I neared the café, I heard that twangy, rubberband sound of a bass, the hammering of piano keys, and the wail of a saxophone. The noise was almost enough to make me turn around empty-stomached; instead I took my "Mozart" to go and ate it with my hands while I walked back to my apartment. When I took the wax paper out of the box to lick off some melted chocolate, the people I passed on the sidewalk looked at me as though I was a barbarian. But it was the loud music that drove me to such savage etiquette. Today, fortunately, the café is not featuring live music. ABBA plays from speakers in the ceiling, but the music isn't turned up loud and there's something about '70s lyrics that go along with the café's atmosphere of mindless, sugar-sweet self-indulgence.

Lona and Carsten are laughing together when I reach their table. Lona sees me first and stops herself to explain she's invited me to join them. I can't tell whether Carsten is happy with the news, and I'm taken more than a little off guard by what he's wearing: a bright orange dress shirt with its collar turned up. Has the boy made a rare fashion faux pas, I'm wondering, or will I hear sometime in the next month that "orange is the new black"?

"We were just remembering a story about Carsten's dad," says Lona. "You know what a workhorse he was, right?"

I sit down, nodding my head. No one, it's true, worked longer hours than Peter Rasmussen. I don't remember his ever taking a vacation in over fifteen years.

"Every new staff member had to hear him tell the story of how the

English create their perfect lawns," says Lona. "It was his favorite illustration for a proper work ethic." She changes her voice to make it sound deeper, more like Peter's. "First you roll the lawn, then you mow the lawn, then you roll it again. Repeat this process for five hundred years and you will then have a perfect lawn."

"You people at the Center had it easy," says Carsten. "You only had to hear the story. I had to live it."

Lona laughs.

"Carsten was just telling me that Peter made him do yard work. I'm trying to imagine a ten-year-old Carsten pushing a steel-drum roller across the old Rasmussen estate in Gentofte."

"My arms are still sore from it," says Carsten. "And now my uncle wants me to take a job with one of the family businesses. He says I can have my choice: either move to Jutland and help manage Thorvaldsen Shipping, or stay in the capital and serve on the Board of Skandia Pharmaceuticals. Before I inherit my parents' wealth, I'm supposed to show the world that I've become a responsible young man. It's part of my image makeover. Well, I don't know. I don't like either option."

"You could work at the Center," says Lona. "I'd hire you."

"Oh, right," says Carsten. "Kierkegaard interests me enormously."

"Or why not pick a charity. Your parents worked with at-risk teenagers, didn't they?"

"Right. For a time. All the rich were following Lady Di's example."

"I remember there was one girl your mom really seemed to care about. She even invited her over to your house, but then she ended up stealing a painting. It was a Rembrandt, right? A miniature."

Carsten nods. He doesn't maintain eye contact with Lona. Instead, he takes out his cell phone and stares down at it. Even I know that this is rude. Lona must be reading Carsten's body language ("uninterested," it screams) and so she turns and looks at me.

"Actually, it's a perfect example of what I was trying to tell Birgit back at the museum. You'd think the girl stole the painting to sell it on the black market, right? To get some kind of monetary profit from it, just as everyone assumes the Kierkegaard manuscript was stolen for money. But that wasn't the girl's motive. She wanted to sit with the painting and copy it. According to Mette, she was a pretty good artist, too. When Mette confronted her about the theft, the girl produced two miniatures and Mette couldn't tell which one was Rembrandt's. She needed an art appraiser to confirm the original."

Lona looks over at Carsten, who's still fiddling with his cell phone.

"Do you remember any of this?" she asks him.

"No. But you're right. My parents loved their charity work. At least my mom did."

A waitress comes over to our table and takes our order. When I ask for "The Mozart," she smiles and tells me she could have guessed. She knows it's my favorite. After she leaves, Lona looks over at me.

"You come here often?"

"Yes," I say. "Once, sometimes twice a month."

"I've often wondered what you do with yourself when you're not at the Center. Now I know: you go on pastry-eating binges."

"And he goes to bed very early," says Carsten. He explains to Lona how he and his uncle found me in my pajamas at six o'clock at night. Then he remembers the bottle of wine. "If you can't sleep and you're looking for something to do at night," he says, "you can stop by with that Château Margaux. I'll split the bottle with you."

I nod. I don't know if he really means that invitation. He may be kidding me. How can one ever tell? Fortunately, the conversation turns away from me.

"About your uncle," Lona says to Carsten. "I'm sure he only means the best for you."

"He wants to keep me busy and out of trouble, if that's what you mean. Uncle Erik is the great protector of the family name, and he's always been that way. If my last name had been Thorvaldsen instead of Rasmussen he would have shipped me away to a foreign port by now. As it is, being his nephew is a little too close to home."

"But you have to do something," says Lona. "You can't just sit around on bags of money."

"I know. It's the curse of the rich. There's nothing you need to do, but you need to think there's something you *need* to do. Kierkegaard: the meaning of life. Yadda. Yadda. I've heard it from my parents since I swam in my mother's womb."

I don't like the way Carsten is talking about his parents, especially his reference to Mette's "womb." But how do you change the conversation in mid-stream without upsetting this delicate balance of friendly banter? The two of them seem so happy saying whatever comes off the top of their heads, but the only thing in my head is the question I want to ask Lona. I try something I've seen other people do.

"So," I say, raising my voice almost to a shout.

Carsten and Lona stop talking and look at me. I'm amazed that it's worked. Just one simple word, "So," and suddenly all previous conversation is obliterated. But now I face another problem: how to begin to say what I want to say.

"What?" asks Lona.

"The manuscript," I say. "You," I say. "How? Where?"

I probably sound like a caveman, but they look at me as though I'm something stranger still.

"Daniel, what are you talking about? What manuscript?"

"Ha!" I say. "Kierkegaard's, of course. How did you get it out of the box? And where did you hide it?"

"Perfect timing," says Carsten.

At first I think Carsten is referring to the way I've blundered onto this subject, but then I look up and see the waitress standing at our table with a tray. We are silent while she passes around our coffees and desserts. When she finishes and leaves, I set my fork into the cake and take the first bite. It is delicious. I start to take a second, but become aware that Lona is staring at me. Red streaks have appeared on her neck. Her face is red, too. When she speaks, it's in a whisper, but not the kind of whisper that's used between friends. There's a hiss in this whisper.

"I can't believe you just accused me like that. It's not fair."

"You're a philologist," I say. "There are only four of you, and one of you had to go into the vault and take the manuscript out of the box. And you told Birgit you'd have the manuscript by this afternoon. How could you know that unless you were planning on making it reappear?"

"Is that what they think down at *Politigård*?" asks Lona.

"Wait," says Carsten. "Wait just a second. Who's Birgit? And what's Daniel been doing down at *Politigård*?"

Lona tells Carsten who Birgit Fisker-Steensen is. It's left to me to explain my activities at *Politigård*, which I do by leaving out everything except the fact that I turned in my shoes to them. I apologize to Carsten for leaving a scuff mark on his mother's wall—now, presumably, his wall.

"I wondered about that," says Carsten.

"I'll pay for re-painting," I say. "I promised Mette I would."

"That's okay. It's already taken care of. I had someone come over as soon as the Police told me they didn't need the evidence anymore."

"But I can still pay."

"That's okay. I can handle it. So, Lona? The manuscript? You'll have it by this afternoon?"

Lona looks at me with that squinting stare of hers but says nothing. I glance away and take another bite of my cake. Am I afraid of Lona? Maybe, a little.

"I *hope* to have it by this afternoon," she says to Carsten, switching into Danish. She turns her back to me and I suddenly remember an event from thirty or more years ago. It happened in my elementary school lunchroom back in Buffalo when a friend, for no reason I could understand, started talking to everyone else at the table except me. Every word he said seemed spoken in order to exclude me, and so I stopped listening. I saw an empty seat at another table and went and sat there, which is the sort of thing I've continued doing for the rest of my life and exactly what I'd like to do now: take my "Mozart" to another table, eat, and leave. But I force myself to stay. Something I overhear might help Ingrid Bendtner.

Lona tells Carsten how she and the other philologists, the day that the manuscript was discovered missing, agreed to leave the empty lock box in the vault. That way, whoever took the manuscript could return it unnoticed. No one was to look inside the box until the agreed-upon time, which was to be this afternoon.

"Once it's returned we can tell the Police that we really don't know who took the manuscript, but that we have it back again. I don't think anyone on staff would steal the manuscript. I'd rather say it was 'borrowed.'"

"How?" Carsten asks. "How do you borrow a manuscript from a locked box?"

"You start by taking the key from Mette's briefcase," says Lona. "Your mother was never all that careful with her briefcase, and lots of people would have had an opportunity to get inside of it for a few seconds without being seen. I think somebody did, maybe one of the philologists, maybe a helper. According to my theory, they did this before your mother left work for the last time. They also slipped in a fake key, in case your mother happened to check her briefcase that night. They probably planned to switch the keys out the next morning, but then came the news of the murder. The person probably panicked and hid the manuscript, somewhere, I don't know where. I'm not accusing anyone. I'm just saying that it might have happened this way because I can't imagine anyone . . . It's ridiculous. No one in the Center would ever."

"Someone did kill my mother, though," says Carsten. He sits with his arms crossed over his chest, directly underneath the saxophone on the wall. He hasn't touched his coffee.

"I know," says Lona. "It's terrible. But I don't think it was anyone from the Center."

"It's been a week now and the Police still don't have a suspect in custody." Carsten pauses briefly, then addresses me. "Did they say whether they had any new leads?"

"No," I say and swallow a bite of cake. "I'm the guy the shoes fit, and that's all they know."

"If they really thought it was you," Carsten says, "you wouldn't be here enjoying that pastry. And you do seem to be enjoying it. Do you always eat that fast?"

I shrug my shoulders and stare down at my plate. My "Mozart" has reached its allegro movement where it must be eaten hurriedly, but it's turned into such a crumble-rubble that I have to use my fingers to slide pieces onto my fork.

"I need to get back to the Center," Lona says. When I glance over at her, I see that she's looking at Carsten, still not talking to me. I sense I've broken some rule of hers. I don't know what the rule is, but the penalty, ignoring me, seems clear enough. "We can talk business another time," she tells Carsten. "There's no hurry."

"Let me know about the manuscript though," says Carsten.

Lona stands up to leave.

"And Birgit wants to know, too," I say. "Don't forget her. The display would be even better with Kierkegaard's originals in it."

"You sure you wouldn't prefer a solo show?" she asks.

"I don't mind sharing," I say.

As she walks away, Lona shakes her head.

Carsten takes out his cell phone again and pushes buttons.

I pinch the last crumbs of cake between my fingertips, lick them off in my mouth, then look down at my empty plate and wonder, "Should I have offered a bite to Lona and Carsten?"

Chapter 4

When Kierkegaard felt exhausted from writing for days on end, he would hire a carriage and ride out to Frederiksberg Gardens or to Gribskov, his favorite woods north of the city. He loved most of all the speed and the blurring landscape, and he would lean out of the carriage window and shout to the driver, "Faster! Faster!" The driver, knowing that Kierkegaard was a rich man and would pay him well, would push the horses to breakneck speed. Satisfied that they were traveling as fast as possible, Kierkegaard would tilt his head upwards and watch as the crowns of trees, the clouds, and the sky all blurred together. Next to writing and, possibly, strong sugary coffee, nothing made him happier.

But I am not Søren Kierkegaard and this is not a tree-lined avenue heading out of the city. Each time Carsten steps on the accelerator and the Jaguar leaps forward past cyclists and other cars, my stomach somersaults, rolls, then stops suddenly when we reach a traffic light. I tell the young maniac in the driver's seat that, for my sake, he might go a little slower.

"What would be the fun of that?" Carsten says and laughs. He's wearing sunglasses with lenses so dark I don't know how he can see the road. And maybe he doesn't. Maybe he's driving blind down Vesterbrogade. What was I thinking when I accepted a ride from him?

I look out my window and watch pedestrians moving in a sane single file down the sidewalk. I should be walking with them. Instead I'm taking the bullet-car. Where are the Police? Why don't they pull this car over so I can get out?

"You really pissed off Lona," Carsten says.

When I glance over at him, I see that his eyes are not on the road. He's turned his head and is looking at me.

"She hasn't had an easy time of it, you know. There's been a lot of speculation about her, mostly on the Web. People think that just because she got the director position at the Center, she somehow must be involved with my mom's murder. They think she stole the manuscript and is just waiting for the best time to ask for a ransom. But you've worked with Lona. You know her. You know she wouldn't do those things, right?"

"Stoplight!" I shout.

Carsten brakes and it's as though he's switched a lever from "High Speed" to "Stop." The tires grab the pavement and we halt within a few inches of another car's bumper. Poor Mette. Poor Peter. Poor whoever had to ride with Carsten when he was learning to drive. And poor me for riding with him now.

"You might want to be careful, too, Daniel. Lona's your boss now, not my mom. You won't be given the same privileges."

"What privileges? I work, I do my job, just like everyone else at the Center."

Carsten laughs.

"You don't know how lucky you've been. My mom was always standing up for you against my father. I never understood why, and I never understood why he always backed down. He knew a hundred translators who could have . . ."

Carsten throws the lever back to "High Speed" and I feel the seat belt pin me in place.

". . . done your job and would have loved to work at the Center. Not that I care much for Kierkegaard, but if you want to keep working on him at the world's premier research center, you might want to watch it with Lona. It's one thing to be accused on Twitter feeds by people who don't know you, but who can blame Lona if she gets upset when one of her own colleagues comes out against her?"

"I'll get out at the next light," I say. "I can walk from there."

"Sure? I don't mind driving you the rest of the way."

"There's a lot of construction around Vartov. I wouldn't want you to scrape up your car," I say, but I'm more worried about being scraped up myself.

We come to Hans Christian Andersen Boulevard and Carsten jerks the car into the right lane. I open the door and start to step out. As I stand up, I can feel the impression the seat belt has made diagonally across my chest. If I took off my shirt, I'd look like a school crossing guard.

"Anyhow," says Carsten, leaning over the empty passenger seat, "if I were you, I wouldn't say anything to the Police about your suspicions. There's no sense getting Lona in trouble."

I nod. I can't quite bring myself to thank him for the ride, or for his free advice.

"Good-bye," I say.

The light changes and I barely have time to close the door before the Jaguar shoots back into traffic, crosses two lanes without a signal, and speeds away. As I join the other pedestrians, I sense them looking at me warily. They're probably wondering if someone who rides with a driver like that is safe to walk beside. I step carefully down the sidewalk trying to win their trust. Along with a silent herd of walkers, I cross the street to Town Hall Square, where most of the foot traffic heads for Strøget. I take my usual shortcut to the Center and am welcomed along the way by jackhammers, cement saws, and front loaders: *thud-thud-thud*, *whine*, *beep-beep-beep*. When I cover my ears now, my hands do double duty: stifling sound, diminishing chill. But it's hard to walk this way and keep my balance. Even in my good Italian shoes I stumble twice before I reach the gate at Vartov.

I'm sitting at my desk with an exercise booklet in front of me and a pencil in my hand, back at the job that Carsten says I'm lucky to have kept all these years. What if he's right and all along I've been mistaken in thinking that Kierkegaard and the Center were the lucky ones? It's true, without Mette I wouldn't have gotten this job. And I always felt something from Peter—a sense that he didn't like me, which I attributed to retroactive jealousy, but maybe he thought I did a poor job; maybe he thought he could have found a better English-language translator if the position weren't occupied by his wife's former boyfriend. It feels unsettling, to say the least, when someone reinterprets your life for you.

Around here, of course, Kierkegaard gets that treatment on a regular basis. Reinterpretation is what makes the scholarly wheels go round. You can't just read Kierkegaard's journals and take him at his word; if you did, there'd be no more words to write, no reason to have a research center. Take, for instance, the famous entry from August 24, 1849, which Kierkegaard titled "My Relation to 'Her,'" and which I am beginning to translate afresh. I glance over at the Danish version propped open on my wooden book stand. The passage is familiar—it's the one everyone quotes in reference to Kierkegaard's relationship with Regine Olsen. Writing some nine years after his proposal to her, Kierkegaard describes his anxious and awkward handling of a delicate situation—telling a lovely and charming eighteen-year-old woman that he wants to marry her, the matter made all the more complicated by the fact that she had no idea she'd been, for quite some time, the object of his affections. He describes the scene using dramatic short sentences, which I try to follow faithfully:

> We met on the street just in front of their house. She said that no one was home. I was foolhardy enough to take this as all the invitation I needed. I followed her. There we stood, the two of us, alone in the parlor. She was a little nervous. I asked her to play something for me, the way she usually did. She plays but it does me no good. Suddenly I snatch up the songbook, close it (not without a certain violence), toss it away from the piano and say, "Oh, what do I care about music; it is you I want, you I have wanted for two years."

Full of passionate feeling, even a little melodramatic at the end, but Kierkegaard was a nineteenth-century Romantic and this was, after all, a climactic moment in his life. It's too bad the last sentence had to be a lie. I, for one, would like to believe the version of this love story in which Regine is Søren's only love in life, the one he sought in secret for two years before declaring his intentions to her. I know it's the version that Kierkegaard wanted people to believe because he went to some length to obscure the name of another young woman who also fascinated him: Bolette Rørdam. That story, the true story if you want to call it that, is told not by Kierkegaard but by one of the Center's philologists who carefully reconstructed deleted and crossed-out passages from other journal entries and blamed the "obfuscation" (Danish: *forvirring*) on Kierkegaard's desire to control the way posterity viewed his relationship with Regine and, to a lesser but still culpable extent, the sloppiness of H.P. Barfod (a.k.a. "The Butcher") who neglected to include an essential scholarly note in his edition of Kierkegaard's posthumously published works.

So it goes with Kierkegaard. There's this version, then this other, then yet another. As if he hadn't made a big enough mess of his life with all those pseudonyms and their contradictory claims, his own personal journals, where you'd expect to get a straight answer, turn out to have more clanging notes than a Philip Glass concert. And what about me? Who am I to believe in the telling of my own story? Is Daniel Peters the most gifted translator of the works of Søren Kierkegaard (source: Mette Rasmussen) or is he a charity case, kept in his job by the magnanimousness of an influential former girlfriend (source: Carsten Rasmussen)? I wish Mette were alive for the sheer selfish fact that I could ask her to reassure me of her version of the truth. While talking with her, if it occurred to me, I might also ask her who murdered her and where the manuscript has gone to, but in my current state of mind, those are secondary concerns.

It happens not infrequently that I get lost in my work and time passes in an unaccountable *swoosh*! After a brief moment of feeling sorry for myself and irritated by the confusion Carsten Rasmussen has cast over my life, I returned to the journal entry, one of Kierkegaard's longest, and translated the entire "official" but widely "debunked" version of his relationship with Regine Olsen. Oh, some of the facts are true enough and corroborated by interviews that Regine gave many years after Søren's death. Both agree that after he blurted out his proposal to her, she sat in stunned silence. He left her that way and sought conversation with her father, who was caught completely off guard. He had no idea Kierkegaard was interested in marrying his daughter and, to make matters more complicated (but also to add interest to the story, as only a love triangle can) Regine already had a suitor, her music teacher, a man by the name of Frederik Schlegel. The father didn't give a definite answer to Søren but, writes Kierkegaard, he was "however willing enough, as I easily grasped." Another scene with Regine ensues, and according to Kierkegaard "I said not a single word to charm her—she said yes." As far as the other suitor goes, when Regine brought up his name sometime later, after she and Søren were engaged, Kierkegaard told her, "You could have talked about Fritz Schlegel until doomsday—it would not have helped you because I desired you!" Stubborn single-mindedness: somewhere in her study of Kierkegaard as an undiagnosed Aspie, Mette must have referenced that quote.

The rest of the story—how the engagement ended and why Kierkegaard felt the need to play mean tricks on Regine (for instance, promising her a carriage ride in the country but turning around after a short distance and taking her back home with the explanation that one must learn to deny pleasure; or sending her his engagement ring along with a note terminating their relationship—then later reproducing the note, verbatim, in one of his books!)—is a source of continued debate and gives scholars adequate reason to make minute study of Kierkegaard's letters to Regine and to pore over any reference in any of his works to a romantic relationship of any kind. Kierkegaard's version of the truth: he wanted Regine to hate him so it would be easier for her to give him up, for her own good. Another version: he wanted to be a writer, not a husband, and he displayed his talents by creating a fiction with the materials of his life, even though, regrettably, one of the main materials was just a sweet, innocent, not extremely bright Danish girl. Yet another version: Kierkegaard was an ass.

Today I have had the pleasure of translating Kierkegaard's account. Tomorrow I will translate the lengthy commentary that sets the passage in its historical and archival contexts and raises the sort of troubling questions that would make Kierkegaard, were he alive, squirm a bit. But for now, hearing the 4:30 chime from the Town Hall clock and realizing that my work day (work *daze*) is over, I will head for supper. Already the thought of visiting *Morfar's Pølsevogn* has my mouth watering.

I am not expecting to see Mette's ghost glide from behind a newspaper kiosk and shimmer in the lamplight only ten yards from where I stand with a hot dog in my hand, about to take my first bite. To say that her sudden appearance spooks me would be quite an understatement. As she moves toward me, I am captivated by her face, more precisely the expression on her face, which is one that I remember her having before, back when she was alive, and which blends amusement and irritation, resolving an emotional contradiction into something like a smirk. She is angry and in love with me at the same time. She does not approve, but she will indulge. The last time she looked at me this way, we were walking along the promenade Langeline, not far from *The Little Mermaid*, and had just decided that we'd both like to have a hot dog. There was a vendor nearby, but I insisted on walking across town to *Morfar's*, the only place I ever have and ever will buy my hot dogs. Mette did not put up much of a fight, but I could tell she wasn't happy about the lengthy walk.

"You knew just where to find me," I tell her as she stands before me, nodding her head as though she'd never died. I can't help myself: I look for the slit in her throat. Miraculously, it's healed.

"I saw you come out of work," she says. "I needed to talk with you."

It's her voice that breaks the spell. Even returned from the dead, Mette would not have Ingrid Bendtner's voice. Only Ingrid Bendtner would have Ingrid Bendtner's voice.

"Tell me how they're taking the news at the Center. Did you notice any odd behavior among your colleagues?"

I shrug my shoulders.

"What news?"

Ingrid stares at me for a few seconds then says, "The manuscript. The Police finally received a ransom letter. Surely you know about this."

I shake my head. Now that I know I'm talking with Ingrid and not a ghost, I have a bite of my hot dog. In the cold air, steam comes out of my mouth and hovers in front of my face. I not only see my breath, I also smell it, and it smells like what I'm tasting. When I swallow, warmth expands in my throat.

"Wasn't there a staff meeting? Lona told us that everyone was informed."

"Not me," I say. "Lona and I aren't exactly on the best terms. She probably doesn't count me as part of 'everyone.'" Between bites, I tell Ingrid about having coffee with Lona and Carsten.

"You shouldn't have done that, Daniel. You shouldn't accuse someone like that."

Great, I think, that's two people who've taken Lona's side against me.

I finish my first hot dog and decide I would like another. I start walking over to *Morfar's*, but two customers arrive ahead of me. I wait in line, and Ingrid waits with me. She is holding her cell phone in one hand and rolling her thumb across the screen. Images flash by vertically and make me dizzy, so I concentrate on the colorful menu posted on the cart's window—all the different kinds of hot dogs with pictures beside their names and prices handwritten on oval stickers that cover up the old prices. The cost has gone up a few times since I moved here, but I don't pay close attention. When it's my turn, I order my usual and smile at the woman who has granted me my wishes for the last several years now, ever since her husband, Morfar, had to quit, or died, I've never thought to ask.

"Let's stand over there," Ingrid whispers. "I only have a few minutes, but I'd like to hear more about your visit with Lona and Carsten. Why did the three of you have coffee together?"

I follow Ingrid away from the crowd, which is a moving mass of people heading in one of two directions: either away from Strøget and toward the crosswalk at Hans Christian Andersen Boulevard, or just the opposite. Hardly anyone stands around and chats. It's too cold for that. Ingrid and I stop in front of one of the griffins guarding the steps of Town Hall and I tell her everything I can remember from what, for me, was an uneventful coffee break, except for "The Mozart" and Carsten's reckless driving, which I leave out of my story.

"Did either of them say what kind of business they had to settle?"

"No, only that it was something they could do later."

"If you can, you might try to get back on Lona's good side. It would be helpful to us, in the future, if you knew a little more about what was happening in the Center."

Something about Ingrid's tone of voice irritates me. She sounds like she did last night when I left *Politigård*, formal and unfriendly.

"What am I supposed to be, your mole?"

"Yes," says Ingrid so directly it startles me. "Wouldn't you prefer that to being a suspect held in custody?"

"I suppose so," I say.

"Do you always have your dinner here?" she asks.

"Monday through Friday, from 4:30 until 5:00. I missed last night because of that DNA test, you might remember."

Ingrid nods.

"And on the weekends?"

"I eat at home. Why?"

"Because, Daniel, you're not an easy person to get hold of. I need to know where I can find you. We would like you to continue to assist us in our investigation. The Copenhagen Police depend upon the help of citizens . . ."

. . . And on and on she goes reciting a page from the Police's Public Relations Manual. I tune her out and enjoy my dinner.

"By the way," she says. "Those things aren't good for you."

"Thanks for caring about my health."

"I have to go. I have a meeting. Please remember what I said about improving your relationship with Lona. It would be helpful to us, especially in the next few days."

I nod and watch her leave. She doesn't walk like Mette, who had a sort of glide, as if she didn't weigh anything and could levitate if she wanted to. Ingrid, on the other hand, hits the ground hard with each step, as if she's mad at something or someone. Then I see it: while she's walking away from me, Ingrid reaches over her shoulder and tucks a loose strand of hair behind her ear. It is exactly the motion Mette used—maybe all women with long straight hair do the same. It doesn't matter. I think it's the most beautiful thing in the world—and now the clock begins its 5:00 chime. Those pealing bells. That hand reaching back and touching hair. This last bite of my Danish hot dog. It's moments like this that convince me I have to stay in this country.

Even if it means being Ingrid's mole.

People with Asperger's Syndrome are often misdiagnosed with other conditions. Depression, because when you can't understand social rules, you make mistakes, and when you make mistakes people laugh at you and tease you, or they simply don't want to be around you, which leads to isolation, and loneliness, and sadness . . . depression! Tourette's, because Asperger's Syndrome is basically a different way of thinking and when that thought is expressed it strikes many people as shockingly non sequitur. Obsessive-Compulsive Disorder, because someone who is single-minded tends to prefer repetition to newness, so follows a rigid schedule; and because someone who doesn't give up easily may appear to act compulsively, even beyond reason, to get what he wants. At the moment, I might be mistaken as OCD, or at least O, because I can't let go of that throwaway comment Carsten made: "He knew a hundred translators who could have done your job." Am I really not that special? Am I not God's gift to Kierkegaard and Danish literature?

As I walk home, I grow more and more anxious to find an answer. What, I ask myself, about Birgit Fisker-Steensen's glowing review of my most recent work? But then I remember: she hasn't seen the originals. How could she know whether I translated the Danish well or poorly? Next thought: Lona called me "the best translator around." Next negation: but now that I've insinuated that she's a thief and murderer, she probably wouldn't stick with that view of me. I shake my head and stare down at my feet. What about Mette? Shouldn't I believe her over her son, who may know a lot about fashion, drugs, alcohol, and fast cars but doesn't know anything about translating Kierkegaard? On the other hand, he lived with his parents. He was privy to their conversations. Where, I wonder, is there an independent and trustworthy assessment of my skills?

When I recall the article about my work in *Translation Review* and remember that I've saved a copy of it somewhere in my desk, my head goes up, my feet move faster. I practically jog the last three blocks to my apartment. In front of the elevator doors I grow impatient and want to pry them open to get inside, shove them closed to start ascending. If there were a Super Boost button to get me to my floor faster, I would push it and hold it in. Finally, the elevator stops. With the key already in hand, I stride to my door and go inside. In an instant I begin rooting through the desk—taking out letters, old calendars, stubby pencils, American currency, my passport and tossing it all onto the floor. When I find what I'm looking for, I carry it over to my bed and fall on top of the covers. Here it is. Here's the answer. Seven crisply printed pages in a peer-reviewed journal. I let my eyes savor the title: "Kierkegaard Reborn in Better Words: New Translations Would Bring a Smile to the Danish Master of Melancholy."

When Mette gave me this article several years ago, I didn't even read it. One look at the title told me that the author had gotten it right. But now I pay attention to its every word and let the objective praise restore me to the person I knew I was until Carsten set my world clattering off its hinges. I suppose all great artists—and translation is most certainly an art—have moments when they doubt their genius. Based on this article, however, I can kiss my doubts good-bye. I'm by far the best translator the Danish philosopher has ever had. The author backs up this claim by quoting long passages from my work and setting them beside Kierkegaard's originals. Time after time he shows that I understood the "most salient features of style" and offered English readers an experience similar to what Danes have when they read Kierkegaard. "Many, practically all, of the previous translators fail in this regard, at one time or another," he writes. "Daniel Peters' attention to the nuances in the Danish language, on the other hand, is uncanny and leaves me without a single criticism of his work."

After these last words there is a superscript, which I follow to the notes at the end of the article. I almost wish I hadn't. "In one instance," the author writes, "I questioned a single word that Peters chose in the famous '70,000 Fathoms' passage in the last section of *Stages on Life's Way*. However, after I discussed the matter with a friend from the Søren Kierkegaard Research Center in Copenhagen, I became convinced that, once again, the translator had gotten it right." The note ends there. Without specifying the word in question. Or, more importantly, the "friend." Was Mette, I wonder, the anonymous source? Did she, perhaps, have something to do with this positive review of my work? Maybe she commissioned it. Maybe she wrote it herself.

Self-doubt is new to me but from my limited experience I would say that it is like a wave, an actual ocean wave, that strikes you full in the body, takes you under the surface, and shows you a murky world where sea monsters open their teethy mouths and grin at you. You are not sure whether to swim away from them or towards them, straight into one of their gaping jaws, just to have the matter settled. Time loses relevance. Darkness becomes your natural light. Resurfacing, your stomach is full of saltwater and you feel nauseated. Somehow you make it back to land, kneel there, and spit up part of the element you just swam in. Your limbs feel heavy. You sleep for ages. When you wake, the tide is coming in, splashing against your bare feet, and there's a taste in your mouth: saltwater and gall.

Maybe I exaggerate. Lying on my bed and staring up at the recessed lights, I am not, I know, sick and dying, stranded on a desert island. It even occurs to me that I could find an answer to my question, perhaps quite easily. If Mette was the author's friend, Carsten might know about it. He often complained about going with his parents to international conferences, but all the same he went. When Peter was alive, he didn't give Carsten a choice. Like it or not, the son accompanied his parents on their annual pilgrimage to St. Olaf's College in Minnesota, which is where, I see, the author of the article teaches. Maybe Carsten remembers him.

This thought is enough to pull me off of the bed. Carsten, whether he meant it or not, invited me over for a visit, and I decide to take him up on it. I walk to the wine rack and remove the bottle of Château Margaux. It is customary to bring a gift to your host, and this is one that I know Carsten will appreciate. I glance at my watch: 8:47. Would he be home this early in the evening? I am not sure, so I go into the kitchen where I keep the key to Mette's house (now Carsten's) in a drawer. Fishing out the key, I see the telephone I promised Ingrid Bendtner I would plug in, but haven't. First I have to read the Instruction Manual, which looks to be fifty or more pages long and is packaged with the phone in a clear plastic bag. Not now, I tell myself, but tonight, when I return from Carsten's with the answer that I need. Some things can wait. Some things cannot.

Nyhavn in the wintertime is like a Christmas tree with most of its lights burned out. The restaurants are still open, and occasionally a customer comes in or out, but the cobbled street along the harbor is otherwise empty and the ships moored to the bank look fast- and long-asleep, the nautical equivalent of hibernation. So much of the place is rendered irrelevant this time of year: the little house where tourists queue to buy tickets for the canal boat tours, closed for the season; the sweet shop with its statue of a waffle cone brimming with round scoops of chocolate, strawberry, and vanilla ice cream and looking like something from another, sunnier world; even the middle of the street where, in the summer, diners sit under umbrellas and sip Carlsberg while waiters squeeze between tables bringing meal orders on trays, is now only unused space—no tables, no waiters, no diners. Walking under street lamps, I don't hear a sound. This is one of the quietest parts of the city, especially the end closest to the harbor, especially now in winter.

When I am within a few yards of Mette's house, I look up. It's the familiar yellow-painted three-story home where Hans Christian Andersen once lived, but which the Rasmussens have owned for the last two decades. Mette moved here a few months after Peter died. She said she couldn't stay in the Gentofte estate all by herself (Carsten was away at college—Princeton, a lot better than I managed) and living in Nyhavn put her closer to the Center. Like me, she walked to work and back. If she were alive today, she might be standing where I am now, having just come home from dinner. She'd see, as I do, that a single light is on in the living room. She'd see a silhouette in the curtain and know that the figure must be Carsten.

He is sitting at a table with his head down, as if he might be reading or writing—two activities I seldom associate with him. I ring the bell and wait. After a minute passes, I step away from the door and look up at the window again. Carsten hasn't moved. A new theory presents itself: he is not reading, but sleeping. I go back to the bell and hold it for a full ten seconds. I wait, but still Carsten doesn't answer. The bell might be broken. Or he may have drunk himself into a stupor. I take out my key and let myself in.

The entryway looks as it did the last time I arrived here, but not as it did the last time I left. The mess I created has been cleaned up, just as Mette said it would be. My last vision of her: she stands on the third step from the bottom holding a brass bracket and some screws in her hand. The railing clings to one bolt in the wall; plaster litters the stairs.

"I'm sorry," I say.

My elbow is bleeding and I feel like the usual fool.

"Don't worry about it. I'm just glad you're okay. All of this can be fixed."

Mette shakes her head. She's actually smiling.

"I'll pay for it."

"If you want to. But go. You better go or you'll miss the bells."

Out I went. Now back I come. And here I am climbing the stairs past the last trace I saw of Mette, and now no trace of her at all. The railing is back on its hinges. The plaster has been repaired. I can't tell where the bottoms of my shoes scuffed the wall. It's strange. A little spooky. Not only has an accident been erased, but with it the life of the one person I could say (could always say, without embarrassment) I loved. Where are you, Mette? Where did you go?

The door at the top of the stairs is unlocked, so I step inside. I look over to my right and see the slumped form of Carsten Rasmussen. His head rests on his arm and his face is turned away from me. There is a book open in front of him. So he actually was reading! He fell asleep reading, just as I have done many times. This realization makes me see Carsten in a new light. Mette often told me that there was more to her son than he let on, but I always assumed she was speaking from a mother's big heart and huge bias. Now I'm curious to see what book Carsten was reading, but at the same time I don't want to disturb him. I put the bottle of wine down on the floor and walk quietly toward him. As my angle of vision changes, I see things on the table I didn't see before: a pen, a knife, a bottle of pills. I stop and stand still. Something, I suppose fear, grips me. My chest constricts. Around my head a field of static electricity vibrates, buzzes. I can both feel and hear my hair stand on end.

"Carsten," I say.

The sound of my own voice comforts me. I speak again.

"Carsten. Are you sleeping?"

I reach over and touch his shoulder, shake it lightly, but his elbow slips off the table, then his body slides off the chair, and he crumples onto the floor.

"Oh," I say, "I'm sorry. I'm sorry."

I look down at Carsten, and I know he must be dead. No sleeping person, not even a drunk sleeping person, would fall quite as he did and not wake up. The color in his face is certainly not right. What do I do now? I can't just leave him on the floor. That's not where I found him when I came in. There was a sense of order to how he sat at the table, dozing off over a book, and that order has to be restored. I bend over and try to lift him, but he's heavy and his limbs flop in awkward positions. It takes me several tries, and before I have him back in the chair I've broken into a sweat. I wipe my brow on the sleeve of my jacket. Then I set about trying to rearrange his arm under his head and to turn his face toward the wall. The items on the table shifted when Carsten fell, so I replace them as nearly as I can remember. For the first time I look closely at the book. It's Kierkegaard's *Stages on Life's Way*, and it's open to the section titled "Guilty? / Not Guilty?"

With a red pen someone has circled the first word: "Guilty."

"Who?" I say aloud, "who's guilty?"

I look at the pen, then the knife, then the pill bottle.

I shake my head.

"No," I say, to myself, to the room. "That's not possible."

I stand for a moment and stare at this perplexing tableau.

Children don't kill their mothers.

But did Carsten kill Mette?

And then, himself?

STAGE III:

The Investigation

Chapter 1

When the Police arrive at Mette's house I am sitting on the couch with my hands on my knees, touching nothing, not a thing, just as I promised Ingrid.

"*Forsigtig*," a male voice says from the bottom of the stairs. I recognize the voice as Rolf Poulsen's, and I know why he's telling someone to be careful. At the foot of the stairs there is a shattered bottle of wine (Château Margaux, 1986) which I kicked over by accident when I fulfilled the other duty Ingrid asked of me: to unlock the house. The bottle went tumbling down the steps and smashed against the front door. I couldn't help it and stepped into the puddle, tracking wine stains up the stairs and into the house. There are irregular-shaped red marks on the carpet inches from where I'm sitting.

I watch as three people enter. Rolf and another man walk directly to the table, bending over it, studying the scene with professional scrutiny. They exchange some words, but I can't hear them. Ingrid, the third person, sits down next to me.

"Are you okay?" she asks.

I nod.

"When you're ready, I need to ask you some questions. We don't have to stay here. If you'd rather, we could sit outside in the car."

I shake my head.

"Okay, then. Tell me, Daniel, what brought you over here?"

"I wanted to ask a question. But now I know it was stupid. It doesn't matter."

"You wanted to talk with Carsten?"

"Yes."

"How did you get inside?"

I reach in my pocket and pull out my key.

"You never told me you had a key to Mette's house."

"You never asked."

"That's true. But normally people volunteer that kind of information. How long have you had a key?"

"A few years. Mette gave it to me after she moved in. She trusted me. When we had dinner together, I'd get things started while she finished up at work. I always quit at 4:30. She usually went later."

Rolf comes over and stands in front of us. The other man is still at the table, talking into a recorder.

"I see you've started the interview," says Rolf. "Have you asked him if everything is just the way he found it?"

"It is," I say.

"Good," says Rolf.

"Or close. As close as I could make it."

I feel Ingrid and Rolf staring at me.

"What?" I say. "It was an accident. I didn't know he'd fall over like that. I was trying to wake him up."

"Take your time," says Ingrid. "Go slowly. Tell us everything you did once you walked in the door."

I tell them, and the whole time I speak Rolf Poulsen shakes his head back and forth, very slowly. He closes his eyes, opens them, and closes them again. I imagine this is what he did when one of his sled dogs was ripped apart in a fight and had to be left to die on the frozen tundra, or when his fuel supply dipped below acceptable levels and it meant he had to sleep in an unheated tent.

"The knife," he says. "Have you seen it before?"

"Yes," I say. "It's what Mette used to carve the pork the last night I saw her."

There is the sound of a cell phone ringing, and both Ingrid and Rolf check their pockets. It's Rolf's. He turns away from us and walks into the other room, speaking in Danish.

"There's no need for you to stay here," says Ingrid. "It's going to get busy soon, and once the media find out they'll be here, too. We won't give them your name, Daniel, and I'd advise you not to speak with them. Just go to work tomorrow as you normally do. Act surprised at the news. When do you go for lunch?"

"Noon," I say.

"Alone?"

"Always."

"I thought so. Meet me at Bjørg's Café. It's just up the street from where you work."

"I know Bjørg's."

"In the morning, while you're at work, try to see as many of your colleagues as you can. I know it's hard for you, but be sociable. Ask them questions. Any questions. Pay close attention. I'll quiz you."

"I like quizzes. I usually do well on them."

Another phone rings, and this time it's Ingrid's. She cups her hand over it.

"Bjørg's at noon," she says.

"It's a . . ." I start to say. "I'll be there."

I stand up to leave. The room is filled with three voices speaking in Danish, none of them to me, and none of them to each other. The officer with the tape recorder is walking around the table, around Carsten Rasmussen's body, not touching anything, behaving as I should have. Somehow he knows the rules for interacting with the dead. Rolf stands in front of the living room window, so it must be his silhouette cast on the curtain now, with Carsten's perhaps in the background. And to my left, in the dining room, Ingrid Bendtner paces back and forth in the very space where Mette and I had our last meal—*flæskesteg*, *brunede kartofler*, *rødkål*, *asier*, my favorite Danish words and flavors. No meal goes together better. But now, in these rooms, nothing seems to go together at all—what I'm seeing or hearing or feeling. Still I have the sense (thank God for the sense!) to walk carefully down the stairs, holding onto the railing, taking one step at a time, so that I do not trip and fall. I even manage to avoid the puddle of wine and the shards of glass. With absolute care I walk into the cold night and head back home.

I am passing by Kongens Nytorv, just about to cross onto Strøget, when I hear the sirens. Their high-pitched pulsations shatter the calm night like an alarm clock on steroids, waking a city full of sleepers. I look up and see the flashing blue lights of "*Politi*" cars heading for Nyhavn, but after a few seconds of watching them I turn back and continue walking.

A group of teenagers, one of them pushing a bike, meanders down the middle of the pedestrian street, talking brightly, reaching out and playfully swinging their arms at each other. All down the street, the fronts of clothing stores and novelty shops are lit for window shoppers looking, I suppose, for gift ideas somewhat late on a Thursday evening in the middle of January. Most of the restaurants are closed; most of the bars are open. A woman with a thick Danish accent sings a Lionel Richie song, karaoke-style. What does any of this matter? What would Kierkegaard, were he here walking his old beat, make of it? That's hard to say. Sometimes he went to parties and appeared to enjoy himself. He never missed a performance of Mozart's *Don Giovanni* at the Royal Theater. But then many nights he kept to himself in his apartment—writing, writing, writing about the hidden inner lives of "single individuals" and brooding over the problems the sheer act of existing presents us. Every day there are everyday choices to make, and the smallest decision, once you look closely at it, is freighted with meaning.

"Excuse me," a voice says in heavily accented English. "Can you tell me where the bus station is?"

I look up and see a dark, cleanly shaven face, smooth as ebony. The man has high cheekbones. His eyes are half-shut and make him look sleepy. He's wearing some kind of religious outfit—it looks like a long robe over pajama bottoms—covered partly by a blue windbreaker zipped up to his chin.

"Mohammad?" I say.

He looks at me, tilts his head to the side, but says nothing.

"We met before," I say. "You asked me that same question about the bus station. I'm afraid I still don't know where it is. No one's been able to tell you?"

"It doesn't matter. I will keep searching. I am a seeker."

"Well, someone ought to know where the bus station is," I say. I look around, but we are the only two people standing in this part of the street. "I can tell you where the train station is, but I never take the bus."

"I am tired. I have family. A wife and two children."

"Yes," I say, "I know. You live in Odense, right?"

Mohammad cocks his head again.

"They have gone, back to Kenya."

"I thought you were from Somalia."

"Yes. But I have a sister in Kenya. I am to meet them there. I must take the bus to the airport. Will you help me find the bus station? I am very tired. It is cold in Denmark. Where is the bus station?"

"I told you, I don't know. I'm sorry."

"That is all right. I understand. I will pray to God for you."

I start to leave, then remember my manners.

"By the way, my name is Daniel."

I hold out my hand and Mohammad shakes it. His grip is weak, barely a squeeze.

"Daniel. Do you have someplace to sleep tonight?"

"Yes."

"That is good. Good night, Daniel."

"Good night, Mohammad."

I start to walk down the street, but something stops me. Here I am only a block from where Søren Kierkegaard grew up, went to church, listened to sermons. I have heard a few sermons myself, not many, back in my childhood when my father insisted that my siblings and I accompany him to the cathedral on special occasions. There was one sermon about "The Good Samaritan," which I remember because it fascinated me to learn how that phrase had made it into common usage. I also remember my brother referring to the title character as a "chump" and saying he'd like to see that guy take a walk down Church Street and try "Good Samaritanizing" (that was his phrase, an unusually good one for my brother) every homeless person he saw there. Although there is no reliable record of it, Kierkegaard is believed to have been quite generous in giving money to the poor. Perhaps here, on this very spot, he reached into his money purse, took out a few rixdollars, and handed them to a beggar. I don't have any money in my pockets but that, I decide, shouldn't stop me.

"Mohammad," I say. "You can stay with me tonight."

His face shows no emotion. He simply turns and follows me down the street.

"I am very tired," he says. "Is it far?"

"Not far," I say. "Just around the corner."

"When I go to bed tonight, I will pray to God for you, Daniel. Daniel, you are a good man to help a weary traveler. I am a traveler. A traveler and a student of the world."

For the rest of the way we walk in silence. When we arrive at my building, Mohammad looks up at it and nods his head.

"You are a rich man, Daniel? God has blessed you? All this, it is yours?"

I point to the top floor where the three dormer windows jut out like maidenheads on a fleet of ships.

"I live up there. I'm not rich. But I know some rich people."

We enter the building and I press the button for the elevator.

"I am hungry," says Mohammad. "It has been days since I have eaten."

"I can fix you something," I say.

The elevator doors open and we step inside.

As I stand next to Mohammad and we begin the ride up to my floor, I suddenly remember that my refrigerator is empty except for a few breakfast essentials. All I have in the freezer is some leftover *flæskesteg* from my last dinner with Mette. I'm not sure what dietary laws guide a devout Muslim. If my guest were Jewish, I wouldn't even make the offer, but since I don't know better I have to ask.

"Do you eat pork?"

"I will be grateful for what I am given," says Mohammad.

That's a relief, I think as the elevator stops and the doors open automatically. I'm so new to this Good Samaritanizing that it's best to start with someone easy and accommodating, like my new friend Mohammad.

After he finishes his pork dinner and drinks the last of his wine (I let him pick the bottle himself, but I wrote down the label and year so I can replace it, along with the Château Margaux), Mohammad stands up from the table.

"I am very tired," he says. "The wine is good, but it makes me tired. I am a weary traveler. Now I must travel in my dreams."

At first, Mohammad will not agree to sleeping in my bed. But I explain to him that I will be up late and that I don't mind taking the couch. Finally, he relents and goes to the bedroom door.

"Before I sleep tonight," he says, "I will pray to God for you, Daniel."

Now I sit alone in the living room reading the instructions for the Bang & Olufsen DXL Cordless Telephone that was in this apartment when I moved in, but has spent the better part of eighteen years in a drawer. I start by studying the diagram and reading the names of the different parts. Each part has a separate number, and when I go to that number I find a complete description of the part's function. Every now and then, when I find a curious phrase in English, I turn to the Danish instructions to see how the translator got it wrong. I can't help thinking that I would have done a better job. Maybe I'm not the best Danish translator in the world, and probably I'll never know, but I love working with words and trying to find the best solution. This work, what I've done for nearly all of my adult years, is the most deeply satisfying part of my life. Translation may not be what Kierkegaard called "That idea for which I would live and die," but it is central to who I am and how I think. Maybe Carsten was right: I was lucky to get the job at the Center. Maybe, like Mohammad, I should be grateful for what I am given.

Because of my frequent flippings between languages it takes me twice as long to read the instructions, but finally I finish and plug the machine into the dusty phone jack, hoping that spiders haven't built webs inside there. I am pressing buttons to set the date and time when, quite surprisingly, the phone rings.

"So you haven't gone to bed yet."

"No," I tell Ingrid.

"Daniel, let me ask you something. The note that Mette left you, the one that was inside the necklace, do you have that at home?"

"Yes."

"I have someone with me from our lab. He'd like to have a look at it. He's not sure if he can determine a date of the writing, but if he sees the note he'll know whether it's worth trying. May we come up?"

"Now?"

"It will only take a minute. We're parked outside your building. I tried calling you earlier, but you never answered."

"I just plugged my phone in," I say. "You're my first caller."

"Lucky me. Now, will you come down and let us in?"

Ingrid's colleague from the lab is leaning over my dining room table and looking at the note Mette wrote me. Fitted over his right eye is a cylinder-shaped magnifying glass, the kind that jewelers and pawn shop owners wear when appraising merchandise.

"Pencil lead is tricky," he says. "And all the erasures will make it nearly impossible. I could try, but I doubt I'll find anything definitive. It would take me a few days to run all the tests."

"Well, we don't have a few days," says Ingrid.

"It may not be worth it, then," he says and lets the magnifying glass drop into his hand. "I have other work I'm in the middle of, and I'd rather not push it back for something as uncertain as this. Unless you think this is critical."

Ingrid shakes her head.

"It's one of many trails we're following. Don't worry about it."

They back away from the table and start to leave.

"I'm sorry we disturbed you, Daniel."

"It's okay."

"I'm glad to see you eat something besides hot dogs. You should go easy on the wine, though."

On the table are the remains of Mohammad's supper. I was going to clear them away as soon as I finished installing the phone.

"Those aren't mine," I say and point to the table setting.

"Really?" Ingrid says. "I thought you lived alone."

"I have a guest tonight."

"Oh."

"His name's Mohammad. He's the one I told you about when we first met. The Somali man with family in Odense. Except they've gone to Kenya. He was just trying to find the bus station. In fact, he's been trying to find the bus station for over a week! You know, that's funny. Kierkegaard was fascinated by the story of 'The Wandering Jew.' Maybe

Mohammad is 'The Wandering Muslim.' But he might not like being called that. It might be offensive to him."

Ingrid and her colleague stand at my door and look at each other.

"Daniel," Ingrid says. "Where is this Mohammad now?"

"In my bedroom, sleeping. He was tired from all his traveling."

"And where did you meet him?"

"On Strøget. Over by the Stork Fountain."

Ingrid nods to her colleague, then walks up to my bedroom door. She doesn't even knock, which surprises me, but what happens next surprises me even more. As soon as she opens the door, Mohammad rushes out, charging right over Ingrid. He starts toward the front door, sees Ingrid's colleague, then takes off through the kitchen and out the fire escape. Ingrid gets up and runs after him. Her colleague follows. I walk into my kitchen, where I am now looking out the window while the guest I invited to spend the night with me, the police officer I've come to know (I thought) pretty well over the last several days, and her colleague who appraised as "not valuable" the piece of paper that means more to me than any other—all three of them run down the spiral staircase (one escaping, two pursuing) as if they were actors on a TV cop show. Before they reach the bottom, Ingrid has caught Mohammad. She holds one arm behind his back and makes him walk in front of her down the rest of the steps and around the side of the building. Her colleague joins them. I shake my head and stare down at the empty courtyard where, for years now, I've taken out my trash but never once seen anything like this happen.

I go back out to the dining room and collect Mohammad's plate, silverware, and wine glass. The phone rings before I make it to the kitchen.

"Look in your bedroom," Ingrid tells me. "See if you're missing anything."

"Okay," I tell her. "I can even take my phone with me. It's a cordless one."

"Most are these days."

"I'm there. Oh, yes. I'm missing some money and my passport. He left me the pencil stubs and calendars."

"Hold on," Ingrid says, then in Danish she asks her colleague if he found an American passport. "We've got your passport, Daniel. I need to take it with me down to the station. I'll return it to you tomorrow."

"I can't believe Mohammad would steal from me. He seemed so nice."

"His name's not Mohammad. It's Jimmy Jones. And he's not from Somalia. He's from Chicago. We've had run-ins with him before. I'll tell you about it tomorrow. I have to go now. I've just added two hours of paperwork to my night."

I hang up with Ingrid and go back to the kitchen. I run hot water and soap into the sink, plunge in the silverware, and start rubbing it clean with a dish towel. When I hear the midnight chimes from the Town Hall clock, I open the door to the fire escape and leave it open. The cold air pours into the kitchen and with it the sound of bells: *ding-dong-ding-dong, dong-dong-ding-ding*. I listen to the twelve tolls, each one clearly struck then reverberating a second and a half before the next one strikes. After the last toll, another chime of bells: *ding-ding-ding-ding, dong-dong-dong-dong, ding-dong-ding-dong, ding*. As the last note fades I spray soap off of my guest's dinner plate. Mohammad, or Jimmy Jones, is the first person I have ever invited into my apartment. He has not been what they call a "model guest." I try to name my feeling. Betrayed? No. Angry? No. Grateful? Yes, actually, oddly. Grateful for what or to whom I'm not quite sure, but I'm sure that's the feeling I have (insofar as one can ever be certain about such things). I turn off the lights and walk to my bedroom, feeling grateful and enjoying that feeling.

It's not until I begin to undress that I remember Carsten. Why don't I feel grief? I wonder. I don't know, but I don't feel it. Maybe grief is a foreign language I'll never learn.

Chapter 2

One of the great advantages about having a telephone is how it allows you to communicate with other people without being in their physical presence. In this regard, a phone book is also quite handy—I would even call it an essential tool—and I'm glad I didn't throw away the one that was in the apartment when I moved in. Sitting in my living room, I look up Thorkild Grønkjær's phone number and call him at home. After reminding him of our meeting at the Royal Library, I get down to business.

"I have a manuscript that needs to be dated. But I need it done soon, before noon if possible."

"That's not much time. How long is the manuscript?"

"About six inches."

"Excuse me?"

"About six inches long and four inches wide. That's only an estimate. I don't own a ruler."

"So, it's a scrap of paper."

"No, I wouldn't call it a 'scrap.' I don't like the word 'scrap.' It connotes 'of little value.' This is an extremely valuable, however small, manuscript. Can I trust you to keep a secret?"

"Yes."

"This may be a clue to Mette Rasmussen's death and to the missing manuscript. The Police can't be sure, and it depends on when Mette wrote it."

"It's a manuscript in Mette Rasmussen's hand?"

"Exactly. The Police lab is pretty busy at the moment, and I don't think they're as equipped for this kind of work as the Royal is."

"I would think they'd have the same technology."

"But they don't have Susannah. I couldn't understand what she did on the Kierkegaard manuscript, but I could tell it was amazing."

"Susannah is amazing. If anyone could date the manuscript, she could. And she works fast. The problem is . . ."

"Yes?"

Thor laughs.

"I love Susannah, but she can be hell to work with. I'll have to convince her to take the job on."

"But you're the Director. You're her boss."

"Oh, I don't think anyone is Susannah's boss. But I'll try. Bring the manuscript by this morning, and I'll see what I can do."

And so, even before I've soft boiled my breakfast egg and had my first cup of coffee, I have begun a productive work day. I want to be completely prepared for the quiz that Ingrid Bendtner will give me over lunch at Bjørg's Café. The subject of the quiz is somewhat vague—whatever I learn from talking with colleagues at the Center—but I have narrowed my study to one essential point: interrelationships. That's the word Ingrid used when we first met in my office. How did my colleagues interrelate with Mette? How do they interrelate with each other? The questions are not dissimilar to ones I ask myself every day when working on translations. It's not enough to know what a particular word means; I must also understand what the word means in the context of others. I must consider diction, whether all the words in a sentence are equally formal or informal. I must listen closely to the sounds the words make together, and not just neighboring words, but also words from, so to speak, the other end of the street, even from different streets in the same town. I must, sometimes, study a passage over and over, waiting for comprehension to reveal itself, much like walking through a foreign landscape and getting lost enough times to finally know your way around.

And as I do with my translations, I must also do with my conversations this morning: be patient, wait, reserve judgment. Leave your pencil on the desk until you've settled the matter in your head—then write what you know is correct, one letter a time, one word at a time. It is a practice I share with Kierkegaard, even though many of the philologists in the Center insist that he wrote rapidly, almost in haste. But that's not what Kierkegaard said, in his own words, of his own work. After a lengthy passage in *On the Point of View of My Work as an Author*, having credited God and inspiration, going further than I ever could, Kierkegaard describes how he wrote, how simple it was for him once he had his own way of doing it. I can't say I'm following obediently after God but something controls my work, just as it did Kierkegaard's. In fact, if you take God out of the equation, we're remarkably similar. In one of the longest passages of his that I have memorized Kierkegaard writes, "I could sit down and write uninterruptedly, day and night, and then another day and night, for there were riches enough. [*And is there ever "wealth enough" in all the work Kierkegaard left behind for me to translate!*] To do that would be the death of me. [*That's for sure.*] But when I learn obedience, do my work as strictly as a chore, hold the pen properly [*Pencil for me, thank you!*], write each letter neatly, then I can do it. And thus many, many times I have had more joy in obeying God than in any of the thoughts I produced."

Yes, I remind myself: the joy is in the work, not in the fact that I'm the one doing the work. All my best moments have come when I've utterly forgotten my own presence, but paid closest attention to the words. Humans are not words—I know that!—but perhaps today I can treat a few of my colleagues as if they were.

The first person I see at the Center, even before I enter the building, is Rebekah. She is sitting on a bench at the far end of the courtyard close to the statue of N.F.S. Grundtvig. I approach her, passing between the two rows of linden trees that have such beautiful flowers in springtime but look, in this season, positively eerie. The black trunks rise up from the cobbled bricks and stretch out their bare, gnarly branches. The branches look like arms ending in clenched fists, and where there would normally be knuckles, long, spiky twigs extend in every direction. Under the gray sky, the word "melancholy" comes to mind. Or perhaps "fatalistic." I believe I have seen this same setting in a movie or two directed by Ingmar Bergman.

At first, Rebekah doesn't notice me. She sits with her head down. On her lap she holds a black notebook, which she writes into using a pen with a fake flower on the clicker end. Her hands are half-covered with mittens—the tips of her fingers jut out the ends. She's wearing the same red scarf I always see her in, but this time she's tied it funny. It's wrapped around her neck like a coil. If I pulled the loose end, she'd spin around like a top. When I stop in front of her, she looks up and I notice that she's been crying.

"Oh, Daniel. It's you. Have you heard? Do you know?"

I shake my head.

"It's terrible. Carsten Rasmussen killed himself."

"No," I say, and to appear surprised (as Ingrid told me I should) I cover my cheeks with my hands.

"Actually, it's even worse. It seems that he's confessed to killing Mette, his own mother."

"That cannot be," I say. "I am shocked at this terrible news."

Rebekah looks at me silently for a few seconds.

"It is terrible news. You're not making fun of it, are you?"

"No. It's just hard to know how to respond. Why would he kill his mother?"

"That's what everyone is asking. Most of the theories aren't very nice. Some say he must have been high. Others think he wanted money so he could go out and get high. *Ekstra Bladet* has a quote from his uncle saying that Carsten was in a hurry to get his inheritance. But you don't kill your mother to get money. That's unnatural."

I make a mental note to read the article in *Ekstra Bladet*. I'd like to know exactly what Erik Thorvaldsen had to say about his nephew.

"What about the Kierkegaard manuscript?" I ask. "If Carsten killed his mother and took the key to the lock box, who did he give it to?"

"That's something else people are wondering about. Personally, I'm not so mystified by it. I should probably tell the Police what I know, but I'm afraid I'll get myself in trouble."

"Why would you get in trouble?" I ask.

Before Rebekah can answer me, Lona calls to us from the main door to the Center.

"Are you two coming in? It's freezing out here. And Daniel, I need to talk with you."

Rebekah stands up and tucks her notebook and pen into her bag.

"Come by my office later this morning," she whispers. "I'll tell you then."

We walk to the door, which Lona holds open for us. As I pass by her, I notice that she's carrying a box of pastries from The Black Horse.

"I brought today," she says. "It was on my way in. There's a peace offering in here for you, Daniel."

I nod at her and we walk down the hallway to the meeting room. Halfway there, I can smell coffee. Anders must have beaten us to work.

For the first few minutes, as we sit and eat our pastries, we talk about Carsten's suicide and his confession to killing his mother.

"I don't care what theories people are coming up with. Carsten would never kill someone," says Lona. "Certainly not his mother. I've known him since he was a boy, and he's never hurt anyone before, even when he's been drunk or high."

"Then why did he leave that message behind?" I ask. "Or do you think he didn't kill himself either?"

I am sitting next to Rebekah. Anders is across from me, and Lona beside him.

"No," says Lona. "I wouldn't be surprised if he killed himself. Mette told me he's tried before. And after what's happened this past week—even if Carsten appeared to take it all calmly, he was shaken. You were there, Daniel. You heard him speak at Mette's funeral."

"I thought he was drunk."

"No, that was grief."

I turn and look at Rebekah. She nods her head. I guess I must have been wrong.

"But why would he circle the word 'Guilty'? What was he guilty of?" I ask.

"I don't know," says Lona. "I've wondered if it might have something to do with the manuscript."

Now our conversation turns to the ransom letter, of which I know almost nothing. Evidently, the thief set a high price (Anders quotes the figure, but it hardly registers with me) and demanded that it be paid by 5:00 p.m. this evening. What the thief didn't say was where and how. That information was expected to come later.

"So far," says Lona, "the Police haven't heard anything new."

"But have the funds been assured?" asks Anders. He is dressed in a short sleeved T-shirt with a cartoon print on the front. Three minimally drawn sharks show their big triangular teeth, but smile as if they are friendly sharks, the kind that might perform a song and dance number in Disney's version of *The Little Mermaid*. There is nothing cartoonish about Anders' muscles, however. They bulge the sleeves of his shirt like rocks pushing up out of the ground.

"We're close, and getting closer," says Lona. "Carlsberg is on board. Augustinus, too. *Politiken* has been taking donations on their website. And there are some impressive grassroots organizations. The word got out quickly that the manuscript is a national treasure. Even people who'll never read it want it protected."

"But isn't that controversial?" asks Rebekah. "Should you give in to someone who demands a ransom? Wouldn't that just encourage more crimes?"

"That was Carsten's position," says Lona. "When I met with the potential big donors yesterday, he was the only one who held to that line. He seemed desperate to convince us that we should not pay the ransom. But what is the alternative? The thief has threatened to burn the manuscript. I can't imagine letting that happen. After seeing it for just ten minutes, I knew it was an extraordinary document. I've never been so excited in my professional life. Søren Kierkegaard wrote poetry! It changes everything we thought we knew about him. But the manuscript won't revolutionize the field if it's reduced to ashes." Lona fixes her gaze on me. "Daniel, what do you think? Is this a widely shared policy in America, never to negotiate with hostage takers?"

I shrug my shoulders and pick at my "Mozart." Lona was kind to buy it for me. Maybe, it occurs to me, she's trying to sweeten me up. But why? What, I wonder, is Lona's interrelationship with me?

"I was only raising a question. I'm not saying I'd rather the manuscript got burned," says Rebekah. "I'd love to study it, especially after reading Daniel's translation."

"Hmm?" I say with my mouth partly full. "You've read my translation?"

"You can thank Anders for that," says Lona. "After he typed your manuscript for Birgit, I asked him to print a few extra copies. I hope you don't mind. We haven't circulated it outside the Center, and we won't without your permission. That's something I need to talk with you about. Are you free anytime today?"

I flatten the last crumbs of my cake with the tines of my fork, then lick them off in my mouth.

"I'm free now," I say. I scoot back my chair. "Lead the way."

Mette's office has changed. Mette's office is no longer Mette's office. It is Lona's office. The books and bookcases have been removed. The long table that held the beginnings of Mette's next book has been replaced by a smaller round one, and instead of an antique desk there is a sleek modern one that would fit right in at Danske Bank or at Danish Immigration. As we sit down to talk, I begin to perceive my new interrelationship with Lona—she will sign my paychecks. She will also, I hope, write the letter attesting to the fact that no one (certainly no Danish citizen) can translate Kierkegaard like I can. Lona equals money. Lona equals permission to stay in the country. I suppose the equation was the same with Mette, but I took it all for granted. Carsten's words to me: "You don't know how lucky you've been." No, I suppose I didn't.

"I've been looking over everybody's contract with the Center," says Lona.

She lifts a manila folder from her desk and holds it on her lap. I don't know if she usually wears reading glasses when she works (because I've never seen her when she works) but Lona is wearing a pair now. They make her look grandmotherly, as if her hands should be holding knitting needles. The tone of her voice, however, is professional—not bossy, but boss-like.

"Your contract differs from the others in two ways I'm not sure you're aware of, Daniel."

"Oh, I've never read my contract. Mette would just put an 'X' beside the line I was supposed to sign, and I'd sign it."

Lona smiles and hands me the file folder. I peek inside. The contract is at least fifteen pages long.

"I highlighted a section on the third page. I think you should read it."

I find the passage. It explains that my salary is paid through matching grants from the National Endowment for the Humanities in the U.S. and the National Research Foundation in Denmark.

"It's nice to know I have support on both sides of the Atlantic," I say.

"But do you understand that if either of those grants is cancelled, you'll lose the other one, too?"

I shake my head.

"I'm afraid, Daniel, that the grant from the National Research Foundation runs out in a year. And it won't be renewed. It was meant to support the Center's main project, *Kierkegaard's Writings*. And only in Danish. I'm not sure how Mette managed to apply funds to your salary, but they won't be available after this year."

Money. I've never understood it, but I've never had to. In college I signed a paper at the bank and they gave me everything I needed for room and board and books. There was usually something left over and I'd dump it in a savings account. By the time I finished graduate school and was asked to pay back my loans, Mette hired me at the Center. She asked me what my debt was. I handed her a letter from the bank. She said, "I'll take care of it." I can't remember if I thanked her or not.

"But," says Lona, "I think we can work something out. I could change this part of your contract to make it standard with the others. All the rest of us are paid through the Center's Endowment. Your salary could come from there, too."

"Okay."

"I'd like to standardize another part of your contract. I highlighted a paragraph on page eleven."

I turn to that page and begin reading.

"I hope you're getting some idea of what it's like to be the Director. Not only do you have to go to meetings and discuss how to handle the return of a priceless manuscript, but you also have to stay up all night reviewing staff matters. Have you read the part I highlighted?"

"Yes."

"It's not like that in the other contracts. I'm not sure why, but Mette worded your contract so you had complete control over your intellectual property. Actually, the work you do at the Center should belong to the Center. It's quite clear in everyone else's contract."

"You mean my translations are not *my* translations?"

"No. Not if the Center is paying you to produce them."

"It's like you're buying them from me?"

"Pretty much, yes. Doesn't that sound fair?"

I nod. I guess it does sound fair.

"Good!" says Lona. "I'm glad you agree. I'll have Anders write up a new contract and put it in your box. Will you sign it by the end of the day?"

"Sure."

I don't see why not. If that's how it works. And Lona would know, now that she's the Director.

"Is there anything else?" I ask.

"Well, I'm not going to insist on it, but Daniel I do think you owe me an apology."

"For what?"

Lona stares at me.

"For accusing me the other day. In front of Carsten. With other people sitting nearby at other tables."

"Oh," I say. "Carsten talked to me afterwards. He was on your side. He said there were people talking bad about you."

"On the Web. Yes. It's true. I can handle what they say. But not from my own friends."

Is that it, I wonder? Is that my interrelationship with Lona? We are friends?

"I jumped to a conclusion. I shouldn't have. Lona, I'm sorry."

"Thank you, Daniel. That's all I wanted to hear."

I stand up to leave.

"I'm not sure why they don't talk bad about me in the Web," I say. "Or maybe they do?"

"I haven't read anything. No one seems to know about your shoes—and I'm not spreading the word."

"I was also the one who found Carsten," I say.

"Really?"

"And I assaulted a Police officer."

"You?!"

"Bloodied his nose," I say with some pride.

Lona shakes her head. But she also smiles. It is hard to know how to read such contradictory body language.

"I'm sure he deserved it," Lona says.

"No," I say as I leave her office. "He didn't."

Sven Carlsen, I remind myself. That's someone else I owe an apology.

I am walking down the hallway stopping at each office door and reading the nameplates, trying to figure out where Rebekah's office is. I see names of people I've never met before. Actually, lots of them. After examining the nameplates beside a dozen doors, I notice a pattern: everyone shares an office. Some offices have three or four people in them. When I reach Rebekah's I discover that she shares an office with Lars Andersen, philologist and resident ironist. That must be a treat. If there's anyone in the Center I would like to avoid, it's Lars. Even when I don't understand how he's teasing me, I still sense that he's teasing me. Nothing that he says means what I think it means. Once he complimented me on my stylish hat, and I thanked him. "Daniel," another colleague turned to me and said, "I think that was meant as an insult." Lars smiled and looked up at the ceiling. "If an insult falls on deaf ears," he said philosophically, "is it an insult?"

I knock but no one answers. The door is unlatched, so I push it open and walk inside. The office is divided in two, but not in half. It's more like one-third for Rebekah and two-thirds for Lars. Determining who has which side is not very difficult. Only Lars would have that particular trio of busts on his bookcase: Socrates looking off to one side, Kierkegaard looking directly at Socrates, and Marx (not Karl but Groucho, with his thick moustache and a big cigar) staring out at whoever's facing the bookcase. Rebekah's section of the office reminds me of certain dorm rooms in college, the ones belonging to the more intellectual students, or the ones who wished to appear intellectual. Instead of posters, they'd have handwritten quotes on their wall, maybe a few postcard-size photos of famous authors. Above Rebekah's desk I find a quote collage, arranged in the shape of a cross. Each quote is written neatly, almost like calligraphy, on a square note card. I sit down in her chair and read them. One of them says,

> All of existence makes me nervous, from the smallest fly to the mysteries of the Incarnation; it is inexplicable, all of it, myself most of all; for me, all of existence is polluted, myself most of all. My distress is enormous, boundless; no one but God knows it, and he will not comfort me

Continuing that theme, another reads,

> Deep inside every person there still lives the anxiety over the possibility of being alone in the world, forgotten by God, overlooked among the millions in this enormous family. A person holds his anxiety at bay by looking at the many who are

around him, his relatives and friends, but the anxiety is there anyhow.

In the center of the cross, I find a quote that is quite different from the others, but it too is by Kierkegaard. It's from a journal entry sometime in 1846, November if my memory is correct:

> I wish to be as small as possible. I want the beautiful, peaceful existence of something very small.

Before I have time to read another quote, Rebekah enters the office. I turn around in her chair and smile at her.

"You're not going to make fun of me, are you?" she says.

"No," I say. "Why?"

"Well, you were looking at my artwork. I guess it makes me the token Christian around here. Lars thinks it's hilarious."

"Lars makes fun of me, too. You don't have to be a Christian to get his scorn. He spreads it around pretty freely."

Rebekah pulls up a chair and sits beside me. I suddenly become conscious that I've done something wrong—taken her chair, the one that sits directly behind her desk, and made her take the guest's chair.

"Sorry," I say and start to stand up.

"It's all right," Rebekah says. "Stay. It's just nice to have someone to talk to. And we don't have to worry about being interrupted. Lars doesn't come in until 1:00. That's also when I leave to teach my class. Mette arranged it that way so I wouldn't have so many run-ins with Mr. Irony."

"You teach?"

"Yes. One class of mostly American students, a few Danes. We're reading Kierkegaard, of course, and trying to understand what he meant by the phrase 'God-relationship.'"

I nod. I'm not sure I want to get into that conversation.

"Can I tell you something about my cross?" asks Rebekah.

She looks at me so sweetly, like a child pleading for permission to go out and play. And before I can disappoint her, she's already out the door—or, in this case, out of her chair, standing up and pointing to her collage.

"They're all Kierkegaard quotes, I'm sure you noticed that. By arranging them in a cross, I'm saying that Kierkegaard's Christian faith is central to all his work. I believe that. I know that Lars would have his ironist reading, and he'd have plenty of sophisticated reasons for holding to it, but I think he's wrong. Kierkegaard, even if he didn't come right out and call himself a Christian, strongly believed in God, the Christian God. He struggled for an authentic faith. He tried in all of his writings, directly and indirectly, to describe that faith, often by presenting its opposite. Now what I've done in the collage is to place the most sincere quotes on the vertical axis. In Kierkegaardian terms, you could call that the Religious stage. On the horizontal axis, I've placed quotes that fall into the Aesthetic or the Ethical stage. They aren't false statements, but they don't point directly to God. Does all this make sense?"

I say nothing. I'm not sure what to say to her.

"I'm sorry, Daniel. I don't mean to overwhelm you with my theory. And I hope you don't think I was trying to proselytize you. I just wanted to explain something that matters a lot to me. And I guess I wanted to prepare myself for a room full of people laughing at me."

"Why would anyone laugh at you?"

"I'm presenting my theory—this collage here—at a conference in May. There's a session called 'The Uses and Abuses of Kierkegaard.' In my mind, the answer is simple: as long as we keep the cross in the center, visually like I have it here, we don't have to worry about abusing Kierkegaard."

"So," I say, somewhat loudly. And the technique works again. Rebekah looks at me expectedly.

"Kierkegaard's manuscript?" I say.

"I hope I can trust you, Daniel. You seem like someone I can trust."

I nod. Perhaps I shouldn't. After all, I'm a mole. Do I have to be a lying mole, too?

"Being a Christian doesn't mean you always do the right thing," says Rebekah. "It wasn't right of me, for instance, to look inside Mette's briefcase before she went home."

"You looked inside Mette's briefcase?"

"I did. Only a few minutes before she left the Center for the last time. The Police think she put the manuscript in the vault, but I know she didn't. It was in her briefcase. I saw it there."

It takes me a couple of seconds to realize what Rebekah has told me.

"That means," I say, "that it wasn't necessarily one of the philologists who took the manuscript."

"I know. It's not fair that they've been the main suspects. Especially Lona. She's been nicer to me than anyone at the Center."

"Why didn't you tell the Police? I'm sure they would have appreciated the information."

"I would have if it had gotten really serious. If they'd taken one of the philologists into custody, I would have come forward, even if it meant getting myself into trouble."

"Does anyone else know that you looked?"

"No," says Rebekah. "You're the only one I've told. You probably think I'm a hypocrite, right?" She glances over at the cross on her wall. "I can understand that. But try to see it from my perspective. Here I am at the world's premier center for Kierkegaard studies, and the most amazing manuscript suddenly surfaces. It could potentially revolutionize everything. But it's off limits. Only you and Mette have access to it. No one knows how long your work will take you. But I'm leaving in the spring, and I really want the opportunity to see the manuscript. Then one day I happen to walk into Mette's office to ask her a question. She's not there, but her briefcase is open on her desk. I would have had to have been an amazingly strong person not to take a peek. And that's all I took: a quick peek. I hope you don't think badly of me."

I'm not sure what to think of Rebekah—Is she a strong or a weak person? A Christian or a hypocrite? But I know she's told me something Ingrid will be pleased to learn. I've done, I feel, some of my best mole work. I stand up to go.

"I have to make a phone call."

"Daniel, may I ask you something before you leave?"

"Yes."

"It has to do with your translation of the manuscript."

"Yes."

"Well, everyone around here is so busy finishing up the last volumes of *Kierkegaard's Writings* or planning events for the bicentenary, and I really don't have that much to do. I'm writing one paper to present four months from now. That's it. I wonder if you'd let me write the commentaries on your translation."

"That would be up to Lona," I say.

"But if you supported it, she'd be more likely to let me do it."

"It's okay with me."

I am out the door and beginning my walk to the main office when I hear Rebekah call out her thanks. Her voice sounds grateful and pleased. Would it, if she knew I was planning on betraying her secret? Something like heartburn rises in my chest and tells me that I may not have the right constitution for being Ingrid's mole for very long.

Chapter 3

"Not yet," Thor tells me over the phone.

I am sitting at one of the smaller desks in the main office. Staff members pass in and out, ask Anders questions, chat among themselves. It's a busy place in here.

"Did she say when she'd be finished?"

"I asked her that. The best way to translate what she told me would be, 'Hold your damned horses.' We're working with Susannah here, Daniel. We'll need to be patient."

After this brief and unhopeful phone call, I leave the Center and walk the few blocks to Bjørg's Café. Either the temperature has gone up several degrees or I'm getting used to walking around without my hat on. My ears don't sting from the cold. The construction noise does them no good, but at least I don't have to use my hands as ear muffs.

A few steps before I reach the restaurant, I see Ingrid crossing the street. The last time I saw her, in the courtyard below my apartment, she had a criminal in custody, force-marching him around the corner of a building, making a bold arrest in the late hours of the night. It's hard to reconcile that image with the woman I see now. She wears a tan coat, her hands stuffed into the pockets, and she walks slower than the other pedestrians. Her gaze doesn't appear to be fixed on any definite thing. It's as if she's being pulled along by an invisible current, without the strength to resist or to outswim. Seeing her looking tired and vulnerable, I feel something for Ingrid. What do I feel for Ingrid? I don't know. I wait for her under the red awning at the entrance of the café. When she arrives, I hold the door open for her.

We wait with a few other groups just inside the restaurant, standing together near a classic American-style lunch counter. In front of it is a row of chrome stools with round red seats, bolted into the floor, just as you'd see in an old James Dean movie. Personally, I've never understood the Danes' fascination with American culture, but I see it everywhere, and usually, like here, it doesn't quite fit in with the rest of the decor. All I have to do is look at a table in the back of the restaurant and I know I'm not in Indiana, circa 1954. What drive-in or burger joint would have white linen table cloths? How many restaurant owners in the States would think to light tea candles and set them in carved glass dishes for their lunch crowd? Even the music played over the speakers isn't quite right—American jazz, not exactly what you'd listen to while sitting on a counter stool and slurping the last straw-fulls of a chocolate shake. But who besides a fellow American would know this?

A waitress leads us to a table near the window. I pull out a chair for Ingrid before I realize that's not what this situation calls for. Fortunately, Ingrid doesn't notice my gesture and walks around to seat herself in the other chair. She starts to take off her coat, and I resist the impulse to help her with a stubborn sleeve. So far, of the three things my mother told me a gentleman should always do for a woman—hold the door, pull out her chair, help her with her coat—I have accomplished only one. That's okay. It's actually an improvement over my last date or date-like situation. When I took Cindy to our high school prom, I managed to neglect all three.

"Oh—I—Am—Tired," says Ingrid, and with each word she musses up her hair. It makes her bangs go frizzy and poof out over her forehead like spun sugar.

"I'm fine," I say. "I slept well last night."

Ingrid gives a weak laugh and an even weaker smile.

"You didn't hear any commotion outside your building?"

"No."

"We arrested three other people right in front of your door. Jimmy had texted some of his friends before we showed up. He asked them to bring a van. They were going to clear out your apartment—all the artwork, porcelain, silver, crystal, and wine. Apparently, you have some expensive wines."

"I don't drink it," I say. "I kick it down stairs or, occasionally, I like to serve it to my pseudo-Somali-Muslim friends."

Ingrid laughs. This time more heartily. I could always make Mette laugh, too. Cindy, on the other hand, was a dud. Hence no dates for me in the past . . . I don't even want to count the number of years.

"Anyway," says Ingrid, "you're probably going to get a commendation. You helped the Copenhagen Police with one of our best arrests in the last six months."

The waitress returns and takes our orders. Ingrid congratulates me on choosing something as healthy as a salmon burger, which comes (in good 1950's diner-style fashion) on a freshly baked artisan roll accompanied by a salad of mixed greens and EU-approved cucumbers (Greece) and tomatoes (Spain). Just the way Richie and the Fonz always had their salmon burgers on *Happy Days*.

"I'm ready for my quiz," I say.

"What?" asks Ingrid.

"You said I should socialize with my colleagues. Ask them questions. You promised me a quiz. I'm ready."

"Okay. What did you learn?"

"That's a pretty open-ended question for a quiz. But how about this: the manuscript may not have been in the vault when Mette left the Center."

Ingrid nods.

"Of course," she says. "We've considered other possibilities. Mette might have left it in her office, or she might have taken it home with her. She might even have given it to one of the staff members. We know that she went into the vault before she left work that night—the CCTV camera tells us that—but we don't know for certain if she left the manuscript in the lock box. And we've never assumed it, either."

I feel my stomach drop. After giving Ingrid my best answer, I think I may already have flunked her quiz.

"Then why did you give me a list of the philologists' names? Why did you want to know if I thought one of them might have taken the manuscript?"

"Because that was, and remains, one possibility. If Mette went into the vault, she probably went there to store the manuscript for the night."

"No, she didn't store the manuscript that night. She took it home in her briefcase."

"Do you know that for a fact?"

"It was told to me as a fact."

"By whom?"

I whisper her name—"Rebekah"—as if speaking in a secretive voice could make me less of a traitor.

"The American from Princeton?"

"No, she's from Indiana . . . but wait, yes, she went to the Princeton School of Divinity. Carsten's been at Princeton for three years now. Did she know him?"

"I was planning on asking her that myself. Some of the last texts that Carsten sent before he killed himself were to a phone we can't identify. Actually, we can identify the phone—the subscription is in Carsten's name. We just can't determine who he gave the phone to. Rebekah is a possibility. When I talk to her, I'll ask her about the manuscript, too. I won't let on that you told me about the briefcase. That's good information, Daniel. You've done some good work for us. Thank you."

It feels like Ingrid has just reached out and stuck a gold star on my forehead. A moment later, as if further reward were owed to me for my fine skills as a citizen police officer, our orders arrive. The waitress slips my plate in front of me and I am immediately taken by the smell of fresh dill and mild fish. I didn't know how hungry I was, but I know now. Though it's no secret to me that the Danes, along with almost all Europeans, eat their sandwiches with a fork and knife, I do my customary rude American thing and snatch up my salmon burger with my bare hands. It makes eating so much easier. Silverware takes too much concentration. That's no good when you're chasing a wild-caught, perfectly flaky North Sea salmon through fields of ferny dill weed, guided solely by your mouth, quickening your pace with delight when an unexpected caper comes into the mix—well, hello there!

"I've never seen anyone eat so fast," Ingrid says.

I lick some mayonnaise-like condiment off of my fingers and nod to her. Looking up, I see that she has nothing in front of her except a cup of coffee.

"Would you like something?" I ask and push my plate towards her. Besides the salad, my order also came with some colorful potato chips—red, blue, and orange.

"I'm not that hungry. But I could eat a chip."

Ingrid reaches out her fork and captures a blue chip between the tines.

"That reminds me of the one time I had dinner with Mette's parents," I say.

"Dinner with Herr and Fru Thorvaldsen. That must have been quite formal."

"It was. I'd never experienced anything like it. The closest I'd come to it was eating in a seafood restaurant near Lake Erie. I was, I don't remember, nine or ten years old, and it was a big surprise to be served fish with bones inside it and its head still on. Until then I'd only known fish sticks. I thought you always ate fish with ketchup. 'Tartar sauce' was a new vocabulary word. But, then, the Thorvaldsens!"

Ingrid smiles. She scrunches up her shoulders and sits up straight, as if she were squeezed between other passengers on a packed Metro. Looking down at the empty table, she pretends to see a complicated setting before her.

"Now this fork, my dear," she says and holds an imaginary fork in her hand, "is used for the smoked herring, not for the dilled. For the dilled, we have this fork." Ingrid puts down the first fork and lifts another which, though invisible, to the trained eye is a quite different fork, an altogether more appropriate fork for the consuming of dilled herring. She laughs. Of all the sounds in the crowded restaurant nothing is quite like Ingrid's laughter.

"Right," I say. "And all the plates. I think there were at least five of them, one on top of the other, and when I was finished with one I wasn't allowed to take it off myself."

"No, a servant would do that."

"A servant did. In fact, there may have been a different servant for each plate. I don't know. It was all so confusing to me. Not just the forks and plates, but the food, too. I wasn't sure how to eat most things, so I kept looking across the table at Mette, who'd give me clues with her eyes. But half the time, I didn't know what her clues meant."

"It sounds to me like her parents were giving you a test."

"I failed it. Royally! The one course I thought I knew how to eat was potato chips. I couldn't believe it when they passed around a crystal bowl heaped with potato chips. Mette's mother told me they'd gotten them especially for me because she thought I might be homesick for American food. At home I would have eaten them right out of the bag, but here comes this expensive-looking carved bowl and with it a pair of silver tongs. I put a pile of chips on my plate—it took a while because I wasn't used to the tongs. Then I thought, okay these are potato chips. You pick them up with your hands and stuff them in your mouth. I was doing that—I can even tell you what brand they were, Lays Original—when I saw Mette's father eating his chips the way you just did. With a fork!"

"So, what did you do?"

Ingrid leans her elbows on the table and rests her chin in her hands. She smiles. There is no mistaking her body language. She is saying, "I am interested in you." Or at least, "in what you're saying."

"I told him how it's done in the States. I tried to teach him some American potato chip-eating etiquette."

"Oh, big mistake!"

"I think it was. I think it cost me Mette."

"He was famous for being domineering. Everyone in Denmark knew that about Herr Thorvaldsen. But wasn't he sick then? Wasn't he dying?"

"Yes. Mette told me he was on oxygen almost all the time. But he made it through dinner without using any. He'd told Mette he didn't want to have tubes in his nose when he met her boyfriend. But I wouldn't have minded. I've seen plenty of sick people before."

The waitress comes by and asks if I'm finished. I let her take my plate. When she asks me if I'd like coffee, I look over at Ingrid.

"I need to leave soon," she says. "We're waiting for further instructions about the ransom. I should be around."

I shake my head and the waitress leaves.

"I'd like to show you something, Daniel. Just tell me if it's familiar to you."

Ingrid reaches into her coat pocket and pulls out a folded piece of paper. I unfold it and read, in Danish, the typed stanza of a poem.

"Kierkegaard," I say. "It's from the manuscript I translated. This one's in a section called 'The Aesthetic.' Mette thought the poem was based on a painting by P.C. Skovgaard. I can't remember the title, but the painting is in the Glyptotek."

"Interesting," says Ingrid. She takes the poem from me and folds it up again.

"Yes. It is interesting. If you'd like to see the rest of the poem, they have copies of it at the Center. Only, it's in English."

"I'm sure the poem is interesting, but I meant the fact that it came from the stolen manuscript."

"Yes, that's interesting, too. Lona told me she couldn't find Mette's transcription in her computer at the Center. Did this come from Mette's computer at home?"

"No. This came from Carsten's iPad. His roommate at Princeton surrendered it to the Police."

"Oh, maybe Mette shared it with him. Can't you send those things with the email these days?"

"Yes. But could she have done that in October of this year?"

"No," I say, "of course not. The manuscript wasn't discovered until December."

"That's what's so interesting," says Ingrid.

After we pay our bill—Ingrid insisted on going Dutch—we walk together down a stretch of Vester Voldgade.

"It complicates things," says Ingrid. "This raises the possibility that the manuscript might be a forgery. What if Carsten wrote those poems himself and sent them to a forger?"

"It would have to be an amazing forgery," I say. "It had to fool Mette and Susannah."

"Who's Susannah?"

I tell Ingrid about Susannah Lindegaard and how I hope she'll be able to date the note from Mette.

"If she can," says Ingrid, "that would be very helpful. I thought my colleague gave in too easily. The technology these days is pretty advanced. It should be possible to get at least a range of dates. Do you have a pen and paper on you?"

"Always," I say.

We step off to one side and let the other pedestrians pass by. Ingrid has me write down a series of dates and tells me that these were the days when Mette accessed the safety deposit box at Danske Bank.

"It may help Susannah to know that those are the dates when Mette *might* have written the note. If she comes to a conclusion, let me know right away. We're working against the clock here."

I nod and we continue walking.

"Have you made any sense of Henriette Lund's letters?" Ingrid asks. "The ones you translated at the Royal?"

"No."

"Well, we have a theory, but only a theory. Do you think it's possible that Mette wanted you to substitute living people for the sender and recipients of the letters?"

"I hadn't thought of that," I say. "I guess it's possible. Who would be Henriette Lund today? Who would be Regine? Who would be Troels?"

"Who are Regine and Troels?"

"Fru Schlegel—that's Regine, Kierkegaard's fiancée. After she and Søren broke up, she married Fritz Schlegel. The first letter is to her. And Troels is Henriette's half-brother. The second letter is to him."

"Are there any half-siblings at the Center?"

"I wouldn't know. I walked down my hallway this morning and realized I've never met half of my colleagues."

"That's okay. We can look into it. To tell you the truth, I don't think the note from Mette is the most important clue we have."

"No," I say. "What do you think is?"

"The fact that she hid the note from her brother."

"Oh, Erik."

"Yes," says Ingrid. "I wish I knew what the Thorvaldsen family secret was."

"I can tell you. I can tell you what they're so ashamed of and trying to hide."

Ingrid stops on the sidewalk. She reaches out and grabs my elbow.

"What?" she asks.

"Me," I say.

Ingrid shakes her head.

"Why would they be ashamed of you?"

I tell her about the original use of the necklace, how it hid my proposal to Mette, and how her parents and siblings (especially Erik) opposed our marriage.

"They don't want to acknowledge that I was Mette's former fiancé."

"No," says Ingrid and resumes walking. "I don't think that's it. I don't think they should have been ashamed, and even if they were, that wouldn't have been a big enough secret. It would have to be bigger. It probably has to do with money or politics."

"Oh," I say, disappointed, "I don't know anything about those areas. I can't help you there."

"You've already helped me a lot today, Daniel. Thank you."

We come to a cross-street, where I will turn left and Ingrid will continue on her way to *Politigård*. I suppose it's the sun breaking through a cloud, the sound of bells, the look of Ingrid's messed-up hair, the fact that lunch seemed to go so well, or my own great loneliness unknown even to myself . . . but something, whatever, causes me to do a foolish thing.

"Ingrid," I ask. "May I kiss you?"

That was how Mette and I arranged for our physical affections during our year of fated love. I didn't like surprises, and I didn't always like the act of kissing, which often felt like we were just smashing our faces together. So the solution to the problem was to ask first. Usually Mette was the one to ask, and if I said no she'd be a little hurt, but she'd get over it. Or at least that's what she told me. Sometimes, though, kissing was pretty nifty. We had a few sessions that lasted several minutes.

It is hard to read Ingrid's face. If it were a painting, it would belong to the school of Abstract Expressionism and would require an entire faculty of art professors to debate possible interpretations over the course of, say, two or three millennia. Given that I don't have that much time on my hands, and since I'm already sensing that Ingrid is not in the mood for a kiss in the middle of downtown Copenhagen with cars and bikes and busses passing in front of us, I shrug my shoulders and turn towards my street. I am halfway across Vester Voldgade when Ingrid calls to me.

"Wait. Daniel. Wait. Don't leave."

Great, I think. Now she wants to kiss, and I'm not sure that I do anymore.

"Let's stand over there," Ingrid says.

She leads the way to a corner building with scaffolding attached to it and blue tarps hanging from the scaffolds. It's not the most romantic spot, but I follow her anyway. I'm suddenly unsure if I even remember how to kiss. As I recall, the fact that both kissers have noses can create some serious difficulty. Then there's teeth. How is it that you avoid bumping teeth? I know about shutting my eyes, but what about my lips? Mette sometimes convinced me to let her put her tongue in my mouth, but that came somewhat later in our relationship, and I never felt like reciprocating. I felt like getting the whole thing over with quickly and going back to reading a book or having coffee and pastries.

Ingrid and I stand inside the scaffolding, hidden in our blue tent, and she places her hands on my shoulders. I don't want to hurt her feelings by refusing to kiss her, so I close my eyes and wait for it to be over.

"Don't do that, Daniel. Don't close your eyes. I'm not going to kiss you, but I want you look at me."

A wave of relief washes over me, followed by something else I'm not able to name.

"I think you're a charming person. I really do. But Daniel, there can be no romantic relationship between us. What we're doing together is entirely professional. You are assisting the Copenhagen Police with an investigation into a serious crime, and your help is much appreciated. We would like to have your continued cooperation."

"I'll help," I say. "I'll still be your mole."

"I don't want to hurt your feelings."

"They're not hurt."

"Are you sure?"

I think for a moment. Maybe they are. Maybe my feelings are hurt. But they're not like my hands or my knees. When I stumble and fall down on the cobblestone, my scraped palms and bruised knees shout out to me, "We are hurt! We are hurt bad! Do something, Daniel! Quick!" But feelings, at least as I've experienced them, float around inside of me. They keep their own counsel. Every now and then I can tag one of them, then off it squirts into some depths I hardly know about.

"I think I'm okay."

"I want you to be," says Ingrid.

We are silent for a few seconds.

"Daniel, let me ask you something. And this doesn't have anything to do with my refusal to kiss you. I'm sure there are a lot of women who would like to kiss you."

"So far just one," I say. "But maybe one is enough for me."

"What I want to ask you is this: at the Center, do your colleagues know that you have Asperger's?"

As I register Ingrid's question, I experience something that is less of a feeling and more the *memory* of a feeling. I remember when Mette asked me to stay in her office after we'd had our usual meeting to discuss my translation questions—this was several years ago. She wanted me to answer some simple questions, yes or no. Do I sometimes feel like jumping over things that stand in my way instead of just going around them? Was I ever teased as a child? When I am in a group, do I ever feel as if there are hidden rules that everyone but me understands? Would I rather follow my usual routine even if a newer one made more sense? Do people, even strangers, comment on my unusual behavior? Is my preference for the clothes I wear more than just a preference? Does touching certain materials feel like torture? To some of the questions I said, "Yes." To others I said, "Yes" and "You know that's true!" After I don't know how long or how many questions, Mette looked up at me and said, "Daniel, I just gave you a self-evaluation quiz for Asperger's Syndrome. You scored in the high zone. You probably have Asperger's." Right there, that moment, whatever I felt and couldn't name: that's what I remember-feel now.

"Mette knew," I say. "But we didn't tell anyone on staff. I didn't want them to treat me any differently."

Ingrid nods.

"How long have you known?" I ask.

"I suspected it from the beginning. I had a nephew with Asperger's, and you remind me of him so much. Sometimes he'd get upset, like you did with Sven, and then he'd flail his arms. He had a quirky sense of humor, though. He made me laugh a lot."

"You're speaking of him in the past tense," I say. "Did he die?"

"Yes. Well. Actually, he killed himself. We were told that suicide isn't that uncommon. He wasn't as well adjusted as you are. He got teased a lot, and he took it hard. He didn't have any friends."

"I have friends," I say. "Last night, I was hosting a sleepover. But the Police broke it up."

Ingrid doesn't laugh at that joke. I'm not sure why.

"Daniel, I want you to be careful. I'm worried that some of your colleagues might take advantage of you. You can be a little too trusting at times. Like last night, with Jimmy."

She pulls her cell phone out of her pocket and looks down at it.

"I'd better be going," she says.

"Me, too," I say. "Lots more colleagues to socialize with! Anything you want your mole to dig up for you?"

"If you can let me know whether the manuscript is definitely authentic, sometime before five o'clock, I'd appreciate that."

"I'll see what I can do."

We exit back to the sidewalk. Ingrid goes her way. I go mine.

Chapter 4

I find Per Aage and Annette standing just outside the gate to Vartov, sharing a smoke break. I usually see them there when I return from lunch, and my customary pattern is to walk right past them, but this time I stop and say hello. After that one word, I'm at a loss for what to say next. Fortunately, Per Aage moves the conversation forward by asking if I'd like a cigarette.

"What brand?" I ask.

"Oh," says Per Aage. "You'll like these. They're American. A classic. Marlboro."

"Sorry, I only smoke Prince."

"I didn't know you smoked," says Annette.

"I quit for twenty-five years. Then I started again after Mette died. I'm not quite back into the habit yet. Actually, I felt sick the last time I smoked."

Per Aage takes a deep drag.

"Cigarettes are bad for your health," he says. "I'd quit too if I didn't have worse things wrong with me."

He and Annette look at each other and laugh. I don't see the joke, wherever they've hidden it.

I decide to set about some mole work. In order to "act normal," as Ingrid told me I should, I place the tip of my index finger on my right temple, creating the illusion that a question has just occurred to me.

"Hmm," I say. "I wonder."

"Yes," says Annette.

"All this effort the Police have put into finding the stolen manu-script. What if it turned out to be a fake?"

"What makes you think it's a fake?" asks Per Aage.

It's a clever response, but I turn it around on him.

"I don't know. If you were me, why would you think the manuscript might be a fake?"

Per Aage laughs.

"I don't know, Daniel. I'm not you. And I don't think it's a fake. Mette spent weeks with the manuscript. If she had any suspicions, she would have been the first to sound the alarms."

"It looked like vintage Kierkegaard to me," says Annette. "I didn't get to look at it for very long—none of us did—but that was the paper Kierkegaard liked to use and his style of filling up the whole page, even the margins. All the herringbone cross-outs. His handwriting—I've seen a lot of his handwriting, and the new manuscript conforms with what I've seen. I even found an instance of 'The Trembling Hand.' I wish I knew when he wrote the part I read. It may contain one of the earliest examples of Kierkegaard's over-caffeinization."

"I'll tell you though," says Per Aage, "if I doubted the manuscript it would be on aesthetic grounds. The part I read had some real howlers. I guess Søren was trying to teach himself rhyme and meter, and he hadn't learned much prosodic subtlety. At least not in the pages I saw. You got it right in your translation, though, Daniel. I saw you rhymed 'love' and 'dove,' equally cliché as the Danish pair. I even scanned part of your translation, and it reminded me of what I'd read in the manuscript: insistently regular, often bordering on sing-song. It must have been difficult for you to translate something so bad."

"I didn't know that it was bad," I say. "I just tried to create the same effect as Kierkegaard's Danish."

"Well," laughs Per Aage as he drops his cigarette butt into a waste bucket, "you succeeded all too well."

Annette finishes her cigarette and all three of us walk up to the entrance. Per Aage waves his key in front of the sensor then holds the door for us. As we walk down the hallway, Annette turns to me.

"I didn't think the poetry in the section I read was so bad. But Per Aage would be the expert."

"To answer your question, Daniel," says Per Aage, "I don't doubt that the manuscript is Kierkegaard's. The fact that some of the poetry is bad explains why he didn't publish it in his lifetime."

"Why didn't he just throw it away?"

"That's one thing we know about Kierkegaard," says Annette. "He didn't throw away anything!"

"Well," corrects Per Aage, "anything *he* wrote. For him, he was his own most sacred cow."

As we pass by Rebekah and Lars' office, Per Aage tilts his head toward the door.

"If you're looking for someone to play the doubting game with you, you know where to find him."

Right, I think. Lars. If anyone would want to laugh at Emperor Kierkegaard's New Clothes, it would have to be Lars Andersen.

"Thanks," I say. "I'll talk to him."

Per Aage and Annette look at me and shake their heads.

"Daniel in the Lion's Den," I hear Per Aage say as they continue walking down the hall.

When I knock on the door, no one answers, so I push it open. I look across to Lars' side of the office and see him seated at his desk with head phones in his ears. He is facing away from me and seems deeply engrossed in whatever he is listening to. Of the three busts on his book-shelf, Lars looks the most like Socrates: a full beard but a receding hairline, nearly bald. I watch him lift a small recording device from his desk and begin to speak into it. In Danish he says, "Against the charge that Kierkegaard's anti-Semitism was not a grievous error in mid-19th century Denmark, one might ask if attitudes that led to the Holocaust are in some essential way innocent of the Holocaust."

"Kierkegaard was an anti-Semite?" I ask.

The question startles Lars, who drops his recorder on his desk and swings around in his chair.

"What are you doing in here?"

"I knocked. You didn't answer. So I came in."

Lars wraps the cord of his headphones around the recorder and places it in a drawer.

"You might not have this custom in America," he says, "out in the Wild West where there are no laws, but here in Denmark if you knock on a door and no one answers, you're supposed to go away and come back later. Or, what's better, don't come back at all."

"I'm not from the Wild West. Buffalo is in Western New York, but it's still on the East Coast."

"I'm surprised to see you out of your mouse hole."

Lars stares at me for a moment.

"And it looks like your Fairy God-Tailor has come and taken back the designer suit he gave you."

"It's at the cleaners."

"You fell down again? Poor thing."

"No. I hit a Police officer and got his blood on my sleeves."

Lars laughs. "Good. Oh, that's good!"

"No, it's bad. I'm planning on apologizing. But it's hard to come up with the right words."

"Daniel, what do you want? As you can see, I'm working."

"Well, I heard you working. Dictating something about Kierkegaard being an anti-Semite. That's new!"

"It is new. And when I present it—if I decide to present it—it will have the effect of the 'Catastrophe' that Kierkegaard thought his little religious pamphleteering was going to have. I think we've overlooked his comments about 'Jew-boys' and 'false religion' long enough. If this is a serious center of intellectual inquiry we should either be honest about who Søren Kierkegaard was or desist. Or maybe we should do both. But I'd appreciate it if you didn't tell anyone about what you heard. If you can do that for me, I might be able to help you with whatever you've come here for."

"I'd like to know what you think of the manuscript."

"What manuscript?"

"Kierkegaard's. The poems."

"Haven't read it."

"What about my translation of it? Does that tell you anything?"

"Sorry, Daniel, I only read works in their original languages. I wouldn't want to hurt your feelings, but you know what the Italians say: '*Traddutore, traditore!*' "

"Which means?"

" 'Translator, traitor!' Or I suppose, closer to your homeland, the old Yankee wisdom of Robert Frost might be worth listening to: 'Poetry is what gets lost in translation.' I grant you, it takes some time to learn sixteen languages, as I have, but at least I have a clear conscience and I can sleep at night. Is there anything else I can help you with?"

"No, I guess that's it. And I won't tell anyone about your theory. I promise."

I start to leave but Lars stops me.

"What exactly do you want to know about the manuscript? Maybe I can help you, if you don't mind talking theoretically."

"Would there be any reasons to suspect that Kierkegaard didn't write it?"

Lars crosses his legs. He pulls on his beard. He still hasn't invited me to sit down, so I stand and wait for what he, in theory, will tell me.

"There are Kierkegaard's own words. In one place he states quite clearly that he would never write poetry because doing so would slow down his thought process. He considered himself a master of Danish prose style, so he didn't have any reason to switch to poetry. That would be like a sprinter deciding to enter the long-distance steeple chase. It doesn't make any sense for him to have written poetry."

"So you think the manuscript might be a fraud?"

"I didn't say that. Kierkegaard did a lot of things that didn't make sense, so it would actually be consistent for him to do something as nonsensical as write a collection of poems. Even hiding them in his desk has a certain Kierkegaardian element of surprise."

"Really? I didn't think that was very original, seeing that the manuscript of *Either/Or* was supposedly found in a desk."

"Exactly," says Lars, who strokes his beard again. "It is unlike Kierkegaard to be so unoriginal, and so it's a surprise to see him repeating himself. Of course, being surprising is something we've come to expect from Kierkegaard, so ultimately his act was unoriginal—that is, its originality bore the seeds of its unoriginality."

My head hurts from listening to Lars. I don't think our conversation is going anywhere, so again I start to leave. And again, Lars stops me.

"Lona told me they can't find the carpenter."

"What?"

"At the museum. They've been trying to find the carpenter who took apart Kierkegaard's desk and found the manuscript inside. But, you know, *deus absconditus.*"

"Okay, no carpenter. Does that fact, in theory, tell you anything about the manuscript?"

"In theory, Kierkegaard might not have put it there. In theory, someone else might have. In theory, I could give you greater details. But first, promise me again that you won't mention that little taping session of mine."

"I promise," I say.

"Do you remember the afternoon when Mette gathered us in the meeting room so she could finally tell us about this new, secret manuscript?"

"Yes."

"For three days she made us wait, without telling us a thing, while she studied the manuscript at the Royal Library. And for that whole time I hoped that the manuscript might be the draft pages to *The Concept of Irony*—the only work of Kierkegaard's for which we do not have his earliest drafts. To me, that's the Holy Grail! But of course, it was only a collection of poems. Poo-hoo. I tried to handle the disappointment like a man. But even in my depression I couldn't help hearing a curious statement from our former director. 'I know this must come as a surprise to you all since no one has ever seriously posited that Kierkegaard wrote poems.' Really, I wondered? Is there anything about Kierkegaard that hasn't been seriously posited after a century of scholarship? We've had Kierkegaard the misogynist. Kierkegaard the masturbator. Kierkegaard the mental patient. Kierkegaard the epileptic. Has no one ever given us Kierkegaard the poet? I realize that I myself have a new theory, but I thought it was the only new theory left. And so I set out on a hunt to determine whether our former, glorious director was correct. What do you think, Daniel? Might Mette have misspoken once in her lifetime?"

"I don't know. It's possible. She never misspoke to me, though."

"Not that you know of, that is. At any rate, she misspoke, knowingly misspoke, in your presence when she said those words about no one ever suspecting that Kierkegaard wrote poems."

Lars reaches into a file drawer and pulls out a document. He hands it to me. It is several pages of typing paper stapled together along the left margin. The text is in blue.

"Mimeograph," he says. "It's a duplication technique that came into existence sometime after the death of the last copyist-monk and sometime before Xerox applied for its patent."

"I'm old enough to have seen mimeograph. What is this?"

"It's an underground publication by some radical students at the University of Copenhagen. In the 1970s, Peter Rasmussen was its editor-in-chief. He wrote an interesting piece in this issue. Have a look."

I turn the pages until I come to an article titled, "What If Kierkegaard Wrote Poems? A Thought Experiment by Peter Rasmussen." I glance over the text long enough to see that it describes the exact metrical form of the poems I translated last month. It even predicts the subjects Kierkegaard would have chosen (actually did choose) for his poems.

I return the document to Lars, who looks at me with a satisfied grin.

"When I showed that to Mette, she was none too happy. She called me a 'rat,' an 'archive rat.' She knew about the article, and she confessed to what I suspected was the case. Peter owned the manuscript he described in there and was just waiting for the right time to spring it on the world. He was a patient man. We all knew that about Peter. And there was plenty of material at the Royal Library to fill his *Kierkegaard's Writings*. The poems, Mette said, were supposed to come later, a way to really celebrate Kierkegaard's 200th birthday and to usher in a new phase of scholarship."

"She never told me that," I say. "She never told me any of that. We worked on the poems together for over a month."

"Oh, the lies we tell. And the truths we don't. Anyway, Daniel, we have an agreement, right? You'll keep my secret? As you can see, even Mette kept secrets. You'll keep this one for me?"

"Sure," I say and back out of Lars' office. I close the door behind me and stand in the empty hallway. Per Aage, I decide, was right. I went into the Lion's Den. And I got mauled.

Mette lied to me? She kept secrets from me?

I stop by the main office to check my mailbox. There's one slip inside. Susannah called sometime while I was out to lunch, and in taking her message Anders has written "Urgent!" But now, after my meeting with Lars, finding out when Mette wrote her note to me doesn't seem all that important. The only thing that really matters would be raising Mette from the dead and asking her to explain herself to me. Somehow I don't think a research librarian, even one as skilled as Susannah Lindegaard, will be able to help me in this regard. Nevertheless, I walk over to one of the phones and dial Susannah's number. When she answers, her voice is hostile, and frankly, I'm not in the mood for it.

"What the hell kind of trick are you trying to pull on me?" asks Susannah.

"I'm not pulling any trick," I say. "If you can't date the note, it doesn't matter. Forget about it."

"I'm not going to forget about it. This thing's driving me crazy. How am I supposed to analyze something so small, wrinkled-up, and smudged with eraser marks? Where did it come from? Can you tell me that?"

"It was rolled up and stuffed inside the clasp to a necklace."

"Well, that explains the traces of silver I keep getting. Why did Mette put it there? But I guess that doesn't matter. . ."

"No, that's the part that does matter. She hid it there for me. She wanted me to see it after she died."

"Huh?"

I try to make it short, but it takes a while to explain the background, and while I'm giving it to her I sense that Susannah is not all that interested.

"We were engaged," I say.

"Congratulations," says Susannah.

"But we had to break it off."

"Sorry for your luck. Look, give me another few hours. I'll go back to the lab."

"Wait," I say, "before we hang up let me give you some more information."

I tell Susannah the dates that Ingrid gave me.

"Interesting," says Susannah. "Is she sure those are the correct dates?"

"She's a police officer. She double-checks everything."

"Look, give me your cell number in case you're not at the Center when I call."

"I don't have a cell phone."

There is a moment of silence.

"Sheez," says Susannah. "Well, a home phone. You're old enough. You probably still have a land line."

"I have a phone, and I have it plugged in, but I don't know the number. Give me a second."

I go over to Anders, who is seated at another desk working on a computer, and ask him what my home phone number is. He pushes some buttons, and in a few seconds it appears on his screen. While he writes the number on a piece of scratch paper, I wonder what other information he has about me hidden inside his computer.

"If I'm not there when you call," I tell Susannah, "you can leave a message. My phone has an answering machine."

"Oh," she says, "that's pretty advanced technology. I'm impressed."

"I read the directions last night. I know how it works."

"Must have been complicated."

"Not really, but I always read the directions first."

After I hang up with Susannah, I call Ingrid and tell her what I found out about the manuscript.

"Can you trust Lars?" she asks.

"No. But he might be telling the truth. It would explain how Carsten had access to the manuscript before it was discovered at the museum."

"That's true. We should probably assume the manuscript is authentic. It makes me wonder, though. You know that teenager you told me about? The one the Rasmussens had over to their house?"

"The girl who stole their Rembrandt so she could copy it?"

"Yes. We've followed up on that lead, and we're learning a lot about her. She certainly was a troubled teen. Theft. Violence. She has quite the record. For a while, she belonged to a girl biker gang and got into plenty of trouble. Her name is Sharlotte Nielsen. Daniel, did you know her?"

"No. I only heard about her from Lona."

"I may need to blow your cover. I may need to talk with Lona, and I don't see how I can hide the fact that I learned about Sharlotte from you."

"If this is the end of my career as a mole, I'm happy to retire."

"You've done a great job for us. Everything I've asked of you, you've done."

After I hang up, it occurs to me that I probably have done a good job for Ingrid and the Copenhagen Police—but there's still one thing I haven't done. I haven't discovered the Thorvaldsen family secret.

Secrets. Lies. Those were Søren Kierkegaard's strong suit, his native tongue, the water he swam in. In the most favorable interpretation, he felt they aided him as a writer. The many pseudonyms he wrote under allowed him to represent a greater variety of perspectives, to carry on his dialectical project, to convey indirectly what could not be communicated directly. Pretending to be a slacker—which he did by hanging around coffee houses or, sometimes, by showing up at the theater during intermission in order to be "seen," then hopping a carriage back home to continue his writing—this created a public image of him that so contrasted with the actual, hard-working person that he was, and only he knew he was, that Kierkegaard got a thrill from playing at the game—and the thrill gave him energy for writing.

But a less favorable interpretation of the lying, secretive Søren Kierkegaard would be this: he lacked utterly the skills to be honest with other people. He was a man so afraid of intimacy that he stationed ranks of guards before the gates of his heart—only one person ever passed, however briefly, through that regiment, and poor Regine Olsen was forced away with the tips of bayonets aimed at her back. Even if Kierkegaard thought that breaking their engagement was for Regine's own good, still that didn't excuse his behavior towards her. For a while he pretended to be a regular Don Juan. He let Regine believe that from the very beginning he only meant to play with her—to seduce her, then toss her aside. Over and over in his journals he writes how difficult it was for him to push her away; only occasionally does he remark on how necessary it was for his own good. In truth, he feared physical intimacy. According to one theory, Søren may have had a curved penis, which would have made sex difficult or impossible; at any rate, embarrassing. And he had some family secrets that he would rather not divulge. His father, it appears from recent research, had a nasty case of syphilis and feared he'd passed it on to his children. Some question whether the family's wealth could really have come solely from hard work and business savvy. If Søren had married Regine, according to how he understood marriage, he would have to expose himself entirely to her and keep no secrets. Oops, decided Kierkegaard a day or so after proposing marriage—I can't quite go there. Or whatever the 19th-century Danish idiom of the day may have been.

I know, and I acknowledge, that I share certain traits with Søren Kierkegaard. Like him, I am an unmarried, unsexed, middle-aged man who lives alone in this harbor town and spends most of his time in the company of words rather than people. Like him, I had one important romantic relationship in my life, and I regret that it had to end. If Mette is right, I also share with Søren a condition that wasn't described until after his death and wasn't detected in me until after my hair started to go gray. But, unlike him, I don't keep secrets. I don't lie. At least not usually—my work for the Police has forced me, for a time, into some unnatural behavior. But what I didn't know, would never have guessed, is that Mette too shared similarities with Kierkegaard: she lied, she kept secrets. I don't know why, but I would like to know why.

As I sit here in the main office and watch people come and go, and hear Anders answer their questions, both reasonable and unreasonable, I recall a piece of advice my father gave me. "When you need an answer," he told me, "go to the person who can give it to you." That was my dad. He didn't mess around with the in-betweeners. He went straight to the source. When my brother broke his leg in a soccer match—a pretty nasty break that ended his playing days—my father arrived at the hospital and pushed through ranks of office staff, administrators, and nurses. He never told us how he did it, but he got himself admitted into the doctors' lounge and spent a half hour talking with my brother's physician. "Will my son be able to play this sport professionally?" he asked. After the doctor finished his hems and haws, my father walked into my brother's hospital room and told him straight. "It's over with soccer. Better find something else to do with your life."

I know what my question is. And the person who can answer it, I decide, is Mette's mother, who lives on the other side of Denmark, in Jutland. By train it will take me just over two hours.

Chapter 5

When Søren Kierkegaard went on his famous "Pilgrimage to Jutland" in July of 1840, at the age of twenty-seven, having recently finished his degree in theology but before approaching Regine with the question that would complicate both of their lives for years to come, he did not, of course, take a train. He left Copenhagen in a boat, a rather homely vessel which he boarded in Nyhavn. He had expected a better ship, a grander one called the *Dania*, and in his journal he complained not only about his transportation but also the company of other travelers: "It is terrible how boring conversation generally is when you are forced to be with other people for a long time. It is just like when toothless old people are forced to turn the food in their mouths again and again—in this instance, a single observation was repeated so many times that it finally had to be spit out."

Poor Søren should have lived in the twenty-first century and experienced the advantages of DSB. My train will reach Jutland four times faster than his old boat, and I will be free from having to interact with fellow passengers. This is because I bought a ticket in the "*Stillezone*" section of the train, literally "The Silent Zone" or more colloquially "The Quiet Area." It's like a library on rails: Shh! No talking—not to people around you and certainly not to people on your cell phone. After what has been probably the most talkative morning and afternoon of my life, I am relieved to settle into my seat with a copy of *Ekstra Bladet*, two pastries from *Lagkagehuset* (they opened a shop in the Main Station just a few years ago; a brilliant idea!), and a cup of coffee. I am reading the front page article about Carsten Rasmussen when the train pulls out at exactly 2:05, precisely according to schedule.

As Ingrid had promised, the Police do not release my name to the press. In fact, my identity is simply passed over in the innocuous passive tense phrase, ". . . once the authorities were notified of Carsten Rasmussen's death . . ." Skimming the article, I find the quote from Erik Thorvaldsen, which turns out to be equally unremarkable. After expressing shock over his nephew's suicide and disbelief over Carsten's apparent admission to murdering his mother, Erik offers two facts that he says wouldn't excuse Carsten's behavior but might make it more understandable: first, he had been fighting drug dependency for many years (meaning, I suppose, that Carsten, could have done something as unnatural as killing his mother or as desperate as taking his own life) and, second, the anticipation of a sizeable inheritance brought greater anxiety to the boy's life than he was prepared to handle. Given the context of Erik's remarks, I think that Rebekah may have overreacted. It's not like Erik was accusing Carsten of killing his mother in order to cash in his inheritance. The MP's phrasing is too diplomatic even to suggest that. But then, Rebekah is newer to reading Danish than I am.

I fold up the newspaper and place it in the empty seat beside me. Gladly I sip my lukewarm, sugary coffee. Even more gladly, I take bites of my fresh pastries. As is often the case, my feelings do not coincide with the circumstances of my life. For me to be happy, all it takes is a little good food and a sense that my life has purpose. The skillful bakers and coffee roasters at *Lagkagehuset* have ensured the former, and now a trip with a mission (however unlikely of success) takes care of the latter. I realize my many good reasons for sadness, but those reasons don't move me to tears. I should mourn Mette's death. I should grieve and be aggrieved by Carsten's suicide and the dreadful message he left behind. But as the train moves through the outskirts of Copenhagen heading for the island of Funen, I can't help smiling like an idiot child with a big round sucker in his mouth. Sugar. Maybe sugar is the answer to the tragic view of life that, however proper to reality, cannot be maintained for long if one wants to exist in something other than a catatonic state. I am reminded of a study some years ago that claimed that the Danes are the happiest people in the world. It pointed to their healthy lifestyle (a diet high in fish and a propensity for regular exercise) and their famous Scandinavian tolerance for difference (allowing, for instance, space on the train for people who want to talk and space for people who want to be quiet). But maybe their happiness is not all that hard to understand. Maybe the researchers should simply have counted the number of bakeries in the average Danish village. When you think about it, who can be unhappy when eating pastries and drinking coffee all the day long as the Danes seem to do?

As I look out the window at the passing countryside, this trip to see Mette's mother and try to wrest from her the great Thorvaldsen family secret begins to strike me as silly. What am I doing? I haven't spoken with Fru Thorvaldsen in over two decades. Before Mette and I announced our engagement, Fru Thorvaldsen seemed fond of me; but afterwards, not at all! Will she even open her door to me? If she does, how do I go about asking whether, in exchange for my once insulting her by suggesting I was good enough to marry her daughter, she might like to divulge an ever greater, darker secret to me? I should get off at the next station and catch a train back to Copenhagen, but I've bought my ticket and something in me refuses to change courses once I've begun. I'm stubborn, even with myself. And besides that, without coming to any final conclusion, I have begun to form a theory.

Frequently in nineteenth-century literature, one finds the figure of the illegitimate child. British, American, Russian, and French novels all provide examples. Even Kierkegaard has a character who, after visiting a bordello, is haunted for the rest of his life by the suspicion that he may have fathered a child. The poor man scans the faces of children he sees on the streets of Copenhagen and wonders if one of them might be his. Since so much of Kierkegaard's work has its origins in his own life, many early biographers conjectured that here, too, Kierkegaard was speaking of himself. But that view has been pretty much decimated. More likely, Kierkegaard was trying his hand at a literary convention of the day—while also processing a related, but not exactly corresponding, family secret. To wit: Kierkegaard's father impregnated a woman out of wedlock. Though the two were quickly married and remained together to raise a large family, still the impropriety haunted Kierkegaard's father for the rest of his life.

Might there be some sexual secret in the Thorvaldsen family attic, I wonder? I never looked closely to see how much Mette and Erik resembled each other, but what if they were only half-siblings? Wouldn't it have caused a scandal if it were known that the proper Herr Thorvaldsen had had relations with someone other than his wife? And if he had, it might also have complicated the inheritance of his fortune. Could Mette not marry me because her family wouldn't support it—literally, financially—seeing that she was not entirely their daughter? But then, of course, it would be odd for them to raise her as if she was. . . .

And so another theory occurs to me. Maybe it wasn't Herr Thorvaldsen of the eat-your-potato-chips-with-a-fork school, but that man's son-in-law, Peter Rasmussen. We all knew that he worked at the Center over the weekend, and we assumed he worked alone. But what if he met someone there in secret? A lover? The mother of his other child, a daughter, Carsten's half-sister? And who might this mother be? Someone on the staff? And the daughter? She could be on the staff, too. In my mind, I run through the possibilities. Would Peter have found Lona attractive? Is Annette young enough to be their daughter? But then if such an interrelationship had occurred at the Center and Mette knew about it, she wouldn't let The Other Woman or The Bastard Child work alongside her, would she? No, she wouldn't. Even her permissiveness and her desire to be liked by others had its limits.

I am about to consider a third unlikely scenario when someone whispers my name. Any sound in the *Stillezone* is amplified, but when it's the sound of your own name you can't help perking up your ears and feeling implicated in a crime. Somewhere the train-librarian will hear this talk. Documents will be checked. You'll be asked to leave for not complying with the law. When I turn from the window and look around the car, I see three passengers: two are reading books and one is closing the cover of a laptop computer and staring in my direction. His face looks somewhat familiar. But I can't place it. He is a medium-build blond-haired Dane in his mid- forties, dressed in a suit without a tie, and looking like a hundred other people I might see in the capital on any given afternoon. He squints his eyes at me and mouths my name. I nod, affirming that I am indeed Daniel Peters and conveying perhaps that I don't know who the hell he is. He smiles brightly and leaves his seat, walking towards me. I feel a panic coming on, thinking he might sit down beside me and want to talk, here in the *Stillezone*, where talking is *strengt forbudt*, strictly forbidden. But instead he touches my shoulder and motions for me to follow him out of the car. We walk down the aisle together. He waves his hand in front of the glass door that separates the cars and it slides open. As soon as it closes behind us, he begins to talk.

"Torben," he says. "I'm Torben Kvist. From Saint Michael's School. You remember me, don't you?"

And fortunately for me, for this awkward situation, I do remember Torben. At the private school I attended during my exchange year, he was our class clown. Watching Torben's antics in the hallways and listening to his remarks in class taught me the Danish sense of humor, which has a surprisingly high regard for slapstick. After seeing the laughs he got for acting foolish, I began to understand why *The*

Three Stooges movies air so often on Danish TV and why, of all the Disney characters, none is loved so much as Daffy Duck (Danish: *Anders And*).

"Are you heading back to Kolding?" Torben asks.

We stand in the aisle of a car that is less than half full. In here, plenty of people talk. I hear a child laugh and squeal, "*Nej, mor! Nej, nej!*" Everyone, it seems, is relaxed and enjoying the ride. They must be Copenhageners going to Funen or Jutland to spend the weekend with family.

"Yes," I say. "I'm going to pay Fru Thorvaldsen a visit."

"Oh, you're bringing her your condolences in person. That's the proper thing to do. Please give her mine. It's a sad situation. Just terrible what happened to Mette. I wanted to go to her funeral, but I was away. I never knew her son—but of course, the news about him is all over the papers and Internet. Personally, I'm interested to hear how things play out with the manuscript. I keep checking my phone for updates, but nothing so far."

"I don't remember you being interested in poetry."

"Gaggh," says Torben and squeezes his neck. "No way! I don't want to *read* the manuscript. Kierkegaard is impenetrable enough in prose. It's hard to imagine what he'd be like in poetry. But I'm an attorney, and my specialty is copyright law. It will be a complex matter deciding who owns the manuscript. Does it belong to the Copenhagen Museum, where it was found; or the Royal Library, where the archives are kept; or the Kierkegaard Center, where it was stolen? And what about the foundations who are paying the ransom? Will they have a say in determining who owns Kierkegaard?"

"It sounds complicated. Maybe the thief won't return the manuscript, and no one will have to argue over it."

Torben makes his hand into a fist and pounds his forehead.

"No, no, no! Don't even say that. I want to see the giants of Danish culture take off their smoking jackets and mud wrestle with each other. I'm also hoping one of them hires me to stand in their corner. Business still isn't back to what it was before 2008. Do you know what I pay to rent an office in Copenhagen?" Torben points to his arm. "One of these," he says. Then he points to his leg. "And one of these."

"I don't pay anything for rent," I say. "I think it's part of my salary. But I don't understand that stuff!"

Torben shakes his head.

"Must be nice. That's how I always remember you from school, too. You never seemed to have a care. You just stared out a window or kept your nose in a book—that is, when you weren't gawking at Mette. Too bad things didn't work out between you. I had you two pegged for early marriage, a double baby carriage, and a nice big summer house in *Blåvand*."

"I couldn't compete with Peter."

"With a Rasmussen? No, most of us can't compete with their like. I suppose it was fated: the daughter of a shipping tycoon marries the son of a pharmaceutical tycoon. Money attracts money, or so they say."

"I'm just glad Peter didn't stand in the way of my working at the Center. I'm grateful to have that job and to live in Denmark."

"What is it you do there?" asks Torben.

As I explain to him my role as translator and, to give him an illustration, share a few things about my work on the new manuscript, Torben listens silently, without interrupting me. I'm afraid I'm boring him with details, but he never looks at his watch (I've learned that trick!) or fidgets. He stands with his elbows propped on the headrest of an empty seat and nods at me while I speak.

When I'm finished he says, "Let me ask you something. What's the intellectual property clause like in your contract?"

"That's funny," I say. "I didn't know I had an intellectual property clause until this morning."

"Oh, it's standard in work like yours. Usually the employee surrenders rights to the employer, or the Institution."

"Not in my case. Or at least not yet. There was an error in my contract, but the new director is going to fix it. I need to sign the revised contract when I get back to the Center this evening."

Torben takes his elbows off of the headrest and stands up straight. He reaches into his back pocket and takes out his wallet. I don't know why he would, but I think he's about to offer me some money.

"That's okay," I say. "I have plenty of money. I don't need yours."

"Well, I might be willing to take some of yours, Daniel. But I promise, I'll save you much more than my fee will come to."

He hands me a business card.

"This advice is free," he says. "Don't, don't, don't sign the contract until you have a competent lawyer review it for you."

I look down at his card, which appears quite professional. When it comes to his career, Torben evidently leaves all joking aside. His face, as he looks at me now, doesn't show the least trace of a smile.

"I'll think about it," I say and slip the card in my pocket.

We start to head back to the *Stillezone*, but just before we reach the glass door, Torben stops and turns to me.

"You know that Fru Thorvaldsen doesn't live in the house on Fjordsvej anymore, right?"

I shake my head.

"She gave that to her second son. He has a large family. She lives by herself in one of the new condos in the city center. It's not far from the station. I'll point it out to you when we step off."

As Torben promised, the walk from the train station wasn't far. Now I stand in front of Fru Thorvaldsen's complex and study the directory. A white button appears across from her name. But before I push it and hear her voice over the intercom, I need to make a decision. Will I lie and say that I've come here to extend my condolences, or will I tell her the truth? I have not enjoyed my mole work at the Center, and I would just as soon that my lies and secrets come to an end. But I also want to know whether there is some family secret that would explain why Mette was not, at all times, honest and forthright with me. If I take the direct approach with Fru Thorvaldsen, what chance do I have of getting an answer to my question? I stand and think for I don't know how long before I finally push the button. After a few seconds, I hear Fru Thorvaldsen's voice.

"What?" she says in Danish. "Are you here already? I'm not quite ready. But come on up."

She switches off before I can even say a word. The front door makes a buzzing sound, and when I pull it towards me, it opens right up. I take the elevator to the top floor and am soon standing in front of Fru Thorvaldsen's door, which is partway open.

"What are you waiting out there for?" she says in Danish. "Come on in. I'm not lifting this bag again, I can tell you that."

I push the door open and find Fru Thorvaldsen seated in a chair in her entryway. She wears a white winter jacket—it looks like fur—and is pulling on a pair of leather gloves. There is an ornately carved wooden cane across her lap. A large black suitcase stands beside a bureau with a mirror attached to it. As I walk in she lifts her head and, seeing me, suddenly jerks her arms and stiffens her back. In the process, her cane falls off her lap and rolls on the floor. I reach down and pick it up.

"Daniel, I wasn't expecting you," she says in English. It is a softer tone than when she spoke in Danish, a little tentative, probably because she doesn't speak English all that often. "Erik is coming to take me to Copenhagen for the weekend. And for the funeral."

I hand her her cane, and she uses it to stand up. She regards me silently for a moment.

"Will you help me with this coat, please?"

"Of course."

I walk around behind her and take hold of the collar and a sleeve. She keeps one hand on her cane, switching from the left to the right, and wriggles out of what must once have been a substantial beast. A polar bear? A mountain lion? I don't know these things, and I feel the way I always did when I went over to Mette's house after school: completely out of place. I was the boyfriend who wasn't good enough to be the butler. And now as I stand with Fru Thorvaldsen's coat draped over my arm and await further instructions, I feel too incompetent even to be her footman.

"You can put it across the chair, Daniel. Thank you. So, have you come to offer your condolences? That is very kind of you."

She pulls off her gloves, one finger at a time, and sets them on top of her coat.

"No," I say.

"Then you've come for some other reason. May I ask what that reason is?"

It is difficult for me to look directly at Fru Thorvaldsen, but I don't want to appear rude by looking down at the floor or off to the side.

"Mette," I say, and with all the power I have in me I make eye contact with Fru Thorvaldsen, "left me a note."

"Oh," she says. And after a silence, she says it again, "Oh."

"Yes," I say.

"Then she finally told you. I can see that. Let's go into the sitting room. I'm sure you have a lot of questions."

I follow her, cutting my usual strides in half so I don't pass her and paying close attention to setting my feet squarely on the floor. If I tripped and bumped into her, we would both fall over. We move through immaculate rooms, with plenty of space around the furniture and framed paintings on the wall. She must have brought only her most treasured items from the house on Fjordsvej, this condo being so much smaller and yet only sparsely decorated.

We settle into upholstered chairs, with a coffee table between us. Through the large glass windows I see the spire of city's oldest church, and off in the distance is *Koldinghus*, the royal castle where Mette and I sometimes walked on weekends, circling its pond or sitting together on one of the benches. And now, how odd, twenty-seven years later, to sit across from Mette's mother and look down on that scene. Across from me, Fru Thorvaldsen sits up straight and holds her hands folded on her lap. She is wearing an elegant blue dress and a pearl necklace.

The word "dignity" occurs to me. Seeing her and the view behind her, I feel as though I am sitting in court with an old queen, overlooking her kingdom. I don't feel comfortable, I don't feel like I belong here, but this is where I have had to come to get my answer.

"I'm sure it came as a shock to you," Fru Thorvaldsen says. "In fact, you look like you're still in shock."

I nod my head and try to manage a small smile.

"I want you to know, Daniel, that I didn't think the secret should be kept from you. From my husband, yes, of course. There was no question about telling him. He was dying. I'm almost certain he would have written Mette out of his will. And we're talking about a lot of money, you understand that, don't you?"

"Yes. I think so."

I try to keep my eyes fixed on Fru Thorvaldsen. Looking at her I notice, for the first time, how much Mette resembled her. In the mouth and nose, but especially in the eyes. I loved looking into Mette's blue eyes, and it is almost as though I'm staring into them now.

"I suppose I should be glad they let me in on it. Mette and Erik were going to keep it all to themselves. They had a plan . . . I'm not sure how much Mette has told you. But you can't keep this sort of thing from a mother. I would have found out eventually. And of course Mette needed my help. She was only eighteen. It was hard to see her struggle so much."

"I wish I could have helped her."

"I'm sure you do. And I believe you had a right to. Except the circumstances wouldn't allow it. I hope you can understand that."

"I'll try to."

"Well, did she give you Sharlotte's contact information? She's still in the States, the last Mette told me. I'm sure you'll want to get in touch with her now. Erik won't be happy, of course. But I always thought you had a right to know. I was surprised that Mette wanted to keep it from you."

"Sharlotte?" I ask.

"Yes, Sharlotte, your daughter. Did Mette give you a different name? That's right: she and Peter changed it after Sharlotte got into some more trouble. But they never told me the new name. All this must be very confusing for you, Daniel. I can't imagine what you must be feeling."

"To tell you the truth," I say and gaze out the window, "at the moment I'm not able to name what I'm feeling either."

"I've probably told you too much. It's overwhelming you, isn't it?"

"No," I say. "Please, tell me more."

"Are you sure?"
I nod.

And so for the next hour, Fru Thorvaldsen unveils the family secret and confirms what I told Ingrid Bendtner—that *I* am that secret,
or at least I am central to it. I learn that Mette's pregnancy wasn't discovered until after I had returned to the U.S. That she, even more than
the others, was against telling me. It was clear that her family would
not let us marry, so why should she involve me? She wanted me to have
a good life. She swore that the whole thing was her fault. Our experi-
mentation, she said, went beyond what I really wanted (and that's true
enough—I only vaguely remember a squishing of bodies, a rush of
fluid, a feeling of deep embarrassment). And so it was left to the mother,
the mother-to-be, and the upstanding older brother to devise some way
out of the situation. First and foremost, Herr Thorvaldsen must not
know. Mette moved to the capital on the pretense of starting her university studies, but in actuality she stayed with Erik and Erik's wife.
They considered, for a time, pretending that Mette was Erik's wife and
delivering the baby under her identification papers—but then Erik's
wife became pregnant, so that wouldn't work. No one else in the family could be trusted with their secret, and by then Mette had passed the
period when an abortion was possible. She would have to carry the
child and put it up for adoption. She lived like a ghost in the guest
room of her brother's house, seldom going out, a new life growing inside her. When it was over, after she'd had the baby and signed the
papers, Herr Thorvaldsen never knew a thing about it. He welcomed
her home for Christmas after her first semester of college. He asked if
she'd come across the Rasmussens' boy, Peter, who was beginning to
teach in the Faculty of Theology. Hadn't she, he teased, become enam-
ored with Kierkegaard during her last year at Saint Michael's? Well,
this Rasmussen, this Peter Rasmussen, this Dr. Peter Rasmussen was a
specialist on Kierkegaard. Maybe she should meet him. Maybe they'd
have things to talk about. Of course Mette never forgot her daughter,
not while the courtship with Dr. Rasmussen accelerated, or later when
a proposal came just in time for Herr Thorvaldsen to give his blessings
(and assure a sizable dowry) before dying, never having met his first
grandchild. It was well into her marriage with Peter before Mette
made him a party to the family secret. He took it surprisingly well.
Theoretically, he said, she'd chosen the better of two options for handling an unwanted pregnancy. However, her choice carried ongoing
responsibility. It was his idea to find out about Sharlotte's progress

through the Danish Welfare System. He, not Mette, raised the possibility of adopting the child. But brother Erik was not in favor. He feared, against Dr. Peter Rasmussen's assurances, that the secret would get out. Brother Erik did not like the way the media might tell the story about one of Denmark's richest families shoving their child-rearing responsibilities onto the State. A reporter might come up with a clever phrase for the opposite of noblesse oblige. And so the search for Sharlotte was postponed several more years. The girl was already a teenager when Mette and Peter first inquired about her and then, under the guise of Lady Di-like volunteerism, visited the group foster home where she was living. The girl was a handful! She'd been kicked out of school half a dozen times, passed from one foster family to another, and twice picked up by the Police for stealing artwork from private residences. Peter took the news of the thefts surprisingly well. Theoretically, he said, she showed a taste for the finer things in life. He and Mette gradually got to know and like her. Occasionally, they invited her to their home in Gentofte. She seemed to settle down and progress well in life. But then she stole a painting from their private collection, one of their favorites, a miniature by Rembrandt. The Rasmussens never pressed charges. Instead, they convinced her to give up crime and devote herself to something better. She needed to start life all over again. It began with a new name, in order to separate her from her past record, then a trip to the United States, where she enrolled in art school, although Fru Thorvaldsen was not sure where that was.

"Did Mette tell you where Sharlotte is now?"

"Not exactly," I say. "But her note gave me a good idea."

"I see. So you think you'll be able to find her?"

"Yes, I think so."

"Can I help you in any other way?"

"Mette didn't say whether she'd told Sharlotte who her parents are."

"I don't believe so. And I'm sure she didn't tell Carsten. She and Peter would have wanted to keep those two apart. Oh, they would have been like gasoline and fire!"

"So Carsten and Sharlotte never met each other?"

"They might have, when Sharlotte went over for visits. You know, Daniel, you'll have to be very careful when you explain things to her. She'll be in shock, just as you were."

I nod.

"Still am," I say.

"Did Mette give you a photo of Sharlotte?"

"No."

"Would you like to see one?"

"Yes," I say, but based on what she's told me I already know what my daughter looks like. I even know what name she goes by.

Chapter 6

Having said good-bye to Fru Thorvaldsen and accepted a photo of "Sharlotte," which I folded up and placed in my jacket pocket, I now head back to the train station for my return to the capital. I walk along familiar streets, unchanged since my days as an exchange student. When I first arrived here as a seventeen-year-old kid from Buffalo, NY, all the streets, all the buildings, all the people, all the clothes they wore, and all the words they spoke were foreign to me. But not now. Now the foreignness is no longer foreign. When I come to the library, I stop in its plaza and gaze over the rows of bicycles. I look at the word on the building: *Bibliotek*, a word that at one time did not mean "library" to me because I didn't know what it meant. Now it means "source." It means "the location at which two persons (Daniel Peters and Mette Thorvaldsen) began their story." Perhaps there are two teenagers in there tonight, standing close together among the stacks, pulling down books by an author their teacher told them they'd better not read; if they did, they'd only regret it. Do I regret reading Søren Kierkegaard? No. Does Mette, in whatever way regret is now possible to her? I doubt it.

"Life can only be understood backwards," our forbidden author wrote, "but it must be lived forwards." This is probably his most often quoted aphorism, but personally it's not my favorite. Not because I doubt its truth, but because I don't like doing two things at once. Like it or not, though, at this very moment I am moving in two opposite directions. Part of me, the part that feels the damp cold penetrating my clothes and starts walking again, this time a little faster, is headed for the train station, then on to Copenhagen, where an important decision lies in my future. Another part of me, the part that sat bolt upright while Fru Thorvaldsen told me the family secret, wanders in the past trying to understand things that will be important for me to know when I arrive in Copenhagen and (I hope, if it's not too late) meet with the daughter I didn't know I had.

Seeing Susannah Lindegaard's photo when Fru Thorvaldsen handed it to me was not, in itself, a surprise. It was something like I experience when I am almost certain that I have found the right word in English for another word in Danish, but I decide to look it up in the dictionary anyway. The surprise comes from the confirmation of just how right the word is. Maybe the Danish and the English share a common etymology, or maybe the word's first published usage is recorded in the *ODS* as "Kierkegaard, S." and so my impulse to create a new word in English, one that cannot be found in the *OED*, seems all the more perfect. Or perhaps it is the way the word fits when I place it among others in a passage. Sometimes a single word can pull the entire translation together. For me, Susannah Lindegaard did just that.

I now understand why Mette sent me to the library. Where else, how else, would I meet our daughter? But someone, Erik, would not have approved, and so Mette had to find a way to get her message to me without his seeing it first. The necklace was the perfect place. But it was also a small place, and so the note inside had to speak volumes to the right person, to the translator she knows I am. Not the fastest, but the most determined. "Daniel," she said to me during one of our weekly meetings, "you never settle for an approximate word!" Which is why she had to find a literal pair of half-siblings so I could match them with Susannah and Carsten. Which is why the manuscripts had to concern a broken engagement, like our own.

There is more that I can infer, but I almost don't want to. A professor in graduate school once asked our Translation Studies class whether any of us who spoke German would agree to translate *Mein Kampf*. The discussion lasted an entire period. The ethical questions got thornier the deeper we trudged into the woods. Mette, I see, has tossed a ball into the brambles and asked me to go retrieve it. If anyone else had asked me, I probably wouldn't. But there's not much I wouldn't do for Mette, and she knew that. As Ingrid Bendtner said, Mette trusted me. She knew she could. And so I do not turn down her translation assignment and I do not settle for an approximate word.

The fact that she placed the note in a safety deposit box, where I'd see it if she died, but wouldn't if she didn't, meant that Mette was uncertain and wanted to keep her options open. She visited the box many times, probably to change the note so that it would always direct me to Susannah, wherever she happened to be at the time. The earlier messages have been erased, but I gave the dates of Mette's visits to Susannah, who may already have solved the riddle and now, like me, has a decision to make. Based on what I can infer her past decisions to have been I fear for my daughter. Yes, that is the word, *fear*. I can feel it in my stomach and chest. It's odd to feel this strongly for someone I hardly know when I couldn't conjure up grief (still can't) for Mette.

I arrive at the station and walk down through a tunnel then up a flight of stairs. The train has already arrived and is boarding. My ticket privileges me to a seat in the *Stillezone*, but I choose the first nearly full car that I see and find a seat there. It is close to 5:00 p.m., and if there is any news about the manuscript someone will hear about it on their cell phone and announce it to the others. It's always that way with important sporting events. A lot depends now on what Susannah decides to do, and for once in my life I prefer the crowd over solitude.

I feel safe in making another inference. Just as the letter from Henriette Lund to Fru Schlegel gave instructions about a book the two had worked on together (Henriette being its main author and Fru Schlegel its most valuable source), Mette was trying to tell me something about the new Kierkegaard manuscript. What was she trying to tell me? I can't be certain, but I think Susannah either copied it (if Lars is right, and Peter owned and saved the manuscript for over forty years—that's a long time even for a patient man like Peter!) or forged it (if Per Aage is right and the poems, some of them at least, are dubious on aesthetic grounds—which might mean that Carsten wrote the poems, just to amuse himself). At any rate, I don't think the new manuscript is entirely legitimate: it's either Kierkegaard-copied or Kierkegaard-forged.

The train pulls out of the station and we are on our way. I become aware that I am the only person in this car without a suitcase above or beside my seat. These are Jutlanders off for a weekend in the capital, many of them to book in at cheap hotels and enjoy the city in its less-crowded season. Most of them are young, teenagers and twenty-somethings. Only a few read books. Most talk with their travel companions or stare down at their cell phones, taking advantage of the train's free wireless system—I have no idea how that works, but I'm depending on it for news updates.

By a simple process of elimination I can conclude that Susannah has the manuscript. If Mette had wanted me to suspect someone at the Center, she would have chosen a different clue for me. I am not sure, however, what Susannah wants to do with the manuscript. According to Lona, Carsten argued against paying the ransom. Did he do that so he would look less guilty? Or did he and Susannah disagree about what should be done with the manuscript after Mette died—no, I tell myself, say it!: after she was murdered? Did Susannah want to collect the ransom, but not Carsten? Was she motivated by money, or did she simply want the pleasure of having her work appreciated by others?

Shortly after the train stops in Odense, the excitement of breaking news grips the passengers in my car. The feeling is palpable, as if the air pressure has suddenly dropped and breathing becomes, if not more difficult, more deliberate. I try to overhear a single conversation, but so many people are speaking at the same time, and their voices are in discord, not harmony that I can't make sense of what anyone is saying. The crowd's tongue is Babel. But I don't speak that language.

I walk down the aisle looking for someone to tell me what's happened.

I stop beside a young woman a few seats ahead of mine. She wears a purple Helly Hansen rain jacket and a green knit hat. Her blonde hair covers her eyebrows and falls down over her shoulders. Most importantly, however, she is staring into a laptop computer placed on her table.

"*Hvad er der sket?*" I ask.

She looks up at me and shakes her head. I don't think she understands what I've said.

"What happened?" I say. "Why is everyone so excited?"

"Oh, it's about Carsten Rasmussen. The boy who killed his mother, then killed himself."

"Yes? What about him?"

"Well, the Police got a package from him in the mail. It had a letter and a video. I'm trying to look at the video now, but I think about a million other Danish people are, too. It's taking forever to download."

"Can you tell me about the letter? What did it say?"

"That he's sorry he killed his mother. He was on drugs. He tried to cover up the murder by stealing a manuscript from her. He wanted to make the Police think someone else killed her."

"Does it say what he did with the manuscript?"

"No. But wait. I think I can watch the video now. That's what everybody's so excited about."

She turns her computer so I can look at the screen. I bend down and lean forward. To steady myself, I wrap my arm around the back of her seat. For about thirty seconds, we watch the video with our faces so close together they almost touch. The image on her screen is grainy, but

I can make out the figure of Carsten Rasmussen seated in his mother's house and holding up pages of an old manuscript. Each sheet is filled with writing that resembles Kierkegaard's and is arranged in stanzas rather than paragraphs. Carsten's hand holds a lighter. A sudden flame appears. His hand moves to one of the pages and sets it on fire. He repeats this with several other pages, dropping each one into a trash can. Finally, he dumps a stack of pages into the bucket and flames leap up over the sides.

"Wow," the young woman beside me says. "That thing was worth a lot of money, too."

"Right," I say. So why burn it?"

"Because he's Carsten Rasmussen. He does the craziest things. My parents are always warning my little brother not to be like him."

I walk through the train looking for my seat in the *Stillezone*. As I pass through cars, I see passengers with their heads bent over cell phones or with their eyes trained on computer screens. Some talk with their neighbors, even laugh, but their amusement doesn't amuse me. Occasionally, I catch a snatch of conversation. It's all the same. Like the young woman who shared her computer with me, everyone is transfixed and excited by Carsten's outrageous act. They see it as a fitting end to his life, one last chance for him to grab the headlines. But as I pass through the glass doors that separate the cars, I worry about Susannah. I don't know much about computer videos, but I think the one I just watched was produced by her. I only hope she wasn't planning on making it her last forgery.

When I arrive in Copenhagen it is just past 7:30. I climb the steps out of the station and onto street level. It takes me less than five minutes to reach my apartment.

In my darkened living room, a red light that I have never seen before flashes like a tiny beacon. I turn on a lamp and walk over to the telephone. The display tells me that I have three messages. I hope that at least one of them is from Susannah. After I press a button, a robotic voice tells me in Danish the date and time of the first message: today at 3:24. It's from Lona:

Hi Daniel. Are you at home? Anders told me you finally plugged your phone in. No one's seen you around here since lunchtime. This isn't an emergency, but it would really help me out if you'd stop into the office sometime tonight and sign your new contract. Birgit needs me to complete a permission form so the museum can use your translations. But as it stands, under your old contract, I don't have the legal right to do so. I know that may sound complicated to you, but, really, all you have to do is sign the new contract and leave the rest to me. I'll be here until 5:00, at least. We're all waiting to hear news about the ransom. Fingers crossed and the manuscript will be back at the Center where it belongs.

At 4:43, Ingrid Bendter called me:

Daniel? Did you skip dinner tonight? I'm standing next to *Morfar's* and you're not here. At the Center they don't know where you've gone. I want you to know what happened here at *Politigård* this afternoon. We got a letter today from Carsten Rasmussen. It's a more explicit confession to killing his mother. And he included a video of himself burning the pages of the manuscript. You may not want to see it, but it will be on TV in about twenty minutes when the Commissioner gives his press conference. It's been a difficult couple of weeks for you, Daniel. You might not know it, but you've been grieving for Mette. I've seen it since the first time I met you. Call me sometime, will you? I care about you. I need to know you're all right.

The last message came from Erik Thorvaldsen, and was made less than half an hour after I left his mother's. He must have called from the train station. In the background, I hear announcements played over a loud speaker.

I guess you caught the earlier train. I wanted to talk with you in person, Daniel. I'm a little surprised to find you have a working phone now. My mother told me about your visit and the conversation you two had. Before you go looking for Sharlotte, talk with me, okay? I can help you find her. But we need to do this the right way. I'll stop by your apartment this weekend.

The messages end there. Without a single word from Susannah.

I am sitting on my couch with only one lamp lit and wondering what I should do next—could I call Susannah? Would her number be in my phone book? No, of course not. In 1994, she would have been eight years old and living in one of the many foster homes she moved in and out of, considered by her "parents" to be a bad girl because they didn't know she had Asperger's—which wouldn't have excused her behavior, but would have made it more understandable. Suddenly, I remember the journal I found in Mette's office, that article about violent tendencies in people with Asperger's. I had thought the "S" referred to Søren. But Mette must have been thinking about Susannah. Or Sharlotte. Her daughter. Our daughter. Someone she shouldn't have trusted, but couldn't help trusting.

An odd feeling comes over me. It is hard to name, but I think it is called loneliness. A yearning to be with others. I want company. Mette's—but she is dead. Ingrid's—but I can't tell her what I know, although how could I be in her presence and not? And then there's Susannah, this stranger who happens to be my daughter and who, I believe, is also a murderer and forger. I recall the first time I met her, how she wouldn't rule out the possibility of the manuscript being a fake—"On the level of the Spanish Forger." She took pride in her work. I know what that's like. But there's so much else I don't know and only Susannah can tell me.

I pick up the receiver and call the one person who may know how to reach my daughter. After three rings, Thor answers. I begin by lying to him, saying that I have to get in touch with Susannah right away. It has to do with dating the note from Mette. It's an urgent police matter, I tell him.

"What?" says Thor. "I thought they finished their investigation. I just saw the Commissioner on TV2. He said they're satisfied that all the pieces fit together. No one's surprised by Carsten's behavior. It's terrible, but he always had to outdo himself. I wouldn't think the note would matter to the Police anymore. Unless . . . has something new come up?"

"No, nothing new . . ."

"So?"

"It's important to tie up loose ends. They thought Susannah would help in that way."

Thor sighs. For a few seconds, he doesn't say anything.

"I could give you her phone number and her address."

"That would be great. Thank you."

I find a pencil and notepad and get ready to write.

"But I don't think you'll reach her. I've tried to since this afternoon. I even went over to her apartment this evening. To tell you the truth, I'm concerned about Susannah."

Thor tells me how he noticed Susannah acting oddly at work. "Odd," he says, "even for Susannah." Sometime after lunch, she locked herself away in her office. When he passed by, he heard her moving boxes around and constantly feeding the paper shredder. He had an afternoon meeting in another part of the Library, but when he got back Susannah's door was open. He walked in. He'd never seen her office look so neat and tidy. The desk was clear except for the note in Mette's handwriting and a brief letter to Thor.

"What did the letter say?" I ask.

"'Sorry I failed you.' Just those few words. But coming from Susannah, it made me worry. You see, she's always completed her work, any assignment I've ever given her. It matters a lot to her. But this job stumped her. I shouldn't have insisted on her doing it. My worst fear is . . ."

"Yes?"

"Oh, it's ridiculous. She probably just needs some time to herself. I hope to see her at work on Monday. Would you mind if I don't give you her contact information? That might upset her further."

"Okay."

"I'll have her call you. That would be better. And there's no urgency about dating the note now, is there?"

"No," I say. "No urgency."

My apartment is filled with an emptiness that perhaps has always been here but which I seem to notice for the first time now. I sit in the half-darkness and look around at the familiar walls and furniture, the wine cabinet, the TV console, the shadowed paintings hanging in their nearly invisible frames. Everything is exactly as it was when I moved in here, and exactly as it will be whenever I move out. Somehow keeping everything in my life the same—a pattern to repeat endlessly, all alone, over and over—no longer feels like such a high aspiration. Loneliness. Is that it? Is that what they call this feeling?

I have not eaten since my train ride to Kolding, and yet I don't feel hungry. Still, I make myself stand up and walk to the kitchen. As I am passing through the dining room, I see something on the table. There shouldn't be anything on it. I cleared off all the dishes and took Mette's note with me when I left this morning. As I turn on a light switch, I feel my heartbeat quickening as I begin to realize that someone has been in my apartment while I was out. And that person sat at my dining room table and wrote me a letter in a hurried, jagged script. It fills one side of a piece of typing paper.

Daniel,

*Or I could call you "Dad." Right? I suppose you've figured
out Mette's riddle. Good for you. Not so good for me. Look,
you're a damned hard person to get in touch with and I've
waited for you as long as I can. I kind of wanted to have one
of those father/daughter talks about how I should handle my
future, but I see I'm on my own as usual. Fine. I'll just ask you
this, as a favor: let everybody think what they think. Don't go
spoiling all the work I've done. Most of it I never intended!
Swear! I lost my head and I'm sorry. But being sorry won't keep
me out of Vestre Prison, with those damned lights they leave on
twenty-four hours a day. I never should have gotten into the
collaborating business. Carsten was a fool, and most of the poems he wrote weren't even that good. And Mette should have
trusted my art and let people see it—no one could have proven
it wasn't Kierkegaard's handwriting. I'm the best at what I do.
You saw that. You called me thorough. Well, hell, yeah. Everything would have been different if she'd just told me a little bit
about my past . . . but then she left you in the dark, too. Jeez!
All right, I have to go. You won't see me. No one will see me.
Like all the best forgery artists, I'm going to disappear. Forever.*

When I finish reading Susannah's letter the last word of it still
hangs in the air. What does she mean, *Forever*? And the word *disappear*—it can mean, "to go away" or it can mean, "to go away . . .
Away!*" Whichever way she means it, I feel certain that our short time
of knowing each other as father and daughter has already come to an
end. In the matter of two weeks, then, I've lost the only woman I
loved, and now the daughter I didn't even know I had.

I leave the letter on the table and turn the light off. For some
reason I don't understand I am drawn to the window and stand there
looking out over the Inner Harbor. Something heavy fills my body. Is
this it? Grief? Finally? Across the water, I can see the steeple of Our
Savior's Church. It reminds me of Mette. It reminds me of the two of
us standing up there together. I think of us and I think of Susannah,
too. In the half-dark, I imagine that I'm filling up with grief; it feels
as though my arms and legs are bloating with it. The point comes
when my skin is so taught from holding in this grief I think I'll burst.
But I don't. I sink to my knees still heavy with the feeling. A voice I
recognize as my own sobs—the sobs that I've wanted to come for
over two weeks now. I feel exactly what a person in my position

should feel. For me, this is some accomplishment, but it brings no relief at all.

Grief, it turns out, is a language I learn by total immersion. For two days I don't eat and I don't feel like eating. I read Susannah's letter over and over, trying to translate her words into something I can understand. But I can't make sense of it. Every word could mean one thing, or it could mean another. I tire from trying to force hope into what is clearly a farewell letter. Or a suicide note. Or a farewell letter.

On Monday I make myself get dressed and leave for work. There is a slim possibility that Thor is right, and Susannah will call me. But it's not likely. I've tried to think through her situation, but I can only see it as an either/or. Two options—and she must choose one of them. I don't think staying around at the Royal Library and making frequent visits to her new-found father is one of her choices. I wish I could promise her that I'd keep her secret. But would I? And would she believe me?

Lost in these gloomy thoughts, I ride down the elevator. When it reaches the bottom and I step out, I see something on the floor, a small envelope with my name on it. I recognize the handwriting and open it immediately. Inside I find a key, similar to the one Mette left me, and a note that reads, "Think of this as your Father's Day present. Hope you like it. –Your Daughter." For a moment, before I come to my senses, I stand in the lobby and feel irritated at Susannah. Didn't she know I would be on my way to work? What, am I supposed to walk across town to Danske Bank and be late to the Center?

But that, of course, is exactly what I do.

Morten Nielsen is standing behind the front desk and smiles at me when I walk in. He is happy to escort me down to the basement so I can access my box. Once we locate it, he steps aside.

"Well, you know how this works. But I don't need to wait for you this time. When you're finished, just slide the box back in. Take as much time as you like."

He leaves and I carry the box over to the table where I viewed the one from Mette. Susannah's box is smaller, but made of the same heavy-duty steel with a hinged lid. I take out the contents and lay them before me. There is a brief note from her. It reads, "You can imagine how much time I spent making this. I couldn't destroy it. But I couldn't keep the Police wondering about it, either. Enjoy, but please don't show it to anyone. –Your Trusting Daughter." I push the note to one side and stare down at an old, yellowed envelope, about the size a small diary might fit into. On the outside are the words "*Digte af S. Kierkegaard.*"

I open the red seal, Kierkegaard's own with the initials "S.K.," and pull out the pages. For I don't know how long (an hour? longer?) I study Susannah's remarkable forgery of Kierkegaard's handwriting, and I feel like I am back in the Old Royal Library, leaning over a manuscript as I did during the first years I lived in Copenhagen and began my work at the Center. I could not possibly tell a difference between her pages and those others. It is beautiful, I think. A beautiful lie. Kierkegaard would envy her. But I am proud of her.

Concluding Postscript:
May 5, 2013

I am seated in my regular place in the sanctuary of Our Lady's Church. I call it my regular place, even though I've only sat here three times. But given church attendance among most Danes, and considering my even spottier record, three times in four months qualifies me for the designation of a "regular." Jesper Olsen, who has seen me attend exactly two funerals and one Easter service, passed me on the path around "The Lakes" last week and said, "Hello, Daniel." It spooked me that he knew my name. I may need to cut back on my visits here.

My pew is next to the statue of John, the beloved disciple. He is holding a tablet in his hand, but he's not writing in it; he's gazing skywards, I suppose "heavenwards" would be the more fitting term. For today, unlike the days in deep winter when I attended funerals, there is a bright ray shining through the skylight in the ceiling. On a day like today if someone wants to tilt his head heavenwards and believe in divine inspiration, the way John seems to, I won't oppose him. And I am indebted to John, or to his amanuensis, or to his follower, or to whomever, in the spirit of John, wrote the Gospel of John, the first words of which brought me back to life when the grief I'd been longing to feel decided to squeeze me in an extra-long bear hug. It has been three and a half months without any word from Susannah. Even so, I can't break the habit of searching the lobby floor for another package from her. Nothing. She has gone away. Or she has gone, period. The last time I bumped into Thor (when I'd gone to the Royal to retrieve Mette's note) he looked glum and seemed to blame himself. "She had no family," he told me. "And no friends. I should have done more for her." I kept my feelings to myself.

They held Carsten Rasmussen's funeral in this church, amid some controversy. The scene was reminiscent of Kierkegaard's funeral (also held here) when a large crowd gathered to oppose the forcing of a Christian funeral service on someone who'd spent his final days rejecting the established Church. But Kierkegaard's brother was a priest, as well as his closest relative, and he determined that Søren should be buried as the good Christian he never claimed himself to be. Similarly, Erik Thorvaldsen planned a funeral that he felt was appropriate to the nephew of a Danish Member of Parliament. He didn't expect to find two rows of motorcycles parked in front of the church revving their engines to drown out the bells, but still, somehow, he managed to see that the service proceeded. It was quiet in the church and I was sitting here next to John (by coincidence or something else?) when Jesper Olsen read the words, "In the beginning was the Word, and the Word was with God, and the Word was God." I didn't hear anything else for the rest of the service. I pondered those words, then and for months to come. I still ponder them. God (whom I've never given much thought to) as a word (which is what I have always loved most). It's an idea I can spend the rest of my life thinking about. Maybe I was wrong when I told myself that "humans are not words." Maybe, if God can be a word, humans can in some way be words too. It changes just about everything in how I look at the world.

The church is filling up for the opening ceremony for SK 2013, the celebration of Søren Kierkegaard's bicentenary. Many international guests are in town for the festivities. A few weeks ago I was in the main office at the Center and happened to look at a flyer, which listed the many activities offered during the coming months. Lona was there and heard me say, "I'm not going to any of that." She squinted at me in her inscrutable way. The next day, though, she called me into her office. "Pick at least one," she told me. "Whether you like it or not, I am going to have you stand up in front of a crowd of people and receive their thanks for the work you did translating Kierkegaard's poems." I picked today's to get it over with as soon as possible. I wish the poems hadn't turned into such a big deal, but they have.

After the manuscript was "burned alive" on television and across the world's widest web, attention turned to that rarest of things: poetry that was not "lost," but was "saved" in translation. The Copenhagen Museum had record crowds (Birgit Fisker-Steensen graciously understood my decision not to make an appearance) and the Center decided to make my translation and Rebekah's commentaries the first post-volume in the *Søren Kierkegaard's Writings* series, the entirety of which will be presented to the University of Copenhagen's Faculty of Theology later this evening at an event I will not be attending. In a related but as yet uncompleted venture, the Center is also sponsoring something called "The Søren Kierkegaard Recovery Project." Lars, who was the first person to point out that the name sounds an awful lot like a twelve-step program for recovering alcoholics, is leading the team of international scholars who are trying to reproduce the Danish originals to *The Poems of S. Kierkegaard*. Using techniques of both "old" and "new" philology, they are assiduously hunting down Kierkegaard's elusive Ur-text. Some members of the team examine the video footage of Carsten burning the manuscript, others interview staff members who saw the manuscript when it first came to the Center, and still others are charged with the responsibility of asking me gazillions of questions. They want to know what Danish word I was translating in this or that line of a particular poem. I try to be helpful to them. Sometimes I make a discreet visit to the safety deposit box and come back with the correct answer, but more than once the scholars have just shaken their heads at me and said, no, that can't possibly be the right word.

I remain the keeper of my daughter's secret. I remain a keeper (one of three) of the Thorvaldsen family secret. On a few occasions I have been tempted to break my bond of silence, but so far I've held. It's hard not telling Ingrid Bendtner, who's made a habit of showing up at *Morfar's* at least once a week and eating a veggie hot dog while I gobble down my usual. But her mole has added muteness to his characteristic blindness. When our conversation turns to the events of mid-January, I simply go silent on her. She says I have a Buddha-look that makes her think I know something she doesn't. "Enlightenment," I tell her, "isn't for every soul." She does not press me further. Tonight, after this ceremony, I am walking back to my apartment and making dinner for the two of us.

A hush comes over the crowd. Lona walks from the side aisle toward the center of the church, where a microphone and a music stand have been set up. I look at her face and see someone who knows exactly what she is doing, exactly what she is about to say, and I am so glad that she is the Director and I am not. Today, on Søren Kierkegaard's 200th birthday, I am happy simply to be alive and to be myself. Whatever word I am, I say, that is enough.

ACKNOWLEDGMENTS

I spent the better part of four years writing *The Stages*, and I had plenty of help along the way. Institutionally speaking, Taylor University has been my greatest financial supporter, employing me as a creative writing professor, allowing me a sabbatical, and more recently creating a non-teaching position for me as their Writer-in-Residence. I want especially to thank Dr. Thomas Jones, Dean of the School of Liberal Arts, and Dr. Steve Bedi, former provost. I would like to thank all of my colleagues in the English Department. While working on this project, I received a grant from the National Endowment for the Arts, for which I am also grateful.

The seeds for this novel go back at least three decades, to my first visit to Denmark. I spent my junior year of high school in Kolding, Denmark, where I lived with the Carlsen family and attended Saint Michael's School. I will always be grateful to Erik and Inge, and to their two children, Niels and Mette. They put up with a pretty bratty American kid back in 1983–84, and they still answer my emails and invite me for visits.

Søren Kierkegaard, although I'm sure I heard his name and read some of his work during my initial stay in Denmark, didn't mean much to me until I studied him in college. I first read the great Danish philosopher and theologian under the direction of Dr. Brian Sayers, who taught a course on him at Houghton College in the spring of 1988.

In preparing to write this novel, I read or re-read a good chunk of Kierkegaard's works, but not all of it. Given the writer's staggering output, who could? I read some of the primary material in Danish, but I am overwhelmingly indebted to Kierkegaard's English-language translators. These include Walter Lowrie, Reidar Thomte, Howard and Edna Hong, and more recently the team of Bruce H. Kirmmse and K. Brian Söderquist, both of whom gave generously of their time in allowing me to interview them.

I read several Kierkegaard biographies, in English and Danish. All helped me appreciate the philosopher's life and gave me details that later worked their way into my story. I am especially grateful to Joakim Garff for his book *Søren Kierkegaard: A Biography* and to Bruce H. Kirmmse for his *Encounters with Kierkegaard: A Life as Seen by His Contemporaries*. Additional help came from scholars currently working in Kierkegaard studies. From Drexel University I want to thank Stacey Ake and M.G. Piety. From the Søren Kierkegaard Research Center in Copenhagen I want to thank the director Niels Jørgen Cappelørn, senior researcher Karsten Kynde, and all of the staff members who joined me for lunch one January afternoon in the Center's break room.

Several Danes agreed to meet with me in person and discuss my novel. I appreciate their hospitality and want to credit them for their aid without implicating them in any way for mistakes that appear in these pages. Anders Borre Gadegaard, Dean of the Cathedral at Our Lady's Church, welcomed me into his study after a Sunday night mass and patiently explained funeral rites as performed in the Danish Lutheran church. I had lunch with Niels-Otto Fisker, Press Chief for Danish National Police, and learned much about the different police agencies in Denmark while also reminiscing over the better days of Leeds United. Jette Sandahl, Director of the Museum of Copenhagen, and Søren Bak-Jensen, Head of Collections, answered my questions about the museum's Søren Kierkegaard Collection, especially the philosopher's desk. They also helped me think through the likely scenario that would play out if an unknown manuscript of Kierkegaard's should suddenly be discovered under their roof. Otto Bering Bryld gave me a tour of Kierkegaard's former home on Nytorv, now a branch office for one of the country's largest banks, and showed me the room where Kierkegaard (probably) slept. He also took me down into the bank's basement so I could view the tidy arrangement of safety deposit boxes and fetch up an idea that would become a central part of my novel's plot. I am grateful to Bruno Svindborg, Research Librarian in the manuscripts department of The Royal Library, for showing me his office and joining me in the "What if?" game of forged manuscripts, theft, and murder. Finally, I could not have written the scenes in *Politigaard*, Copenhagen's police headquarters, without the assistance of Vice-Inspector Jens Møller Jensen and homicide detectives Birgit Maagaard and Britta Almfort. I can't say for sure whether suspected criminals are served coffee and pastries after being led through the maze-like halls of *Politigaard*, but these officers certainly looked after me with genuine Danish hospitality, coffee being a natural part of it.

This novel underwent several major changes during its composition. I would like to thank those people who read earlier versions and offered their feedback. I would like to thank all of them by name, but the list would grow very long and I'd probably leave someone out. For simplicity's sake, I will mention only my father, Doug Satterlee, my brother, Danny Satterlee, and my sister, Dea Browning, who each encouraged me by their responses. I also want to thank Ellen Geiger, my agent at the Frances Goldin Literary Agency, for the hours she spent reading what really amounted to three novels before it finally arrived, with much guidance from her, at its current state.

In situations like this one—writing the acknowledgments page for your first novel—it's best to save the most important person for last. And that's just what I've done. Without the support of my wife, I'd be in an existential crisis the size of which Kierkegaard (even at his most brooding) never imagined. But love saves the day. Thank you, Kathy. I love you. I'm grateful to you for twenty-three years of blessed marriage, and I look forward to what lies ahead. Hey, let's celebrate our 25th anniversary in Scandinavia . . . we can go sailing together down a fjord!